MR. MONSTER

TOR BOOKS BY DAN WELLS

I Am Not a Serial Killer
Mr. Monster

MR. MONSTER

DAN WELLS

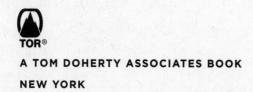

TOR®

A TOM DOHERTY ASSOCIATES BOOK

NEW YORK

MR. MONSTER

Copyright © 2010 by Dan Wells

Edited by Moshe Feder

A Tor Book
Published by Tom Doherty Associates, LLC
175 Fifth Avenue
New York, NY 10010

www.tor-forge.com

Tor® is a registered trademark of Tom Doherty Associates, LLC.

ISBN 978-0-7653-2248-7 (hardcover)
ISBN 978-0-7653-2790-1 (trade paperback)

First Edition: October 2010

Printed in the United States of America

0 9 8 7 6 5 4 3 2 1

To my wife, because this is her favorite.
How lucky am I?

ACKNOWLEDGMENTS

As always, this book would not exist without the awesome help of my agent, Sara Crowe, and my editor, Moshe Feder. This book owes particular credit to Moshe because he's the one who suggested, in his very first call, that I turn *I Am Not a Serial Killer* into a series, and helped brainstorm ideas of how to do it. I am very pleased with the result, and I hope you like it.

This manuscript was read, and greatly improved, by a lot of wonderful people. First thanks go to the Rats With Swords: Karla Bennion, Drew Olds, Ben Olsen, Janci Patterson, Brandon Sanderson, Emily Sanderson, Isaac Stewart, Eric James Stone, and Rachel Whitaker. Other readers include Dave Bird, Steve Diamond, Nick Dianatkhah, Bryce Moore, my brother Rob, and various other family and friends. Special consideration must be given to my friend Janella, who asked to be killed in a horrifying way, and to my mother-in-law, Martha, who secretly called my wife to ask if she felt comfortable being alone with me. These are the memories I treasure.

If you helped with this book and I forgot to mention you, I apologize. I had to save room for Danielle Olsen, who took no part in the production of this novel whatsoever.

From childhood's hour I have not been
As others were—I have not seen
As others saw.

—"Alone," EDGAR ALLAN POE

PROLOGUE

I killed a demon. I don't know if it was really, technically a demon—I'm not exactly a religious person—but I do know that my next-door neighbor was some kind of monster, with fangs and claws and the whole bit. He could change back and forth, and he killed a lot of people, and if he'd known that I knew who he was, he would have killed me too. So for lack of a better word, I called him a demon, and because there was no one else who could do it, I killed him. I think it was the right thing to do. At least the killing stopped.

Well, it stopped for a while.

You see, I'm a monster too—not a supernatural demon, just a messed-up kid. I've spent my whole life trying to keep my dark side locked away where it couldn't hurt anybody, but then that demon showed up, and letting my dark side loose was the only way to stop it. And now I don't know how to lock it back up.

I call my dark side Mr. Monster: the side that dreams

about bloody knives, and imagines what you'd look like with your head on a stick. I don't have multiple personalities and I don't hear voices or anything, I just . . . It's hard to explain. I think about a lot of terrible things, and I want to do a lot of terrible things, and it's just easier to come to terms with that side of me by pretending it's someone else—it's not John who wants to cut his mother into tiny pieces, it's Mr. Monster. See? I feel better already.

But here's the problem: Mr. Monster is hungry. Serial killers often talk about a need—some driving urge that they can control at first, but that builds and builds until it's impossible to stop, and then they lash out and kill again. I never understood what they were talking about before, but now I think I do. Now I can feel it, deep in my bones, as insistent and inevitable as the biological urge to eat or hunt or mate.

I've killed once, and it's only a matter of time before I kill again.

1

It was one a.m., and I was staring at a cat.

It was probably a white cat, but here in the dark I couldn't tell for sure; what little moonlight filtered through the broken windows turned the room into an older version of itself, a scene from a black and white movie. The cement block walls were gray, the dented barrels and stacks of wooden planks were gray, the piles of half-used paint cans were gray; and there in the center, refusing to move, was a gray cat.

I played with the plastic jug in my hands, turning it back and forth, listening to the gasoline as it sloshed around inside. I had a book of matches in my pocket and a pile of oily rags at my feet. There was enough old wood and chemicals in here to fuel a spectacular fire, and I desperately wanted to light it, but I didn't want to hurt that cat. I didn't even dare scare it away, for fear that I might lose control.

So I stared at it, waiting. As soon as it left, this place was gone.

It was late April, and spring was finally winning its battle to transform a dull, frozen Clayton County into a cheerful green one. A big part of this, of course, was the fact that the Clayton Killer had finally left us alone—his vicious killing spree had lasted almost five months, but he'd stopped very suddenly, and no one had heard from him since January. The town had huddled in fear for another two months, barring their doors and windows every night, and waking up each morning hardly daring to turn on the TV and see another shredded corpse on the morning news. But nothing had come, and slowly we'd started to believe that it was over for real this time, and there wouldn't be any more bodies to clean up. The sun came up, the snow melted away, and people started smiling again. We'd weathered the storm. Clayton had been tentatively happy for almost a month now.

I was the one person, in fact, who hadn't been worried at all. I'd known for certain that the Clayton Killer was gone for good, way back in January. After all, I'm the one who killed him.

The cat moved, turning its attention from me to drop its head and lick its paw. I held completely still, hoping it would ignore me or forget me and go outside to hunt or something. Cats were supposed to be nocturnal hunters, and this one had to eat sometime. I pulled my watch from my pocket—a cheap plastic wristwatch that I'd torn the straps off of—and checked the time again: 1:05. This was going nowhere.

The warehouse had been built as a supply dump for a construction company many, many years ago, back when the big wood mill in town was new and people still thought Clayton County might turn into something. It never did, and while the wood mill still struggled along, the construction company had cut its losses and gone home. In the years since, I wasn't the only one who'd made use of this long-abandoned building— the walls were covered with grafitti, and the ground inside and out was littered with beer cans and empty wrappers. I'd even found a mattress behind some wooden pallets, presumably some vagrant's temporary home. I wondered if the Clayton Killer had got him, too, before I stopped him; either way, the mattress was musty from disuse, and I figured nobody had been out here all winter. When I finally got a chance, that mattress was slated to be the core of my carefully crafted fire.

Tonight, though, there was nothing I could do. I followed rules, and those rules were very strict, and the very first one said "Do not hurt animals." That made this the fourth time the cat had stopped me from burning down the warehouse. I suppose I should have been grateful, but . . . I really needed to burn something. One of these days I'd take that cat and—no. I wouldn't hurt the cat. I'd never hurt anyone again.

Breathe deep.

I set down the gas jug; I didn't have time to wait for the cat, but I could burn something smaller. I grabbed a wooden pallet and dragged it outside, then went back in for the gas. The cat was still there, now sitting in a ragged square of moonlight, watching me.

"One of these days," I said, then turned and walked back out. I drizzled a little gas on the pallet, just enough to make it easy, then placed the jug by my bike, far away from where the fire would be. Safety first. The stars were out, and the trees in the forest loomed close, but the warehouse was in a clearing of gravel and dead grass. Somewhere through the trees the interstate rumbled by, filled with late-night semis and the occasional drowsy car.

I knelt down by the wooden pallet, smelling the tang of gas in the air, and pulled out my matches. I didn't bother to break up the planks or build a proper fire, I just struck the match and dropped it on the gas, watching it flare up bright and yellow. The flames licked up the gas and then, slowly, started in on the wood itself. I watched it closely, hearing the little snaps and pops as the fire found pockets of sap. When it had a firm grip on the board, I grabbed the pallet by a safe corner and turned it on its end, letting the fire spread, and then flopped it down on the other side so the flames could reach up and spread to the rest of the boards. It moved like a living thing, probing the wood with a thin yellow finger, tasting it, then reaching out greedily and lapping it up.

The fire caught well, better than I expected. It seemed a shame to waste it on just one pallet.

I pulled another pallet from the warehouse and dropped it on top of the fire. The blaze was big enough now that it roared and crackled, jumping on to the new wood with obvious delight. I smiled at it, like the proud owner of a precocious dog. Fire was my pet, my companion, and the only release I had left; when Mr. Monster clamored for me to break my rules and hurt someone, I could always appease it with a good fire. I watched the blaze tear into the second pallet, hearing the dull roar as it sucked in oxygen, and smiled. It wanted more wood, so I went inside for another two pallets. Just a little more wouldn't hurt.

———

"Please don't hurt me."

I loved it when she said that. Somehow, for some reason, I always expected her to say "Are you going to hurt me?" but she was too smart for that. She was tied to the wall in my basement, and I was holding a knife—of course I was going to hurt her. Brooke didn't ask stupid questions, which is one of the reasons I liked her so much.

"Please, John, I'm begging you: please don't hurt me."

I could listen to that for hours. I liked it because it got right to the point: I had all the power in the situation, and she knew it. She knew that no matter what she wanted, I was the only one who could give it to her. Alone in this room, with this knife in my hand, I was her entire world—her hopes and her fears together, her everything at once.

I moved the knife almost imperceptibly, and felt a rush of adrenaline as her eyes twitched to follow it: first left, then right; now up, now down. It was an intimate dance, our minds and bodies in perfect sync.

I had felt this before, brandishing a knife to my mom in our kitchen, but even then I'd known that Brooke was the only one who really mattered. Brooke was the one I wanted to connect with.

I raised the knife and stepped forward. Like a partner in a dance, Brooke moved in unison, pressing back against the wall, eyes growing wider, breath growing quicker. *A perfect connection. Perfect.*

Everything was perfect—exactly as I'd imagined it a thousand times. It was a fantasy become real, a scenario of such utter completeness that I felt it begin to gather me up and sweep me away. Her wide eyes focusing completely on me. Her pale skin trembling as I reached toward her. I felt emotions surging, roiling inside me, spilling out and blistering my skin.

This is wrong. This is exactly what I've always wanted, and exactly what I've always wanted to avoid. Right and wrong at the same time.

I can't tell my dreams from my nightmares.

There was only one way it could end; only one way it ever ended. I shoved the knife into Brooke's chest, she screamed, and I woke up.

"Wake up," said Mom again, turning on my light. I rolled over and groaned. I hated waking up, but I hated sleeping even more—too much time alone with my subconscious. I grimaced and forced myself to sit up. *I made it through another one. Only twenty hours before I have to do it again.*

"Big day today," said Mom, pulling open the blinds in my window. "After school you've got another appointment with Clark Forman. Come on, get up."

I squinted at her, bleary-eyed. "Forman again?"

"I told you about this last week," she said. "It's probably another deposition."

"Whatever." I climbed out of bed and headed for the shower, but Mom blocked my path.

"Wait," she said sternly. "What do we say?"

I sighed and repeated with her our ritual morning phrase: "Today I will think good thoughts and smile at everyone I see." She smiled and patted me on the shoulder. Sometimes I wished I just had an alarm clock.

"Corn flakes or Cheerios this morning?"

"I can pour my own cereal," I said, and pushed past her to the bathroom.

My mom and I lived above the mortuary in a quiet little neighborhood on the outskirts of Clayton. Technically we were across the municipal line, which put us in the county rather than the town, but the whole place was so small that nobody really noticed or cared where any of the lines were. We lived in Clayton, and thanks to the mortuary we were one of the only families that didn't have at least one person working in the wood mill. You might think that a small town like this wouldn't have enough dead people to keep a mortuary in business, and you'd be right—we were on the ropes most of last year, struggling to pay the bills. My dad paid child support, or more correctly, the government garnished his wages to pay it, but it still wasn't enough. Then last fall the Clayton Killer had shown up and given us plenty of business. Most of me thought it was sad that so many people had to die to keep our business solvent, but Mr. Monster loved every minute of it.

Naturally, Mom didn't know about Mr. Monster, but she did know that I had been diagnosed with Conduct Disorder—which is mostly just a polite way of saying that I'm sociopathic. The official term is Antisocial Personality Disorder, but they're only allowed to call it that when you're eighteen or older. I was still a month shy of sixteen, so Conduct Disorder it was.

I locked myself in the bathroom and stared in the mirror. It was encrusted with little notes and Post-its Mom left to remind us of important things—not daily things like appointments, but long-term words to live by. I could sometimes hear her recite them to herself as she got ready in the morning: things like "Today will be the best day of my life," and other crap like that. The largest was a note she had written specifically for me, compiling a list of rules written on lined pink notepaper and taped to the corner of the mirror. These were the same rules I'd created years ago to keep Mr. Monster locked up, and I'd followed them just fine on my own until last year when I had to let him out. Now Mom had taken it upon herself to enforce them. I read the list while I brushed my teeth:

RULES:

I will not hurt animals.

I will not burn things.

When I think bad thoughts about someone, I will push the thoughts away and say something nice about that person.

I will not call people "it."

If I start to follow someone, I will ignore them as much as possible for a full week.

I will not threaten people, even implicitly.

If people threaten me, I will leave the situation.

Obviously, the one about burning things had already been tossed out. Mr. Monster was so insistent, and my mom's supervision so restrictive, that something had to give, and that was it. Lighting fires—small, contained fires that wouldn't hurt anyone—was like a release valve that let out all the pressure building up in my life. It was a rule I *had* to break to have any hope of following the others. I didn't tell Mom what I was doing, of course; I just left it on the list and ignored it.

Honestly, I appreciated Mom's help, but . . . it was getting very hard to live with. I spat out the toothpaste, rinsed my mouth, and went to get dressed.

I ate breakfast in the living room, watching the morning

news while Mom hovered in the hall behind me as far as her curling iron could reach. "Anything interesting going on at school today?" she asked.

"No," I said. There was nothing interesting on the news, either—no new deaths in town, at least, which was usually all I cared about. "Do you really think Forman wants to see me for another deposition?"

Mom paused for a moment, silent behind me, and I knew what she was thinking—there were things we still hadn't told the police about what happened that night. When a serial killer comes after you, that's one thing, but when that serial killer turns out to be a demon, and melts away into ash and black sludge right before your eyes, how are you supposed to explain that without getting thrown into an asylum?

"I'm sure they just want to make sure they have everything right," she said. "We've told them everything there is to tell."

"Everything except the demon who tried to—"

"We are not going to talk about that," said Mom sternly.

"But we can't just pretend—"

"We are not going to talk about it," said Mom. She hated talking about the demon, and almost never acknowledged it out loud. I was desperate to discuss it with someone, but the only person I could share it with refused to even think about it.

"I've already told him everything else twenty-seven times," I said, flipping to another new channel. "He's either suspicious or he's an idiot." The new channel was as dull as the last one.

Mom thought for a moment. "Are you thinking bad thoughts about him?"

"Oh, come on, Mom."

"This is important!"

"I can do this myself, Mom," I said, putting down the remote. "I've been doing this myself for a very long time. I don't need you reminding me constantly about every little thing."

"Are you thinking bad thoughts about me now?"

"I'm starting to, yes."

"And?"

I rolled my eyes. "You look very nice today," I said.

"You haven't even seen me since you turned on the TV."

"I don't have to say sincere things, just nice things."

"Sincerity will help, though—"

"You know what will help," I said, standing up and taking my empty bowl into the kitchen, "is for you to stop bugging me all the time. Half the bad things I think about are caused by you breathing down my neck every second of the day."

"Better me than somebody else," she called from the hallway, unfazed. "I know you love me too much to do anything drastic."

"I'm a sociopath, Mom, I don't love anybody. By definition."

"Is that an implicit threat?"

"Oh for the—no, it was not a threat. I'm leaving."

"And?"

I stepped back into the hallway, staring at her in frustration. We recited it again: "Today I will think good thoughts and smile at everyone I see." I picked up my backpack, opened the door, then turned around and looked at her one last time.

"You do look very nice today," I said.

"What was that for?"

"You don't want to know."

2

I left my mom and walked downstairs to the side door, where our upstairs home met the first-floor mortuary. There was a small space there, a landing between the doors and the stairs, and I paused there for a moment to take a deep breath. I told myself, as I did every morning, that Mom was only trying to help—that she recognized my problems and wanted to help me beat them in the only way she knew how.

I used to think that telling her my rules would help me follow them—that it would somehow make me more accountable to them—but her level of control was too overbearing, and now I couldn't see any way out of it. It was driving me crazy.

Literally.

The rules I followed were designed to protect people—to stop me from doing anything wrong, and to keep me out of situations where I might hurt somebody. And the potential was definitely there.

I was seven years old when I first discovered my life's greatest passion: serial killers. I didn't like what they did, obviously—I knew that it was wrong—but I was fascinated by it, and by how they did it, and why. What intrigued me the most was not how different they were, but how similar—to each other, and to me. As I read more and learned more I started to check off all the warning signs in my head: chronic bedwetting. Pyromania. Animal cruelty. High IQs with low grades; lonely childhoods with few or no friends; strained parental relationships and dysfunctional home lives. These and dozens more are predictors for serial killer behavior, and I had every one. It's a pretty big shock to realize that the only people you can identify with are psychopathic killers.

The thing about predictors is, they're never set in stone: most serial killers show these signs as children, but most of the children who show these signs will never become serial killers. It's a step-by-step process to move from one to the other, moving from one bad decision to another, doing just a little more and going just a little farther until finally you're caught with a basement full of corpses and a shrine made of skulls in the den. When my dad left, and I was so mad I wanted to kill everyone I knew, I decided that it was time to do something about myself. I made rules to help me stay as normal and happy and nonviolent as I could.

A lot of the rules wrote themselves: "Don't hurt animals." "Don't hurt people." "Don't threaten animals or people." "Don't hit or kick anything." As I got older and understood myself better, I started making my rules more specific, and attaching self-punishments where necessary: "If I want to hurt someone, I have to compliment them." "If I start to fixate on a specific person, I have to ignore them for a week." Rules like that help me drive out dangerous thoughts and avoid dangerous situations.

Once I hit adolescence, my whole world changed and my rules had to change to keep up: the girls in school grew hips and breasts, and all of a sudden my nightmares were full of young, screaming women instead of old, screaming men. I instated a new rule, "Don't look at breasts," but in general I find that it's easiest just not to look at girls at all.

Which brings us to Brooke.

Brooke Watson was the most beautiful girl in school, and she was my age, and she lived two houses down from me, and I could pick out her scent in a massive crowd. She had long blond hair, and braces, and a smile so bright it made me wonder why other girls bothered smiling at all. I knew her class schedule, her birthday, her Gmail password, and her social security number—none of which I had any business knowing. I had anti-stalking rules that should have prevented me from knowing any of that, or even from thinking about her at all, but . . . Brooke was a special case.

The thing was, my rules were designed to keep Mr. Monster in, but they had the brutally efficient side effect of keeping everyone else out. A guy who forces himself to ignore people anytime he starts to get to know them is not a guy who's going to make a lot of friends. I used to be okay with this, content to ignore the world and stay far away from any temptation, but Mom had other ideas, and now that she was taking an active hand in my sociopathy she was forcing me into situations I wasn't sure how to handle. She insisted that the only way to learn social skills was to practice them, and she knew that I

liked Brooke, so she pushed us together every chance she got.
Her latest ploy, now that I had my learner's permit, was to loan
me a car and tell Brooke's parents that I could drive Brooke to
school every morning. Brooke's parents thought it was a great
idea, partly because the nearest bus stop was about eight blocks
away, but mostly because they didn't know how many times
a week I had dreams about embalming their daughter.

I pulled out my keys and went outside, walking to the car.
Mom had bought the cheapest possible car she could find for
me to use—a 1971 Chevy Impala, baby blue, with no AC and
no FM radio. It was built like a tank and handled like a cruise
liner, and I figured you could melt it down and make at least
three Honda Civics, but I wasn't complaining. It was good just
to have a car.

Brooke came out of her house before I could even get the car
in gear. I always wanted to drive to her house and pick her
up—it seemed more polite that way—but every morning she
heard me start the engine and met me halfway.

"Good morning, John," she said, climbing in the passenger
side. I didn't look at her.

"Good morning, Brooke," I said. "Ready to go?"

"All set."

I pulled away from the curb and got up to speed, carefully
keeping my eyes on the road. I didn't look at her until the end
of the block, stopping at the corner and catching a quick glance
as I checked for traffic. She was wearing a red shirt, and the top
layer of her hair was tied up in a pony tail. I stopped myself
from looking at her clothes any closer, but from the flash of
skin on her legs I knew she was wearing shorts. It was pretty
warm this time of year, so she'd be fine by lunchtime, but it

was just chilly enough this early in the morning that I reached out and flipped on the heater before continuing down the street.

"Are you ready for social studies today?" she asked. It was the only class we shared, so it was a frequent topic of conversation.

"I think so," I said. "I didn't want to read the chapter on peer pressure, but some friends convinced me to."

I heard her chuckle at that, but I didn't look to see her smile. Brooke was the big anomaly in my life—the twisted knot that messed up all of my rules and disordered all of my plans. Any other girl, of course, I wouldn't even talk to, and if I ever had a dream about any other girl I wouldn't allow myself to even think about her for a week. That was the safe way—that was the way I'd lived for years.

Because of our situation, though, I had to stretch my rules to accommodate my enforced proximity to Brooke. I'd made a long list of exceptions to cover the area between "ignoring her completely" and "abducting her at knifepoint." I couldn't ignore her, but I couldn't just stare at her either, so I'd developed a set of acceptable options:

I could say her name once, in the morning, when she got in the car. I could talk to her while driving, but I had to keep my eyes on the road. At school I could look at her three times during class, and talk to her once during lunch, but that was it—between classes I had to avoid her, even if it meant going out of my way. I could not follow her, even if we were going to the same place, and I could not, under any circumstances, think about her during the day. If I started to, I made myself recite number sequences in my head to drown out the thoughts: 1, 1,

2, 3, 5, 8, 13, 21, 34. Perhaps most important of all, I could not touch her or anything that belonged to her, for any reason.

Before I'd made that last rule I'd actually stolen something of hers, just to have it—a hair clip that managed to end up on the floor of the car one day. I kept it for a week, like a good luck charm, but it made the "don't think about her" rule almost impossible to follow, so I'd put it back on the floor and pointed it out to her the next morning, as if I'd just found it. Now I shied away from everything, to the point that I didn't even touch the passenger door—"her" door—unless I absolutely had to.

"Do you ever think he'll come back?" asked Brooke suddenly, interrupting my thoughts.

"Who?"

"The killer," she said. Her voice was distant and thoughtful. "We act like he's gone, just because he hasn't attacked anybody in months, but they still haven't found him. He's still out there somewhere, and he's still . . . evil."

Brooke usually avoided talking about the killer; she hated even thinking about the subject. Something must have been bothering her if she was talking about it now.

"He might still be out there," I said. "Some serial killers can wait years between attacks, like BTK, but they're usually a different kind of killer. Our killer was . . ." I almost looked at her, stopped myself, and glared at the road. I had to be very careful not to freak her out—people usually got really creeped out when they realized how much I knew about serial killers. Even Agent Forman had been surprised in our early interviews—he was a criminal profiler, and yet I'd read an essay on Edmund Kemper that he'd never even heard of. "I don't know," I said. "It's hard to think about."

"It is hard," said Brooke. "I don't like to think of it, but with Mrs. Crowley right there, it's kind of hard to forget. She must be so lonely." I checked my blind spot just in time to see Brooke look over at me. "Do you ever have nightmares about it?"

"Not really," I said, but it wasn't true. I had nightmares about it almost every night—it was the main reason I hated sleeping. One minute I'd be nodding off, fighting to fill my mind with happy thoughts, and the next I'd be back inside the Crowley's house, beating Mrs. Crowley with a clock. I had nightmares about finding Dr. Neblin, my therapist, dead in the Crowley's driveway. And I had nightmares about Mr. Crowley—the Clayton Killer himself—impossibly transformed into a demon, slashing and killing a long parade of victims before finally coming after Mom and me. I'd killed him then, but that only made the nightmares worse: most of them were about how much I enjoyed killing, and how much I wanted to do it again. That was a lot more frightening.

"I can't imagine what it must have been like for you to find that guy," said Brooke. "I don't think I could have done what you did."

"What I did?" Did she know that I killed the demon? How?

"Trying to save Neblin," said Brooke. "I would have just run."

"Oh yeah." Of course: she wasn't thinking about killing, she was thinking about saving. Brooke always saw the positive side of everything. I'm not sure I had a positive side, but at least around her I could pretend.

"Don't think too much of it," I said, pulling into the school parking lot. "I'm sure you'd have done the same, and probably done a better job. You have to remember, I didn't even save him."

"But you tried."

"I'm sure he appreciates the effort," I said, and pulled into the one parking spot that still had enough room for my massive car. It was kind of funny, actually—this thing probably out-weighed 99% of the vehicles here, even though half the kids drove trucks. "Well, here we are."

Brooke opened the door and stepped out. "Thanks for the ride," she said, "I'll see you in social studies," then ran off to join a friend. I permitted myself one long look as she walked away, jogging to join a friend on her way to the building. She was gorgeous.

And she was so much better off without me in her life.

"Shut up," said Max, walking up next to me and dropping his backpack on the ground. Max Bowen was the closest thing I had to a friend, though it was more a matter of convenience than actual friendship. Serial killers tended to be withdrawn from the world as children, with few if any friends, so I'd told myself that a best friend, even a fake one, would help keep me normal. Max was the prefect candidate—he had no friends of his own, and he was just self-absorbed enough to not care about my various eccentricities. He was, on the other hand, very annoying—like his new habit of starting every conversation with "shut up."

"You are just a delight to be with these days, you know that?" I said.

"This from the walking dead boy," said Max. "We all know you're a goth waiting to happen—why don't you just wear black and get it over with?"

"My mom buys my clothes."

"Yeah, so does mine," he said, forgetting the string of insults and squatting down to open his backpack. "Pretty soon I'm going to fit into my dad's clothes, though, and then I'm going to look awesome—I can wear his combat fatigues and everything." Max worshiped his dad, even more so now that he was dead. The Clayton Killer had ripped him in half just after Christmas, and everyone in town had been extra nice to Max ever since, but I figured he was better off this way. His father was a jerk.

"Check this out," he said, standing up and opening a thick cardboard folder. Inside were several comic books, carefully sealed in plastic, and he gingerly took one out and handed it to me. "This is a limited edition," he said, placing it carefully in my hands. "Convention-only Green Lantern issue number zero—it's even got a foil stamp in the corner. It's numbered."

"Why do you bring these to school?" I asked, but I knew the answer. Bragging about his expensive comics was the whole reason Max bought them—they weren't any good to him if they stayed at home in a locked drawer where no one could see how cool he was for owning them.

"What this?" asked Rob Anders, stopping next to us. I sighed. *Here we go again.* This happened almost every day: Rob would mock Max, I'd mock Rob, he'd threaten me, and we'd go to class. Sometimes I wondered if I bugged him on purpose just to feel the thrill of danger again—to feel just a taste of the driving terror I'd felt over the winter. But Rob was not a killer, and he was definitely not a demon, and his threats were thin and hollow. He was sixteen years old, for crying out loud. What was he going to do?

"Good morning, Rob," I said. "It's always good to see you." Mr. Monster desperately wanted to stab him.

"I wasn't talking to you, freak," said Rob, "I was talking to your boyfriend."

"It's a comic book worth more than anything you own," said Max, taking it back protectively. Max always knew exactly what not to say.

"Let me see," said Rob, and shot out his hand to grab the comic book. Max was at least smart enough not to fight over it, and let go immediately.

"Hold it carefully," said Max, "don't crease it."

"The Green Lantern," said Rob, holding it up in front of him. His voice was different now—more deliberate than normal, and a little more dramatic. I'd learned through experience that a voice like that meant the speaker was mocking something. "Is this who you dream about at night, Max? The big, dreamy Green Lantern swooping down into your bedroom?"

"Is homosexuality really all you talk about?" I asked. I knew I shouldn't antagonize him, but Rob never did anything to me, just to Max—I think he was still scared of me after the Halloween incident.

"I only talk about gays around gaywads like you," he said, flexing the comic and its cardboard support.

"Please don't bend it," said Max.

"Or what?" asked Rob with a smile, "your commando dad's gonna beat me up?"

"Wow," I said, "did you actually just make fun of his dead father?"

"Shut up," said Rob.

"So you're tough because somebody else killed his dad," I said. "That is a gutsy claim, Rob."

"And you're a fag," he said, slapping the comic into my chest.

"You do realize that highly vocal homophobes are far more likely to be gay?"

Rob sneered. "And you realize that you're asking me, in very plain terms, to beat your face in? Right here. You're handing me a signed request form."

Chad Walker, one of Rob's friends, walked up behind him. "It's the freaks," said Chad. "How are you today, freaks?"

"I'm wonderful, Chad," I said, not taking my eyes off of Rob. "Nice shirt, by the way."

Rob stared back at me a moment, then dropped the comic book into my hands. "Take a good look, Chad," he said. "Living proof of how messed up fatherless children can get. Two dysfunctional families in action."

"Having a father has obviously done wonders for you," I said.

Something finally snapped in Rob's mind, and he shoved me in the chest. "You want to talk about dysfunctional, freak? You want to talk about cutting people open? They bring you in to the police station almost once a week, John—when are they finally gonna arrest you for the psycho you are?" He was shouting now, and other kids stopped to watch.

This was new—I'd never pushed him this far before. "You're very observant," I said, struggling to find some kind of compliment. I couldn't think of anything else to say, but Mr. Monster was whispering something in my ear and it slipped out before I could stop it: "But think about it this way, Rob—you're either wrong, in which case all these people staring at you think you're an idiot, or you're right, in which case you're physically threatening a dangerous killer. It doesn't seem very smart either way."

"Are you threatening me, freak?"

"Listen, Rob," I said. "You're not scary. I've been scared before—really, legitimately scared—and you're just nowhere in the same league. Why do we have to go through this every day?"

"You're scared of getting caught," said Rob.

"We've got to get to class," said Chad, pulling Rob away. His eyes said that he was worried—that Rob had gone too far, or that I had. Rob took a step back, flipped me off, then walked toward the school with Chad. I handed Max his comic book, and he studied it carefully for damage.

"One of these days he's going to hurt one," said Max, "and then I'm going to sue him for damages—my dad said these things are worth, like, hundreds of dollars."

"One of these days you're going to leave your hundred-dollar comic books at home where he can't hurt them," I said, angry at him for attracting Rob's attention. I shouldn't break any of my rules—not even the simple ones like this. A year ago I would never have provoked Rob like that. Mr. Monster was getting too strong.

Max slipped his comic back into his folder, and then into his bag.

"See you at lunch," I said.

"Shut up," said Max.

3

School was, as predicted, uninteresting, and I spent my time thinking about Agent Forman. He was the FBI investigator assigned to the Clayton Killer case, and he'd been living in town since around Thanksgiving. Even after the rest of the FBI team left in March, Forman had hung around. He'd made us his pet case—he was one of the first people on the scene when we called to report Neblin's body, and since that time he'd interviewed me half a dozen times at least. It had been a while since the last one, though, and I'd assumed we were done. What did he want now?

I'd already told him everything I could possibly tell him, all except for three important things. First, there was the unspoken secret between Mom and me: that a demon had attacked us, that I had stabbed it, and that it had melted away into sludge right there in the back room of the house. We figured no one sane would be-lieve us, and we didn't want to be "the weirdos who say they saw a monster," so we just cleaned it up and kept it quiet.

The second secret was something that Mom didn't even know: the demon who attacked us was actually my next-door neighbor, Mr. Crowley. He'd been killing people and stealing their body parts to replenish his own body, which was falling apart. I'd stalked him for weeks trying to find a way to stop him, though when I finally did it I was minutes too late— maybe just seconds too late—to save Dr. Neblin. Being partially to blame for your own therapist's death is a tough thing to deal with, especially because you don't have a therapist anymore to help you through it. Sometimes irony just kicks you in the teeth like that.

The third secret was good old Mr. Monster himself. Sure, Mr. Monster had come in very handy when I'd needed to kill a demon, and when I'd needed to lure the demon by threatening its wife, but how do you explain that to the cops? "I stopped a supernatural force you don't believe in, and of which I have no evidence, by calling on the power of my inner serial killer and beating an old lady until she passed out. You can thank me later." I may have some big mental problems, but I'm not crazy enough to tell that story to anybody.

So yes, I was keeping a lot of secrets from Agent Forman, but the story I did tell him made perfect sense without those secrets, and there was absolutely no evidence to link me to anything else—Crowley's remains had never been found, so they couldn't even prove he was dead, let alone that I had killed him. I'd even destroyed the cell phones the victims and I had used that night, just in case. What did I possibly have to worry about?

After school I drove Brooke home—stealing three good looks at her face—and then I drove alone to the police station downtown, where Forman had set up an increasingly permanent office. The front receptionist, a blond woman named Stephanie, greeted me with a smile.

"Hello John," she said as I came in. She looked about my sister's age, in her early twenties, but my sister, Lauren, was usually more somber and preoccupied. Stephanie was like a bubbling pot of cheerful.

"Hi," I said. "Forman wanted to see me again?"

"Yes." She looked at her list. "You're right on time. Sign in and I'll tell him you're here."

She handed me a clipboard with a piece of paper, mostly empty, and I wrote down my name and the time on the first empty line. The metal chain on the pen was broken, so I clamped it into the clipboard and set it back on the counter.

The Clayton County police station was small and sparse, really only designed to handle the occasional DUI or domestic abuse call. Behind Stephanie was the large glass window of the sheriff's office, and inside I could see Sheriff Meier—a stern, weary man with a long, gray mustache—talking on the phone. The pane of glass was woven through with metal wires, like a chain link fence, and there was a bullet hole in the lower right section of it. I could never get anyone to tell me the story of how it got there.

"Hello, John, thanks for coming in." Agent Clark Forman was a short man, balding, with glasses and a thin moustache. He reached out his hand and I shook it dully.

"What is it this time?" I asked, following him into the side room where he'd made his makeshift office. His "desk" was oversized and thick, and I assumed it had started life as a conference table. Under Forman's care it had become covered with loose sheets, bulging folders, piles of photographs, and more. A map of the county hung on one wall, with each of the Clayton Killer's probable crime scenes marked with a pin. It always pleased me to see that there was no pin out by the lake—that was one of Crowley's victims that I knew about that they hadn't found yet. I couldn't tell them about it without incriminating myself, of course, but it's not like I was impeding an important investigation. The killer they were looking for was already dead.

"Have a seat," said Forman, pointing at one of the conference room chairs shoved into the corner. He smiled as I pulled up the chair and sat, and gestured to his window. "Pretty nice weather out there today. Is your mother waiting outside?"

"I drove myself."

"That's right," he said, nodding his head. "You've got a learner's permit now. You turn sixteen in . . . two more months?"

"One more."

"Right around the corner then," he said. "Don't worry—you'll have a real license soon enough, and then you'll be out there terrorizing the streets."

There was that phrase: "terrorizing the streets." I'd never heard that phrase in my whole life until I started taking Driver's Ed., and now I'd heard it four times in the past month. It was one of those filler phrases, like "hot enough for ya?," that didn't mean anything—they just spill out of people when they don't take the time to think. I wondered how much of this conversation was going to be real thought, and how much was going to be parroted filler.

"What do you need me for this time?" I asked.

"Just a routine follow-up," he said, then paused for a moment before reaching for a folder and pulling out a photograph. "Let me get your opinion on something first, though, as long as you're here. This will be on the news in a few hours, so it's not proprietary information." He slid the photo across the table, and I could see even from a distance that it was the face of a corpse. The eyes were open, but dull and lifeless.

Another corpse. And that meant there was another killer. I felt a rush of excitement boiling in my chest and making me feel lightheaded. Another killer.

I looked up at Forman. "Here in Clayton?"

"She's not from here, no, but we did find her here. Just this morning."

I leaned forward to look more closely, noting the pale skin, the slack jaw, the stringy hair. There was a fleck of something black on her cheek, and another on her forehead. Pieces of bark, perhaps.

"She was underwater," I said, peering at the photo. "There's sediment all over. You pulled her out of the lake."

"An irrigation canal," said Forman.

"Do you know who she is?"

"Not yet," said Forman, glancing down at the photo and then back up at me. "We really don't know much at all, except that the body's covered with small wounds: burns, abrasions, punctures, that kind of thing."

"Are there any pieces missing?" I asked. The Clayton Killer had always taken something—a limb or an organ—from each of his victims. The police just thought he was a serial killer saving mementos of his victims, but in reality the demon was dying, and used the pieces of other people's bodies to replace his own. Mr. Crowley was supposed to be dead—I had seen him die—but maybe he *had* come back? Maybe he could regenerate his body even better than I thought?

Or maybe it was another demon?

"Would you believe that missing organs were the first thing we looked for too?" asked Forman. "The victim was nothing like the Clayton Killer's victims, the scene was different, the methods appeared to be different, but still . . ." He shook his head, then showed me another photo of a blackened foot. "Same victim—that crater in the sole we think is an electrical wound, and probably the cause of death. So no, there's really no similarities at all, but we just . . . I think maybe we want this to be him, because that would mean there's only one killer to deal with. But in the end, no—there was nothing missing. There's no evidence to link this killing to any of this winter's."

I studied the photo, analyzing the situation in my mind. After a moment I looked up at him. "You said you wanted my opinion," I said. "If this is unrelated to the other killings, what does my opinion have to do with it?"

"Just grasping at straws, really," said Forman, picking up the photo. "You're the only witness who got a good look at the Clayton Killer and lived. You've already stated that you didn't see a weapon, but in light of this new corpse I'm wondering if maybe you can remember seeing any tools? Maybe a work belt?"

"What kind of tools?"

"Well," he said, putting the photo back down and pointing

to the corpse's shoulder, "for example, we think this wound was made by a screwdriver."

I looked closely; the wound was small, barely a blip on the skin, but if they suspected a screwdriver it was probably a deep puncture. An image flashed through my head, more visceral than visual, and I imagined myself stabbing someone with a screwdriver, feeling it sink into the muscle and jar against the bone. Mr. Monster smiled, but I kept my face blank and pushed the thought away.

Agent Forman was looking at me, waiting.

"Nothing I can remember," I said. I knew for a fact that it wasn't the same killer, but I had to play this carefully so I didn't give myself away. "There was certainly nothing like a tool belt, but it was cold, and he had a big coat, like I said. He could have had anything in those pockets."

"Think hard," said Forman, watching me intently. "Try to remember everything, even things you might not think of as weapons: a box cutter, a pair of pliers, a cigarette lighter."

I breathed deeply. Had this body really been wounded by all of those things? What kind of damage would they do, and how would you use them? Would they work in an attack, or would the victim have to be restrained first?

Forman was still watching me.

"I don't remember seeing anything like that," I said. "He was a just a man in a coat; I didn't even see the blade that he used to kill Dr. Neblin."

"I understand," said Forman, taking back the photo and sliding it back into the folder. "It was a long shot, but I figured as long as I had you here I might as well ask."

I wanted—I needed—to see this body up close. And even as open as Forman was being, there was no way he'd take me in to see it—but when they were done with their forensic autopsy they'd probably send it to the mortuary for embalming. If they did, I could see it then.

What if the autopsy found a missing organ? Would that mean this was a new demon? Mr. Crowley had killed because he was dying, and stealing organs helped keep him alive, but what if the new demon killed for other reasons? What if he just enjoyed it? My skin went cold at the thought.

But then, if he didn't kill to stay alive, there would be no reason to steal organs at all. So it might be a demon even if nothing was missing.

I pushed the thought away. One body wasn't even a pattern, let alone a serial killer, let alone a serial killing demon. It was probably just a standard murder—a botched robbery, or a domestic dispute gone wrong. It was common enough in the rest of the world, and even in a little town like Clayton people had to die sooner or later. After all, if we could have a supernatural serial killer, we could have anything.

I looked up at Agent Forman and saw him sitting calmly, watching me. "Sorry to take up all that time," he said. "Do you still have a minute for the real reason I brought you in?"

I tried to focus on the moment, forgetting my thoughts of demons and corpses and serial killers. There would be time for that later.

"Sure," I said.

"Just routine stuff, like I said." Forman pulled another piece of paper from a stack and looked at it. "It's a standard questionnaire, really; you just happened to have your follow-up scheduled on what turned out to be a particularly interesting day. Lucky you."

Yeah. Real lucky.

"Do you remember anything new about the night you called the police?

"No."

"Do you remember anything new about the man you saw that night, whom you believe to be the Clayton Killer?"

"No."

"Do you remember anything new about the body you pulled from the car—Dr. Benjamin Neblin?"

"No."

Forman looked up. "You're absolutely sure? We've examined the body in detail of course, but you saw it before it was moved—was it arranged in any particular way, or was anything placed on it or in it?"

"No," I said. "It was just slumped over in the passenger seat. The face was hidden, so I didn't recognize him at first, but I told you that before."

"You did," said Forman, nodding. "Just one more question: Do you remember anything new about your own feelings that night—why you did what you did, what went through your mind, that sort of thing?"

"I probably remember it worse now than I did then," I said.

"Then that's it," he said. "Sorry for the anticlimax, but that's really all I've got for you today. If you do remember anything new, you'll be sure to call me?"

"Absolutely."

"Excellent," he said, and stood up. "Well, until then."

I stood up and shook his hand, my mind already racing with

the possibilities. Was this new killer connected to Crowley, and through him, to me? Was it Crowley himself, back from the dead? Or was it something completely new? At the same time, Mr. Monster was thinking as well, sorting through the facts and building a plan; where I saw a danger, Mr. Monster saw a rival. I'd killed the last killer that came to Clayton, and Mr. Monster wanted more.

4

In my dreams they hunted me, not with guns or knives or claws but with sheets of paper, thin and immaterial, which passed from person to person like a virus. It started with Agent Forman, who waved the paper in my face and I knew, through the iron logic of dreams, that it was my arrest warrant, my conviction, and my death sentence all in one. I turned to run but there was Sheriff Meier, waving the same paper, and beside him were Rob Anders and Brooke, each with a paper of their own. I ran out and found Max, my sister, my aunt, and even my mom—the whole town behind them— all advancing on me slowly with their intangible, invincible papers. They weren't angry, they weren't sad, they were . . . disillusioned, perhaps. Betrayed.

I did it for them, and now they were going to kill me.

I never slept much, but after my meeting with Forman I began sleeping even less. Mom and I would watch the news, hearing arguments and speculation and no real information about the new corpse, and then she would go to sleep and I'd stay up to watch a talk show or a late movie, and then when there was nothing tolerable left on TV I drifted into my room and read—books, magazines, anything I could find to keep my mind active, because as soon as I drifted off, I relinquished control, and something inside took over. Something deep and dark.

Because when I wasn't using my mind, Mr. Monster was.

Mr. Monster's thoughts were like the grating background static of my own thoughts. When there was something else to drown them out they were just a low buzz, but as my other distractions faded their static grew louder, harsher, and more chaotic. Random white noise devolved into nightmare shapes and sounds, bodies and limbs and screams that never let me rest. At three or sometimes four in the morning I'd surrender to them, hoping to get at least a little rest, however fitful, before Mom woke me up at six-thirty and I started a new day. During those few hours Mr. Monster reigned, and I was a captive audience to his thrashing horrors.

The police kept a tight lid on their investigation, revealing virtually nothing about the autopsy results. If there was a stolen body part to link this victim to another demon, I didn't know. I was desperate for facts, but there were none to be had.

I'd have to go back to the warehouse soon. I really needed to burn something.

"Calm down," said Margaret, chopping lettuce in the kitchen. She was my mom's twin sister, and her partner in the mortuary. "You act like you haven't seen her in years."

"I barely have," said Mom, tweaking the placement of a fork on the table. "Not socially, I mean—the mortuary doesn't count, we barely talk."

It was Mother's Day, and my sister was coming. This was a big deal, because she never came to anything. I'd even baked a cake.

I'd taken up cooking as one of my many hobbies designed to occupy my mind and keep Mr. Monster down. Mom was a big fan of the Food Network, and I was a big fan of food, so one day when I was daydreaming about corpses and trying to clear my head I happened to catch a special on chocolate chip cookies, and decided to follow along. It grew pretty quickly from there, and soon I was making all kinds of food for every different meal. Mom wasn't much of a chef anyway, so she didn't mind.

The cake was already done and cooling on the counter, so I was browsing through the paper. I noted with pleasure that Karla Soder had been admitted to the hospital for extended care; she was one of the oldest people in Clayton, and I'd been waiting for her to die for a while now. We hadn't embalmed anybody in more than a month.

"Lauren was here at Christmas," said Margaret, laying out silverware, "and our birthday."

"She got here half an hour late for the birthday party and left early," said Mom. "Of course *you're* not nervous—she likes you. Do you have any idea what it's like to be estranged from your own daughter?"

"Just don't overdo it," said Margaret, placing the lettuce onto salad plates. "Don't try to be her mother, just be her friend. Work your way up from there."

"Maybe she *needs* a mother," said Mom, garnishing each lettuce pile with a wedge of tomato. "I don't even know what she does outside of work."

A knock sounded from the door, and the two women froze. I shifted on the couch to get a better view of the door.

"Come on in," said Mom, "it's unlocked."

The door opened and Lauren walked in, smiling bigger than I'd seen in a long time. Mom grinned back, wide-eyed, as if she didn't know what was so wonderful but wasn't willing to let it slip by uncelebrated.

"Guess what?" said Lauren, practically dancing. Mom shook her head in a daze, and Lauren gestured at the open doorway. I could hear someone waiting just outside. "I brought someone for you to meet. Please say hello to my boyfriend, Curt."

A huge man barreled through the doorway and swept Lauren up in a massive hug. He twirled her around while she shrieked, then set her down and grinned wolfishly at Mom and Margaret. He was tall and wide, like a football player, with short sandy hair and a rough swath of sandy five o'clock shadow.

I hated him instantly.

"Lauren wanted to surprise you," he said, "so I figured I may as well make it exciting. Holy hell, you really are twins." He looked back and forth from Mom to Margaret, sizing them up, then laughed loudly. "I give up. Which one's Mom?"

Mom stepped forward, trying to get her bearings, and extended her hand. "That would be me," she said. "It's very nice to meet you . . ." She trailed off, not remembering his name.

"Curt," said Curt, "with a C, like Curtis, but I'll smack anyone who calls me that." He laughed again, gregarious and authoritative. This was a man who was accustomed to being the center of attention.

Mom's face had become a mask—stiff and smiling, which meant she was upset and trying to conceal it. I glanced at Lauren to see if she saw the same thing, but she was too busy smiling at Curt. I looked back at Mom and saw her walk stiffly to the table.

"This is such a surprise," she said. "We'll have to . . . set another place. Margaret, could you get another plate, please?" While they shifted the table around, trying to find the best place for a fifth person, Lauren finally noticed me.

"John!" she said, grabbing Curt by the shoulder and turning him to face the living room. He resisted the pull, delaying just long enough to make it obvious it was his own choice to turn, and not Lauren's. "Curt, this is my little brother, John. You've heard me talk about him."

"Nothing good," said Curt, and winked at me. I stared back, not certain what to say.

"Whoa, we got a shy one here," said Curt, laughing. "Don't worry, sport, I don't bite . . . hard." He laughed again, and elbowed Lauren a little harder than was strictly necessary. My reflexes kicked in and I started searching for something to compliment him on.

"That's a very nice shirt," said Mom, and I shot her a stunned look. She glanced back at me, shrugged, and turned back to her work. "John, honey, can you grab the folding chair by my computer?" I retrieved the chair from her bedroom while Curt loudly proclaimed the merits of his shirt.

I took the folding chair into the kitchen and set it up next to Lauren's seat, leaving that side of the table just slightly crowded with two chairs. Curt, not even looking at me, sat down at the head of the table, on Lauren's other side. I glowered and sat in the folding chair myself; it was an inch or so lower than the kitchen chairs, and I felt short and awkward.

Every rule I had seemed to cry out to me to do something—compliment him, shake his hand, show him how normal I was—but I couldn't bring myself to do it. Something about him made me so mad, but I couldn't figure out what it was. He was rude and loud and boorish, certainly, but I knew a lot of people like that, and I could talk to them just fine. Why was Curt different? His comment that I was too shy to talk burned in my ears, but I didn't correct him; if he thought I was shy he might leave me alone, and I could ignore him.

Ignoring him proved even more difficult than speaking to him, because he barely ever stopped talking.

"I can't believe I'm still driving around in that old piece of junk," he said, jerking his thumb in the general direction of the curb and shaking his head. "It was a nice enough truck when I bought it, but it's ancient now—I'm embarrassed to be seen in it."

"It's only four years old," said Lauren, "and it's gorgeous."

"It might be good enough for you," he said, "but you haven't seen the new ones. I know it's Japanese, but that new model truck they've got at the lot makes this one look like a piece of crap. It's like a luxury car in there—driver-side memory settings that adjust the seat and the steering wheel and the mirrors automatically, so I wouldn't have to fix it all myself every time Shorty here drives it."

He waved at Lauren with a smile. Lauren laughed at the

comment, and Margaret seemed to be listening closely, but Mom was still at the counter carefully rearranging our four salads across five plates. I watched as she placed each leaf of lettuce slowly, deliberately, not stalling for time but honestly trying to make each salad the best it could be. Her mouth was a thin, frozen smile; she was determined to make this dinner work.

"The seats are all leather, and they're heated," said Curt, "and the stereo system has Bluetooth—standard, not optional—"

"Your seats are leather," said Lauren.

"But not heated," said Curt. He looked at me. "She wouldn't know a nice car if it bit her, eh sport?"

Mom brought the reapportioned salads to the table, passing them out and then sitting down next to me—and as far from Curt as possible. It was the only seat left, of course, but I could tell by the way she sat subtly sideways, focusing on Lauren instead of on him, that she was grateful for the distance.

"Eat up," she said. "The chicken's ready to eat as soon as we're done with the salads."

"Lauren didn't cook it, did she?" asked Curt, grinning like a cat. Lauren smiled and shook her head. "She's beautiful," he said, "but she can't cook to save her life."

Mom set down her fork abruptly, staring at Curt. "That's no way to talk about your girlfriend."

"Hey, I'm just calling it like I see it," said Curt, stabbing another piece of lettuce and shaking his head dismissively. He'd already moved on; if he'd noticed how upset Mom was, he didn't show it.

Mom started to talk again, jumping into the empty space

while Curt chewed, but Margaret caught her eye and shook her head almost imperceptibly. Mom and Margaret could communicate completely wordlessly sometimes, after knowing each other for so long. Mom stared back, her nostrils flared, and I could tell she was mad. Lauren, when I glanced at her, was looking at Curt and ignoring the two women altogether.

"Course, she can do a damn fine bag of popcorn," said Curt with a smile. "It's just anything with a stove that gives her trouble."

"You remember how bad I am with baking," said Lauren. "Remember that time I tried to make brownies in junior high, and they ended up burned on the edges and raw in the middle?"

"Yep, she still does that," said Curt, picking up his water glass and taking a long drink. I found it fascinating the way he responded to her in the third person, answering her comments directly but without addressing her or looking at her—or at anyone else, for that matter. He wasn't talking to us, singly or as a group, he was simply talking, and we were the nearest audience. Mr. Monster perked up his ears, shifting restlessly inside my mind. He wanted to crush this blowhard's veneer of security and confidence and make him cry in terror; he wanted to make him beg for mercy.

I retreated deeper into myself, forcing myself to ignore Curt and the dinner. I thought about Agent Forman instead, wondering what his plan was; was he focused on me as a suspect, or did he have others? Was he even suspicious at all, or just trying to scare me into divulging some other information? Nothing that incriminated me, maybe, but something that might give him a clue he'd missed so far. There were unanswered questions galore in this case, and I knew they must have been bugging him more and more as time went on. How long had Mrs. Crowley been tied up? Could the same person have done that *and* killed Dr. Neblin? Why had Mr. Crowley's body never been found, when all of the previous killings had left behind a dismembered corpse? Even if Forman didn't suspect that I did it, he must have suspected I knew more than I was telling.

"Actually," said Mom, "John baked the cake."

I looked up and saw all four people looking at me. How much had I missed?

"Jim?" said Curt.

"John," said Mom, Margaret, and Lauren in unison.

I nodded.

"Well I'll be damned," said Curt. "Home Ec assignment or something?"

"He does most of the baking around here," said Mom. "He's really very good, and he loves to do it."

"Baking," said Curt, balling his fist in a show of mock solidarity. "It's a manly pursuit."

"It is," said Lauren. It was the first time I'd heard her take a defiant tone with Curt. "I wish you'd cook for me sometime."

"That's because there's no good restaurants in this podunk town," said Curt.

"And," insisted Lauren, "it's because women appreciate it when men take time to do things for them."

"I bought you that pair of shoes," said Curt.

"I *love* those shoes," said Lauren, rolling her head back in ecstasy.

"I hope so," said Curt with a laugh, "they were expensive."

"We're going to have girls beating down our door once they find out how well John cooks," said Mom, getting up to clear the salad plates.

"Well, bring it on," said Curt, spreading his arms. "Guy food's usually better anyway, right? No whining about calories and fat and crap like that—just great big piles of the good stuff." He looked at the counter and sniffed deeply. "He make the chicken too?"

Mom and I looked at each other, suddenly wary of what to say. I'd stopped cooking meat six weeks ago because it ruined the whole point—instead of getting my mind off of dead bodies, it made me think of them more and more, chopping up soft red meat with a cleaver and squishing my fingers into bloody mounds of ground beef. I'd stopped eating meat altogether.

"John's a vegetarian," said Mom.

I didn't really think of it in those terms; "vegetarian" seems so much more zealous than "doesn't eat meat." I didn't think meat was murder or anything, I just . . . well, actually I guess I did. For me, anyway. But how many other vegetarians fantasized about murdering their own meat?

"A vegetarian!" cried Curt. "What on Earth would possess a sane man to do that?"

It's so I don't hurt idiots like you, I thought.

"He bakes the desserts and I do most of the meals," said Mom, serving chicken breasts from a baking pan one by one onto plates at the counter. "I barely eat meat anymore these days, either, just because it's easier than making two meals, but I still like it for special occasions." She gave each plate a scoop of rice and placed them two-by-two on the table; the last to come was mine, the meat replaced by a lentil soup I'd really started to like.

"Dude," said Curt, leaning seriously over the table. He was staring at me intently. "That's not even food. That's what food eats." He burst into laughter at his own joke, and Lauren laughed along. Margaret smiled politely, and I could see now from the way she smiled—curling the edges of her lips, but without moving a muscle around her eyes—that her close attention was all an act, and she really didn't care about anything Curt said. I smiled, and ate a piece of broccoli.

"Seriously, though," said Curt, glancing at Lauren. "Maybe you ought to be eating the same as him; you're never going to fit your skinny jeans if you keep eating like this."

"Honestly!" said Mom, slamming down her fork again. "Who talks like that?"

"It's true!" said Lauren, "I haven't fit my skinny jeans in months—Curt's never even seen me in them."

"That's no excuse for talking to you that way," said Mom.

"I don't need an excuse when it's true," said Curt. I could see from the way he was grinning that he thought he'd said something funny; a joke to cut the tension. Amazing—even *I* knew that was a stupid thing to say.

"She's sitting right here," said Mom, gesturing to Lauren. "Show a little courtesy, for crying out loud!"

"I knew this was going to happen," said Lauren, closing her eyes. "Dammit, Mom, why can't you be civil for one meal? For even half a meal? We've only been here twenty minutes."

"I'm the one who's not being civil?" said Mom. "He hasn't stopped insulting you since you got here."

"Oh come on!" said Lauren, throwing down her napkin and

standing up. "He's trying to liven this place up! The rest of you are dead in here—John hasn't said word one the entire time!"

That's not because I'm dead, it's because I'm smart.

"She told me you two didn't get along," said Curt, glaring at Mom, "but I had no idea how bad she had it."

"Amazing," said Mom, folding her arms and staring at Lauren. "He's the most sensitive man in the world. Where did you find such a catch?"

"Don't you dare talk to me about choosing men," said Lauren, jabbing her finger at Mom. "Don't you dare tell me you're some kind of expert at the dumbest thing you ever did!"

"I don't have to take this," said Curt, standing, "and neither do you." He took Lauren by the elbow and herded her to the door.

"Don't you walk away from me!" shouted Mom.

"Why on Earth would I stay?" shouted Lauren. She broke away from Curt's grip and stomped back to the table. "You have been cutting me down my entire life, like I'm some kind of . . . what do you even think of me? Can I make any good decisions at all? Am I just a . . . mistake machine that spits out stupid all day?"

Mom folded her arms. "How am I supposed to talk to you when you take that attitude?"

"You talking to me is the *last* thing I need," said Lauren. Curt took her elbow again and guided her to the door, ominously quiet now that the two women were fighting. This time Lauren didn't break away, and he led her outside and closed the door behind him.

"Come back here!" shouted Mom, then whirled around and slammed the palm of her hand as hard as she could into the door of a cupboard. "Not again," she sobbed. "I've lost her again." She hid her face in her hands, leaning against the cupboard, and cried.

5

It was nearly six hours later when Mom finally went to bed and I slipped out of the house, pedaling my bike in a beeline for the old warehouse. She'd spent the afternoon sobbing and talking to Margaret, going over the situation a thousand times: Lauren was right, Lauren was wrong, Lauren was making a huge mistake, Mom had made a huge mistake, and on and on and on. I hid in my room and pulled my ski mask down to cover my ears and muffle the noise.

It was just like the old days, when everyone fought and everyone cried and everyone walked out of our lives as fast as they could go. Just like the old days but worse—I had Forman trying to get inside my head, and Mr. Monster desperate to claw his way out. I didn't know how far I could stretch before I snapped. Plans seemed to form themselves in my mind: how to find out where Curt lived; how to incapacitate him; how to cut him, slowly and carefully, in order to cause the most pain I could possibly cause. I started pacing the room and singing snatches of whatever music I could remember—old songs my dad used to listen to, new stuff Brooke played on the radio in the mornings—anything to fill my mind and keep my thoughts as far from death as possible. Nothing worked.

It was the *need*—the desperate urge that built up inside of a serial killer and drove him to kill. What was it? Where did it come from? I had always been able to control my dark side before, keeping it locked up for years, but it was stronger now. I'd killed the demon, and Mr. Monster had gotten his first taste of death, and now he wanted more. Could I still control it? How strong would it get? How intense would the need get before it exploded and killed somebody else—my mom, or Margaret, or Brooke?

I paced back and forth in my bedroom, feeling caged; the slats of my blinds were like bars, and looking out between them I could see Mr. Crowley's house, large and dark. How many nights had I spent creeping around the walls, peeking in the windows, studying my prey? I missed that part of my life— I physically missed it, like a severed limb that still itched intrusively. Couldn't I do it again? But Crowley had been a demon, not a person; it was okay to stalk him because it was all for the greater good. I had weighed the implications carefully, and I had made my decision, and now I couldn't justify that kind of behavior for anything less.

But what if there *was* a new demon?

It was foolish to assume that Crowley was the only one, but it was also foolish to assume that they all worked in the same way. The new body didn't have any pieces missing, but it did have dozens of minor wounds and a single huge wound on its foot. Was there some kind of new supernatural menace that needed to electrocute people to stay alive? And did the fact that the victim was a woman suggest, somehow, that the demon was also a woman?

But no—just as I was misleading myself by assuming that the demons' methods would all be the same, I couldn't assume that their motives would be the same. Mr. Crowley had killed men who matched his own physique because he needed to replace pieces of his own body. It was about survival. The new demon might be killing for food, for sport, for personal expression; there were any number of reasons. Just like me, the demon would have a need—some kind of emotional hole that needed to be filled.

How could I discover the demon's need if I didn't even know my own?

I thought about Curt again, and how satisfying it would be to electrocute him, like the dead woman had been electrocuted—watching him scream and writhe until the charge had burned a massive crater in his flesh. I shook my head to clear the thought. I couldn't go on like this. I needed to burn something.

It was time to visit the warehouse again.

On my way out of the house I grabbed some chicken from the fridge—no one had finished their dinner, after all—and sealed it in a plastic bag and shoved it into my coat pocket. That cat wouldn't stop me this time.

It was just after midnight, and dark enough to make my bike a bad idea, but the car would make noise; it might wake up Mom, and it would definitely make me easier to trace if the arson was investigated. I rode my bike through the darkened streets for nearly a mile, then got down and walked along the uneven trail through the trees, feeling my way through the dark patches where the moon couldn't penetrate. The tank of gas sloshed in my hand.

The fire was calling to me.

The warehouse reflected bright gray moonlight from its cinder block walls, shining dully in the clearing. I was grinning now. This was the time when the lines inside of me blurred, and Mr. Monster became simply John Cleaver: not a killer but a boy; not a monster but a human being. Fire was my great catharsis, but this prelude moment was my purest freedom—the one brief respite when I didn't have to worry about what Mr. Monster wanted to do, because he and I wanted the same thing. Once I'd made my decision to light a fire, I wasn't at war with myself anymore; I was just me, and everything made sense.

The cat greeted me with a silent stare, perched in the sill of a shattered window that granted him a lordly view of his entire domain, both inside and out. I dropped my bike by the trees and walked forward quietly, pulling out the chicken and tearing off a small piece. The fibers separated cleanly, layers of cooked muscle peeling away from each other in easy strips. I reached up to the window and waved the chicken as close to the cat as I could, letting him smell the meat, then dropped the torn-off piece on the ground and tossed the rest several feet away. The cat's eyes tracked the meat as it arced through the air. He focused on it like a laser. I slipped into the warehouse through the empty doorway.

When I glanced up at the window again the cat was still there, and it turned to look at me as I came through the door. It watched me for a moment, then turned back to stare at the meat outside. *That's right,* I thought, *go and get it.*

I pulled the old mattress out from behind the stack of pallets. It was thick and musty, covered with dirt and animal tracks, and the bottom was damp; the smell when I flipped it over was a slow, moldy cloud. I flipped it back, dry side up, then thought better of it and flipped it back over again. I could use some of these other pieces, like the wooden pallets, to prop up the mattress and create an oven underneath it. The dry bottom side would catch quickly and help dry out the top, and the smoke from the wet patches would escape into the air without suffocating the flames below.

The cat was still perched in the window, watching me with interest. I stopped moving, trying to make myself as uninteresting as possible, and stared back at it. It didn't move.

I waited a moment longer, but the cat stayed still. I started gathering material for my oven; the cat had to move sooner or later.

Along one wall of the warehouse there was a row of metal barrels, though as near as I could tell they were all empty. They weren't flammable, and they didn't contain any flammable chemicals, so I ignored them and moved on. The far corner held a pile of paint cans, and more were placed around the rest of the room seemingly at random. On previous visits I'd managed to catalog them all: most were latex paint, which wouldn't burn, but there was a nice stack of white enamel paints that would go up like rocket fuel. I used my keys to lever one can open, and smiled at the acrid puff of alcohol that rose up from inside. The paint was old—several decades, probably—and the pigment had settled out and congealed on the bottom, leaving a thick alcoholic soup on top. I hauled the cans over to the center of the room, two at a time, dreaming about the massive blaze I would create.

The cat was still in the window, watching me. I frowned. I went outside and found the chicken breast, untouched in the scrub and gravel. The little piece I'd torn off was untouched as well. I picked it up and held it out to the cat.

"Don't you want it?"

It stared at me.

"It's food, cat, don't you eat food?" I had to stop myself from calling it a name—any abuse, even verbal, was against the rules. I tossed the food up in front of it, letting it arc right in front of the cat's face and then fall back to the ground. "Get out of the window."

My chest felt tighter, and I took a deep breath. *Don't freak out*, I told myself, *it's still okay. You can still have your fire. The cat will go away and everything will be fine.* I was breathing more heavily now, and squinted my eyes harshly against . . . I don't know what. I just needed to squint them, two, three, four times in a row. I walked back inside quickly, casting around for something to do. Wood! There was some wood in the center; I could stack it up.

The construction company that used to own this place had left behind several boards and planks, two by fours and one by eights, and over twenty-something years of seasonal cycles the wood had grown warped. Some were slightly curved, other were bloated, and some had cracked and split. Past visitors had moved some of them around, restacking them or simply knocking them over, but most were still stacked in their original piles. To build my oven I grabbed three of the one by eights and propped them up on six open cans of enamel paint—the paint wouldn't do much until the fire got really big, but when the flame finally reached them they'd flare up spectacularly. I arranged these in neat rows and laid the mattress over the top, working so quickly that I knocked all the boards off the cans the first time I tried to lift it. The cat, still sitting in the window, was making me too nervous. I needed to calm down. I reset the boards and then raised the mattress more carefully, dry side down, before setting it on top of the boards. The mattress was wetter than I thought, soaked through, and I ran my hand through my hair uneasily. After a moment I simply picked up my gas can and poured some over the top of the mattress. It wasn't the most elegant solution, but it was probably the simplest.

The cat was still there. I dropped the gas can and kicked a stack of two by fours. "Get out!" The noise echoed through the empty room, and the cat hissed and arched its back aggressively.

I squeezed my eyes shut again, feeling sick. "I'm sorry, I'm sorry, I'm sorry." I took a few steps, then turned and stepped back, pacing erratic patterns in the dirty floor. I turned back to the cat and looked it straight in the eyes. "I'm not going to hurt you," I said. "I'm not going to let anything hurt you." I paused. "Maybe I can help—maybe you just don't know what to do."

I could climb up and carry the cat out myself—gently—but I'd need something to stand on. I ran to the metal barrels and grabbed one by the top rim; even empty it was still heavy, and I braced myself against the wall to tip it over. It hit the floor with a hollow clang, and I rolled it impatiently to the other side of the room, navigating carefully around the piles of wood and cans and garbage that filled the warehouse.

"I'm not going to hurt you," I repeated, rolling the barrel,

"I'm just going to help you. I'm going to take you somewhere safe."

I pushed away a couple of pallets leaning against the wall under the window, and maneuvered the barrel into place. It seemed nearly impossible to stand it back up, but I steadied it against the wall and got my hands under it, heaving it up into place. The cat watched everything impassively.

I carefully climbed on top of the barrel, standing up slowly from a crouch. When I drew close to the cat it hissed again, baring its fangs and staring me down. I paused, trying to reassure it.

"Don't be scared. I'm just going to pick you up, very gently, and take you outside." I stood up straighter and it hissed a third time, louder. "Listen, this whole place is about to be on fire, and you don't want to be here. You don't understand fire, but it's very scary. It's very bad."

I straightened further and the cat arched its back, hair standing on end. Standing this close I could see the familiar lines of a housecat in its face, but there was something deeper; traces of leopard and tiger burned through from inside, reawakened remnants of the cat's primal ancestry. Wherever the cat had come from, whatever civilization it may once have had, it was all gone now. The creature threatening me was a wild, dangerous animal.

I held myself motionless, peering into its face like a well of memory. It hissed again, crouching on its forelegs in preparation to pounce.

I backed away.

I shouldn't be doing this. I allowed myself to break one rule—to burn things when I needed the release—but this was going too far. I couldn't break any of my other rules, and if I touched this cat it would attack me, and I'd fight back, and by hurting it I'd be breaking my biggest rule of all. I couldn't do it, and I was going to stop.

I jumped down from the barrel, edgy and drained. I felt light-headed, and sat down on a stack of boards to catch my breath. I wasn't going to hurt anything.

I wasn't going to burn anything.

My tension was still there—my rage, my fear, my desperation—but I couldn't let it out. Not like this. This was too loose and uncontrolled; I think somewhere, deep down, I'd *wanted* to provoke the cat to attack so I'd have an excuse to hurt it. But I would not allow myself to hurt it.

Trying to release my tension in safe, little doses like this was becoming too dangerous; there had to be a better way. But bottling it up, never to be released at all, wasn't working either, and I definitely couldn't just pull out the stops and let it run uncontrolled. There had to be a middle ground.

What I needed was another demon.

I'd never been as comfortable as I had been over the winter, hunting the demon that stalked my town. I'd had focus and direction; I'd had a purpose that gave everything meaning. I'd been able to let Mr. Monster out, and because of that, I'd been able to live at peace with myself for the first time in years. Now that the demon was gone, my psychological outlet was gone, too.

I walked out of the warehouse slowly, breathing in a controlled, steady rhythm. We had another victim, but no killer to hunt; it was not a demon, it was not a serial killer, it was just a drunk husband or a jealous boyfriend . . .

A jealous boyfriend. Forman had said that the body was

covered in small wounds—stabs and scrapes and burns and blisters and who knew what else. An angry, jealous boyfriend could have done that easily; an angry, jealous boyfriend who had no respect for women and, as such, treated them like dirt. A man like that would have no qualms about inflicting that kind of pain on a woman.

And I knew exactly where to find a man like that.

It was a long shot, I knew, but it was something. It was a clear, attainable goal: to follow a man who *might* be the killer to determine if he really was. I could live the way I had before; I could serve Mr. Monster's needs without endangering my own.

It was time to get to know Curt much, much better.

6

The victim was eventually identified as Victoria Chatham. Since she hadn't come to us for embalming, there was no chance to examine the body or study the wounds. That left me no direct way of learning more about the man who had inflicted those wounds, so my study of the killer would have to begin elsewhere.

And since I was stuck in school for a few more weeks, "elsewhere" meant a lopsided conversation with Max in the lunch room.

"The central question of criminal profiling," I said, "is 'what does the killer do that he doesn't have to do?'"

"Oh please, not again," said Max, rolling his eyes.

"This really works," I insisted. "And it works better to have someone else to bounce ideas off of. You were really helpful last time."

"If I was so helpful, why didn't you catch the bad guy?"

Actually, I did.

"The FBI agent at the police station called me in and showed me the crime scene photos before they went public," I said. "He asked for my help."

"Shut up."

"No, seriously."

"John, we are two tables away from three incredibly hot girls in incredibly short shorts, and I *so* don't have time for another analytical conversation with you."

I closed my eyes. Brooke was sitting just two tables down with two of her friends, Marci and Rachel, but I'd already used up my one allowed lunchtime conversation and my two allowed lunchtime looks. Brooke had her hair up in a ponytail, tied with some kind of pink ribbon or elastic. She was wearing a pink T-shirt with white stripes, and a pair of jean shorts that showed off her long, slender legs. I wasn't even allowed to think about her anymore, which was the whole point of analyzing the killer instead.

My fingers itched to burn something.

"The body was covered with wounds," I said. "They said it on the news and I saw it in the photo. The killer hurt her before he killed her; he tortured her. Why would he do that?"

"I don't know," said Max, "you're the scary weirdo. Why would *you* do that?"

"That's insulting, but yes, putting ourselves into his place is more or less what we're doing here."

"I'm serious," said Max. "If you were going to kill someone that way, which I'm not entirely ruling out, why would you do it?"

This is better than nothing. "Because I want something," I said, "and killing her, in that manner, would help me get it."

"So what do you want?"

"I don't know what I want," I said. "That's the whole thing we're trying to figure out. We have to work backward."

"Okay," said Max, looking at the ceiling and waving his hands slowly. "What do you . . . get, when you . . . kill someone in a way that . . . gets you whatever it is that you want?"

"What do I gain by killing someone in this way," I said.

"That's what I said."

"I gain . . . satisfaction."

"That's really sick," said Max.

"It's not really me. The killer gains satisfaction."

"It's still sick," said Max. "What else?"

"The killer gains revenge. The killer gains power."

"The killer gains peace and quiet," said Max.

"Probably not," I said. "If all you want to do is shut someone up, there are easier ways to do it than torturing them to death."

"What if it's someone who's been nagging you your whole life, and you just can't stand it anymore, and you want to make them suffer for it before they die? Then your reward is peace and quiet."

"Actually," I said, "in that case your reward would be power, revenge, and satisfaction. You'd be taking control of your life, and getting revenge on the person who'd taken it away from you."

"And when you're done with all that," said Max, "you'd have peace and quiet. I'm telling you, it keeps coming back to that."

"Does it, though?" I asked. "If I want peace and quiet, the last thing I'm going to do is dump a dead body in the middle of an ongoing serial killer investigation. This death is going to get more coverage, more attention, and a lot more investigation than any other dead body in any other nowhere town."

"All right already," said Max. "I give up, I don't get peace and quiet. I get the exact opposite of peace and quiet; I get . . . war and noise. I get a noisy war; I'm a terrorist."

Pieces clicked together in my mind. "Maybe you are," I said, leaning forward eagerly. "I mean, not a standard terrorist, but it's the same general idea—you use violence to get attention."

"So I'm a four-year-old?"

"You're doing this on purpose," I said, "because you want people to notice you. You kill someone in a weird way, leave them in an obvious place, and that's how you get your message out."

"Why is this suddenly me instead of you?"

"Me then. Whatever. The killer. The killer is trying to say something. 'I hate women,' or 'I'm better than you,' or something like that."

" 'I can do whatever I want.' "

"Exactly."

Max took a bite of his sandwich. "So who's he talking to?"

"I . . . don't know. Everyone, I guess. The police. The FBI. We have an agent in from out of town who does this for a living, he might be talking to him."

"What if it's the Clayton Killer?"

"The methods are completely different," I said.

"No, I mean what if he's talking to the Clayton Killer?"

I stared back. The Clayton Killer was dead, but Max didn't know that. Nobody did. Including the new killer.

What if this was one killer's way of saying "Hi, I'm new in town?" to another?

"Holy crap, here she comes," said Max.

"Who?" I looked up sharply and saw Brooke coming straight toward us. That was three looks during lunch; I wasn't allowed that many. I had to follow my rules as strictly as I could, even if she initiated it. They were my first and last defense against Mr. Monster, and if I could do anything I wanted, then so could he. I couldn't let that happen.

"If she asks what we're talking about," said Max, "please say cars."

Brooke stepped up to the table. "Hey John."

"Hey." I wasn't allowed to talk to her again during lunch either, after saying 'hi' on the way into the lunch room.

"You have English next?" she asked.

"Yeah." I tried to be as polite as I could, watching the wall behind her, looking just to the right of her face.

"Mrs. Barlow said we're starting the same new unit as your class," Brooke said. "*Beowulf* and *Grendel*."

"Yeah," I said, hoping for the conversation to end. Then, desperate not to seem rude, I added, "They sound really interesting." I gritted my teeth. *I shouldn't have said that.*

"They do," said Brooke. I could see in my peripheral vision that she was smiling. I glanced down at the table, then back up at the space just beyond her other shoulder.

"I think it would be great to talk about it," she said, "you know, like in the car and stuff. Since we're there everyday anyway."

"Sure," I said. I wasn't supposed to contribute to the conversation, but . . . what else could I do? "That would help a lot in class, since we're in different classes."

"Exactly," said Brooke. "We can share all the brilliant insights from each other's classes, and then sound like geniuses in our own."

I looked down at the table again. "Yeah." *Please leave.*

"Great!" she said. "I guess I'll see you in the car?"

"Yeah."

"All right, see you there!" She walked away. *Finally.*

Max stared as she walked away. "Goodbye, beautiful butt. I'll miss you." He turned back to me and clapped his hands silently. "Effing brilliant, by the way. I'd never picked you for that kind of romantic subtlety."

"What are you talking about?" I said, shaking my head. It felt prickly and wrong, like it was caught in a spiderweb.

"Brushing her off like that," said Max. "If the second-hottest girl in school walked up to me, wearing those shorts and begging to be my study partner, there's not a chance in hell I could have played it so cool. I don't think anyone in school could have played it that cool."

" 'The *second* hottest girl?' "

"She's no Marci," said Max. "But seriously: I'm very impressed. You've got her wrapped around your finger."

"I don't know what you're talking about," I said.

"Don't be modest, dude, it's a great plan." Max leaned back and gestured broadly with both hands. "You give her just enough attention to show what a nice guy you are, and then you back off and let her fill in the blanks herself. It's really starting to work; the 'hard to get' thing is paying off."

"That's not what that was."

"Oh come on," said Max. "You think nobody notices? You drive her to school every morning, you gaze longingly as she walks away, and then you practically avoid her the rest of the day. Yesterday at lunch you walked up to her, chatted about her *shoes*, of all things, and then just one period later you walked right past her in the hall and pretended not to notice when she smiled at you."

That was the break between fifth and sixth period; English and math. She had a class right on my path from one to the other, so I usually walked around the other hallway to avoid her. That day I'd been held up talking to the teacher and didn't have time, so I walked straight down the hall staring at the floor, just so I wouldn't see her.

And apparently she liked this? How could I ever hope to understand people?

It had to stop. I couldn't let her get any closer to me than she was now; not like this. Mr. Monster wanted her so much it hurt.

"It doesn't mean anything," I said. "She's just the girl I drive to school, nothing more."

"Are you kidding me?" asked Max. "I think even people in other countries can tell you're in love with her."

"I spend too much time with her already."

"What does that mean?" Max asked. "She's a fox, man. When I say that she's the second hottest girl in school, I assure you that I have devoted a *lot* of time to a detailed comparison. You need to get over yourself and ask her out."

I stared at him. "Are you crazy?"

"No," said Max, "You're crazy. I actually think you're playing hard to get a little too well. She probably would have asked you out herself by now if you made yourself a little more available."

"Why do you say that?"

"Because I pay attention," said Max. "She is, as mentioned, very hot. And when you're busily ignoring her she sends a lot of interested glances in your direction. I think she finds you mysterious, though I'm starting to think you're just a clueless idiot."

I didn't need this. I had enough trouble keeping Mr. Monster under control—living through his fantasies at night, and then spending my days building a cage of rules and behavior patterns to keep those fantasies from becoming reality. He wanted to hurt people, sometimes very badly, and the things he'd planned for Brooke were almost too horrific to think about. He wanted to possess her, wholly and completely, and he couldn't do that until she was dead. It was all I could do to look at her and smile with this black pit of intent roiling inside me. And now here was my friend, my only friend, telling me I should focus on her even more—spend more time with her, think about her more often, and do more things to attract her to me.

Something had to change, and soon, or nobody around me would be safe.

7

For my sixteenth birthday I got a dead body to play with: Mrs. Soder, the oldest woman in Clayton County, finally died. The corpse was laid out on the stainless steel embalming table, the body bag removed and the body motionless. It had died in the hospital, and they'd shipped it to us in a hospital gown. This made it a lot easier; rather than wrestle with real clothes, or try to get the family's permission to cut them off, we could just snip a tie here and there and have the hospital gown off in seconds. The embalming would be almost too easy—I wanted to take as much time as possible, so I could really enjoy it.

Mom was in the office, signing some papers with Ron, the coroner, and Margaret wasn't here yet. Lauren was technically our office assistant, but she still wasn't speaking to Mom and, naturally, wasn't here either.

All the more time for me.

I touched its hair, long and white and very fine, like cornsilk. Mrs. Soder had been nearly a hundred years old when she died, and the body curved oddly on the table thanks to the old-age hump in its spine. The first thing you do with a body, naturally, is to make sure it's dead: it's definitely going to be dead by the time you're done with it, so you'd better make sure it's not alive when you start.

We had a small makeup mirror in one of the drawers, and I held it in front of the body's nose. A living body, even in a coma, would start to mist it up with its breath. I counted to twenty as I held the mirror, but nothing happened. It wasn't breathing. I put the mirror back and pulled out a sewing needle, small and sharp but large enough to keep a solid grip on. I poked the body in the fingertip—not deep enough to break the skin, but hard enough to shock the nerves and spark an involuntary reaction. Nothing moved. It was dead.

I pulled over a portable sink, basically just an elevated bucket on wheels, and placed it under the head. Step two in an embalming was to wash the body, and the hair was one of the most important parts because it was one of the most visible. It didn't look like anyone had washed or brushed this body's hair in a while, but that was fine with me. More time for me. We had a small rubber hose hooked up to our stationary sink, and I pulled it over and sprayed it just enough to wet the hair. We didn't have a special shampoo for corpses, just a bottle of the same stuff we used upstairs, and I squeezed a bit onto the upper side of the head, near the forehead. Then I started to brush it through.

"Hey John," said Mom, bustling into the room in green medical scrubs. She had on her flustered face—eyes slightly wide, mouth slightly open, teeth clamped together—but she was moving loosely, almost casually. Sometimes I think she enjoyed being flustered, and acted like it even when she was relaxed. "Sorry to leave you alone so long; Ron had some kind of new state form I'd never seen before."

"That's okay," I said.

Mom paused, turned, and looked at me. "Are you okay?"

"Sure," I said. "I'm just washing its hair."

"Her hair," said Mom, turning back to the counter.

"Her hair," I repeated. "Sorry."

I always called corpses "it," because . . . well, obviously. They're dead. But apparently that kind of thing really bothered normal humans. It was just so hard for me to remember.

"Where's Margaret?" I asked.

"I told her not to bother," said Mom. "This is an easy one—you and I can do it without her, and she can take care of all the service planning with the family."

"Don't you usually do that?"

"Maybe I just want to spend some time with my son," she said, scowling in what I had come to learn was a humorous way. "You ever think of that?"

I looked at her earnestly. "My favorite part of family togetherness is when we aspirate body cavities. What's yours?"

"My favorite part is when you don't talk like a smart aleck," she said, and pulled a bottle of Dis-Spray down from a shelf. "Check for cradle cap. She was in the hospital nearly two weeks, and goodness knows if they washed her hair at all."

I looked at its head—her head—and parted the hair to peer in at the scalp.

"There's some kind of muck in there."

"Cradle cap," said Mom. "It's oil and dead skin cells, and it's a bear to get off. Try this." She stepped over and squirted the area with Dis-Spray. "That should eat through it. Just keep brushing."

I pressed a little harder with the brush, scraping gently at the scum on her scalp. After a few minutes the Dis-Spray started to break it down, and I brushed it out. When I was content that the hair was mostly clean I sprayed it again with water, soaking it more thoroughly this time, and brushing it even more to help rinse it all clean.

I timed my brushes to the beat of my own heart, one stroke per beat. Both were slow and measured; calm for the first time in weeks. Embalming was a job, like any other, but the people who did it for a living each had their own way of going about it. For my dad it had been a form of respect, a way to honor the lives of those who had passed on. For my mom it was service—she got to spend hours helping someone who was truly helpless, and even more time with the family helping to arrange the funeral and the burial and the services that went with each. For both of my parents embalming was a good thing—an almost reverent thing. It was their shared sense of deference for the dead that had brought them together in the first place.

For me, embalming was a form of meditation; it brought a sense of peace that I had never found in any other aspect of my life. I loved the stillness of it, the quietness. The bodies never moved or yelled; they never fought or left. The dead simply lay there, at peace with the world, and let me do whatever I needed to do. I was in control of myself.

I was in control of them.

While I brushed the hair, Mom cut away the hospital gown

and replaced it with a towel for modesty. She washed the limbs and body, and when I finished the hair I pulled out a razor. We shaved the face of every corpse, no matter the age or gender, because even women and children had a bit of peach fuzz here and there. I massaged a dab of shaving gel into the cheeks and upper lip, and gently slid the razor across the skin.

A few minutes later I set the razor down. "I'm done shaving," I said. "Are we ready to set its features?"

"Her features," said Mom.

"Her features," I repeated.

"We go through this every time, John," she said. "You have to think of them as people, not objects. You of all people should recognize how important that is."

"I'm sorry," I said, putting away the shaving things.

"Look at me, John," she said. I turned to look at her. "I'm not kidding about this."

"I'm sorry," I said. "*Her*. Let's set *her* features."

"Don't slip up again," she said, and I nodded.

She had died so recently that *her* body was still stiff from rigor mortis, and before we could arrange *her* face we had to massage *her* body back into mobility. Rigor mortis was caused by a natural buildup of calcium in the muscles; living bodies used that calcium for various things, but in dead bodies it just built up and built up until the muscles grew rigid. In a day or so she'd be loose again from decay, but for now we had to knead the calcium out by hand, stroking and pressing and rubbing the flesh until it was soft and pliable.

Once we could work with her again we started on her features: positioning her head, closing her mouth, and so on. We put tufts of cotton under the eyelids to keep them from looking sunken, and then sealed them closed with cream. We embedded two small hooks in her gums, one behind her upper lip and one on her jaw, and then cinched the mouth closed with a small black string. It was important to place the hooks carefully, and to tie the string just right: too loose and the mouth would flop open; too tight and the nose would look pinched and unnatural. The last thing a family wanted to see at a viewing was their dead grandmother sneering at them from her coffin.

Once the features were set we started the first internal phase of the process, called arterial embalming. While Mom gathered the proper chemicals and mixed them in the pump, I used a scalpel to cut a small hole near the body's collarbone, then used a blunt hook to fish out a pair of slick purple blood vessels. Each was about as wide as a finger, and I cut them open carefully to avoid slicing all the way through. The whole process was very bloodless, since there was no beating heart to provide pressure and pump the blood out. I attached each vessel—one artery and one vein—to a metal tube, then connected the arterial tube to the pump when Mom wheeled it over. The tube in the vein connected to a hose, which we snaked down to a drain in the floor.

Mom turned on the pump and it went to work, pumping in a cocktail of detergents and preservatives and perfumes and dyes, and forcing as much of the old blood as possible down the drain. I looked up at the ventilator fan as it churned steadily overhead.

"I hope the fan doesn't give out on us," I said. Mom laughed. It was an old joke—our old ventilator was so bad, and the embalming chemicals were so toxic, that we used to have to step outside while the pump worked. The fan never actually gave out, but Margaret said the same thing every time. After all the extra business we'd had over the winter, though, Mom and Margaret had invested some of their profits in a new ventilation system. The new fan was high-tech and reliable, but we still had to make the same comment. It was practically a ritual.

Cavity embalming has the same general purpose as arterial embalming: you take the old fluids out and put new fluids in, to kill bacteria and halt decomposition long enough for a viewing and a funeral. But whereas arterial embalming used the body's natural circulatory system to make the job easy, cavity embalming involved a lot of individual organs and unconnected spaces that had to be dealt with one by one. We accomplished this with a tool called a trocar—basically a long, bladed nozzle attached to a vacuum. We used the trocar to puncture a body and suck out the gunk, a process called "aspiration," and then once we'd sucked everything out we cleaned the trocar and attached it to a different tube, so it could drizzle in another chemical cocktail similar to the one we put in the arteries.

A trocar, overall, was a very handy tool. I'd even used one to kill Mr. Crowley.

I hooked up the vacuum hose while Mom added a second modesty towel, rearranging them both to expose the body's abdomen. I put my hand on her stomach, feeling the rough, wrinkled skin, and probed for the right place to insert the trocar. The ideal spot is above the navel, a few inches up and to the right. I braced the skin with my fingers spread, placed the tip of the trocar in the right place, and drove it in—just a little at first, enough to prick the skin and anchor the blade, then deeper into the abdomen, shoving hard to punch through one layer of muscle, then another. A small bloom of red bubbled out of the hole, then sank back in as I thumbed the button and activated the suction. The vacuum wasn't strong enough to suck up an organ, but it would suck out fluids, gasses, and even bits of food in the stomach and intestines. I probed around in the body, listening to the gurgle as the cavity contents trickled up through the hose.

This was good. This was how life was supposed to be: simple, peaceful people doing the things that made them happy. The troubles of the last few weeks seemed to melt away, and I was calm. There was a sense of rightness to the world that made me smile for no reason at all.

I could do this; I really could. Not just the embalming, but life—I felt, in that moment, that I had a handle on it. That I could control it. Even Mr. Monster seemed to fade, until he was so small I almost forgot about him. What had I been so worried about? I was strong, I was in charge of my own mind, and nothing bad was going to happen. I wasn't a threat to anyone.

I thought again about Brooke, and about what Max had said. Maybe he was right—maybe it was time to ask her out. I liked her, and she apparently liked me, so what was the problem? I'd spent years training myself to look and act completely normal. And normal teenagers went on dates. In a way I owed it to myself to go on a date.

I adjusted my hand on the stomach of the corpse, moving the sharp trocar carefully and puncturing another organ. Yes, I would ask Brooke on a date.

In a way, I owed it to her.

———

All night I tried to come up with a plan, and all day at school I wracked my brain for ideas. I had to move carefully, saying the right words at the right time; I decided it was best to wait a few days and come up with something perfect. I am not, as you may have noticed, an impetuous person.

Brooke was silent on the way home from school, which was normally fine, but today it worried me. Was she sad? Was she angry? I checked my blind spot on the next street, stealing a glance at her as I did. The sun lit up her hair like a halo of white gold. What would I do just to touch that hair? The thought terrified me.

A few blocks before our street she spoke up suddenly.

"Do you think the killer's back?" she asked.

"You mean because of the body?" I asked. "I . . . well . . . It doesn't seem like the same killer at all, I mean, the victim is different, the methods are different; you know what they say on the news. It's probably just a random murder."

Brooke tapped her finger on the window, softly. "But what if it is the same guy?" She tapped again. "What would you do?"

"I think I'd. . . . Well, if he was just back, in general terms, I don't know that I'd do much of anything. Not anything different, I mean—just live my life as normal."

"And if he came back here?"

We turned another corner and I glanced at her again, catching a quick look at her face—thin and delicate, eyes intense, mouth closed and thin. She was looking right at me, but what was she thinking? There was some kind of emotion behind those eyes, but what was it? She was a cipher to me. How could I explain what I was thinking if I wasn't even sure how she was perceiving it?

The Crowley's house came into view ahead, lonely and ominous at the end of the street. All the memories came flooding back—a night of darkness and violence, and of victory. "If the Clayton Killer came back here," I said, "and he was attacking someone I knew, then I'd fight back." I was being more honest than I usually allowed myself to be. Why? I glanced at Brooke's face again, involuntarily, and saw her staring back earnestly. She was listening. It was intoxicating. "If it came down to him or us, to kill or be killed, then I'd kill him. If it would save somebody, I'd kill him."

"Huh," said Brooke again.

I pulled up in front of Brooke's house—it was only two doors away from mine, but I never wanted to make her walk all the way back when it was just as easy for me to let her out here. I wanted more time, but I didn't know how to ask for it.

Brooke didn't move. What was she thinking about me? About what I'd said? I let the tension grow until I got too nervous—just a couple of seconds, really, and then turned toward her. I kept my eyes on her door handle, avoiding her face and body.

"It's so weird," she said, as if prompted by my look. "You live in a small town like this and you think you're so safe, and then something like that happens right here, right on our own street. Like a horror movie come to life. I was terrified when I found out what happened, but I was a hundred, two hundred feet away. You were right in the middle of it." She paused, and I stared silently at her door. "You never know how you'll react to something like that until it happens," she said. "I guess I just . . . feel safer, knowing that people—that you—are ready to do what you have to do. To do the right thing. You know?"

I nodded slowly. "Yeah." This was not what I'd expected.

"Does that make any sense?" she asked. I could tell that she was staring right at me, so I pushed my rule a bit and turned my eyes to meet hers. She was so beautiful.

"Yeah," I said again. "It makes perfect sense."

"Anyway," she said. "Thanks again for the ride." She unlatched her seatbelt and pushed open the door, but before she could step out I spoke up to stop her. It was now or never.

"Hey," I said, "are you going to the Bonfire?"

The Bonfire was a big party they held every year at the lake, on the last day of school. Only sophomores, juniors, and seniors were invited, and here I was, asking Brooke to go with me. I was asking her on a date.

"I was thinking about it," she said, smiling. "It sounds like a lot of fun. Are you going?"

"I think so," I said. I paused. This was it. "Do you wanna go together?"

"Sure," she said, smiling even wider. "I've been hearing about the Bonfire since kindergarten, you know? I can't wait to see what it's really like."

"Cool," I said. Was I supposed to say anything else?

"Cool," she said. We sat there a minute, unsure what to do. "Awesome," she said, laughing and getting out of the car. "I'll see you then."

"Yeah," I said. "I'll see you then."

8

They found the second woman's body on Saturday, lying in a ditch on Route 12, covered with a similar array of torture wounds. It was the same place where the Clayton Killer's second victim was found, less than ten feet from the exact spot. It was now obviously a serial killer, and it seemed just as obvious that this new killer was trying to communicate something, but what? Was he saying "I'm the same," or "I'm different"? Was he telling us he wanted to be like the first killer, or was he hinting that he already was? More than anything else, I wondered who he was talking to: the police? The whole community? Or was he sending this message to the only other killer in town?

Was he talking to me?

I needed to see the body up close, to see what, if anything, the killer was trying to tell me. It could be as simple as "I'm here," or as dangerous as "I know what you did, and I'm coming for you." If I could examine the corpse I'd know just what to look for: claw marks, missing organs, specific lacerations that would point to a knowledge of the previous crimes. The previous body's location had been all over the news for days, and anyone in the world with a good Internet connection could have looked it up and planted this body in the same place, but the specific details of the previous attack had never been released to the public. If certain things were the same, I'd know for sure the attacks were related.

Unfortunately, the police weren't likely to release the details of this attack either, so I had to wait for an embalming—if we got to do one. I spent Saturday waiting, trying to be patient, but by Sunday afternoon it was too much. I had to know something about the body—anything—and I didn't dare just sit around until the body was shipped away like the last one had been. My only hope was Agent Forman: he'd talked to me about the last one, and maybe he'd talk to me about this one, too. It was worth a shot, but I had to be careful not to look too interested. I couldn't give myself away. I needed an excuse, but what?

A memory—he'd specifically asked me to contact him if I remembered anything new about the night Neblin died. I'd ignored the request, because I didn't want to share anything else about that night, but now it was the perfect excuse to get into the station and talk to Forman. All I needed was a memory, either real or very plausible. I pored over my memories of that night, analyzing each bit of information, comparing what was true to what I'd already told them.

I'd gone into the house through the cellar door, using a key I'd stolen previously, but I'd locked it afterward and no one had ever known. I could point them down there, but any evidence they might find would point to me. I discarded the idea and moved on.

After the attacks that night I'd smashed and hidden all three cell phones: Mrs. Crowley's, Mr. Crowley's, and Dr. Neblin's. If I suddenly "found" one of the pieces, by accident, I could take it in and identify it as a piece of Crowley's phone . . . but that was no good either. No one but the police, and me, knew that the phones were a key part of the investigation. My mom didn't even know. Turning them in would look too suspicious.

What could I do? What could I tell him? I'd described the killer in vague terms, describing a large, dark shape that suggested neither Mr. Crowley nor a demon. I'd described my own actions, hiding Mr. Neblin's body behind the Crowley's shed and hoping the killer didn't find me. I'd described the sound the killer made that brought my mom out of the house to find me—a kind of strangled roar. These were things they already knew, and they were virtually the only things I felt confident enough to reveal. Anything else would point back at me as a liar, or as a criminal in my own right.

What I needed to do was to find more details in the information I'd already given. If seeing the killer from my bedroom window was innocent, then suddenly remembering an extra detail—the style of coat he was wearing, maybe—should also be innocent. I needed something specific, so I got on the Internet and looked up a few department store catalogs, browsing through men's coats until I found a good one—thick and rugged, like a rancher's coat, all straight lines and sturdy fabrics. It would look imposing on a large, shadowed figure, and had no bulges or hoods to make it distinctive; it should be entirely acceptable that I'd forgotten it until now.

Now all I had to do was tell Forman. I didn't bother waiting; I just got in my car and drove straight to the police station.

"Hey John," said Stephanie the receptionist. I'd come in often enough since January that she, and many of the cops, knew me by sight. I didn't know much about her because I did my best not to look; she was very attractive, and my rules against looking at women were just as strict with women as they were with high school girls.

"Hey," I said. "Is Forman around?"

"He is," she said. She spoke more slowly than normal, and her words trailed off a bit at the end. She was probably tired from the frenzy of activity over the weekend; normally she didn't even come in on Sundays, but a corpse like this one was sure to mean a lot of extra hours. "He's very busy," she said. "Do you need to talk to him?"

"I do. He told me to contact him if I remembered anything new about the Clayton Killer case, and I did. I know you're busy right now, but he told me to come in as soon as I had anything new."

"Sure thing," said Stephanie. "Sign in." In my peripheral vision she picked up a phone and held it between her ear and her shoulder. One hand dialed while another one made a few clicks with her mouse. "Hello Agent Forman, I have John Cleaver here to see you." Pause. "He says you asked him to come in. Apparently he remembered something important?" She glanced up at me and I nodded. "Thank you, I'll send him in." Stephanie hung up the phone and pointed at his door. "He's only got a few minutes, but you can head on in."

I nodded and walked to his office, in an old conference room just off the lobby. Forman looked up briefly when I entered, then dropped his eyes back down to the stack of papers in front of him. The conference table was still covered with files and folders, just like always.

"Have a seat, John," he said. "You say you've got something new?"

"I do," I said, sitting at the end of the table. "I know you're busy, but you seemed really anxious to hear anything I might remember, so I thought I'd better come in."

Forman looked up and watched me for a second, his head cocked to the side. "I did," he said after a moment. "I did indeed. I was actually going to call you yesterday, but then we found this new body and things went all haywire."

"You were going to call me?"

"A new avenue of inquiry has opened up in our investigation, but that can wait. What did you want to tell me?"

"A new avenue of inquiry?" I didn't want to play my hand just yet, in case he was thoroughly unimpressed and sent me away; better to draw him out and try to learn as much as I could first.

"Yes," he said, "even before the new victim was found. That makes two solid leads just this weekend. You could say it's been a great week—just please don't say it in front of the victim's family."

"So you've already identified the new victim?"

He smiled. "Just a tasteless joke. Thanks for not calling me on it."

He paused, as if waiting for me to say something. I decided the easiest way to avoid suspicion was to ask the most obvious question.

"Everyone's saying the Clayton Killer's back, because of where the body was found. Do you think it's the same person?"

"I don't," he said, still watching me, "but I do think it's someone who was involved in the earlier killings. Maybe not the Clayton Killer himself, but someone who knew him. Maybe someone who worked with him."

"Serial killers don't often have accomplices."

"Not often," he said, "but it's not unheard of. And a relationship between them doesn't have to imply a close one, or even a good one. They could have been antagonists, or maybe rivals. It may be that the new killer is showing the old one how he would have done it better."

I started to ask another question, but Forman cut me off.

"Enough small talk," he said. "What have you got?"

I laid it out for him, hoping that a smooth flow of conversation might get him talking about the new victim again later. "The killer's coat," I said. "He was wearing a big coat, like a workman's coat. I can't remember the color, because it was so dark, but the outline was pretty recognizable." The real killer, Mr. Crowley, didn't actually have a coat like that, but I wasn't trying to help the investigation—just build trust with Forman.

"Interesting," he said. "What sparked this memory, if I may ask?"

I'd prepared for that question. "It was in a commercial— some people caroling in big heavy coats in the middle of summer. I don't remember what it was for, probably a cell phone or a truck or something, but as soon as I saw the coat on one of the guys it struck some kind of chord in my head, and I knew I'd seen it before."

"Interesting," said Forman. "So you're saying the guy in the commercial is the Clayton Killer?"

What? "No, of course not; there's probably a million coats like that," I said. "Of course I'm not saying that. But you asked what sparked the memory, and that was it." His comment worried me—it meant he probably wasn't taking me seriously. Why not? Had I said something to tip him off that I was lying?

"Yes, yes," he said, "I know. I'm just in an odd mood today, honestly; lack of sleep. Just forget about it." He swiveled in his chair and picked up a thick folder from a low table behind him. "Now we'll be happy to follow up on that information, but first I wonder if you have a minute to discuss this other item?" He swiveled back to face me, holding the folder.

I nodded warily. "The new avenue of inquiry."

"Exactly. You see, we've subpoenaed Dr. Neblin's case files."

His expression was flat and passive, but his words hit me like a sledgehammer to the gut. Dr. Neblin was the man who'd diagnosed me with Conduct Disorder, and one of the three people in the world who knew about it; if they had his files, the confidentiality laws I'd been hiding behind for months had just evaporated. I can only imagine Forman's surprise when he found out that a key witness in his case was also a sociopath.

"There are a lot of interesting things in there," said Forman, setting down the folder and opening it carefully. "I kind of wish we'd been able to pull this sooner."

"I'm kind of surprised it took this long," I said, trying to sound casual.

Forman nodded. "How much of this were you planning to tell us?"

"Only the parts that have a bearing on this case," I said.

"And how much is that?"

"None of it."

Forman nodded again. "Dr. Neblin was found dead across the street from your house. You were covered in his blood, though you claim you were trying to help him escape the Clayton Killer. That all seemed pretty believable, especially given that you were the one who called the police that night. But this . . .'" He tapped the paper. "This changes everything."

"Now that I'm a sociopath I'm suddenly a suspect? Isn't that some kind of disability discrimination?"

Forman smiled. "Yes, he does suggest that you may have sociopathic tendencies, but there's a lot more than that in here. Neblin points out several major changes in your behavior after the killings started last fall. Changes that could be read, in a certain light, as being common to the behavioral shift between a potential killer and a practicing one."

I wanted to protest immediately, to tell him I was not a killer, but I stopped. If I protested too much I'd look guilty. It might be better to go straight for the sarcastic approach.

"You've got me," I said. "I killed Dr. Neblin. With an axe. *Dipped in poison.*"

"Very cute," he said, not smiling, "but no one is accusing you of killing Dr. Neblin."

"Most people don't use poison," I said, ignoring him, "because they think a big axe blade can do the job on its own. And they're right, but I say they have no style."

Forman shrugged his shoulders and spread his hands out. "What are you doing?"

"Confessing," I said. "Isn't that what you want?"

"Dr. Neblin wasn't killed with an axe."

"Then it was a good thing I put that poison on there."

Forman studied me, as if he was watching for something—or listening, to something only he could hear. After a moment he said, "Did you ever want to kill anyone?"

"You're going to have to arrest most of Clayton County if wanting to kill someone is suddenly a crime. They practically lynched one of the suspects, you know."

"I was there," he said, and an odd look came into his eyes. "Mobs can make people think and feel some pretty crazy things. Your case is different, though, as I think you have to admit."

"I didn't kill anybody," I said, trying to sound as casual as possible, like I was letting him in on a joke instead of protesting my innocence. "I'd be pretty stupid to come straight in to the police station if I had." I knew as soon as I said it that it was a bad argument—serial killers often involved themselves in their own investigations. Edmund Kemper even volunteered at the police station, and was good friends with most of the cops on his case. I waited for Forman to call me on it, but he didn't mention it.

"What fascinates me the most," he said, almost to himself, "is that I didn't see it earlier." He was furrowing his brow and scrunching up a corner of his mouth, which usually meant the person was confused. "I'm a criminal profiler, John—I identify sociopaths for a living. How were you able to hide it from me?"

Because of my rules, I thought. *I don't want to be a killer, so I have rules to help keep me just as normal as everyone else.*

Well, normal on the surface. Somewhere inside, Mr. Monster was just waiting for me to make a mistake. And so, it seemed, was Forman.

"I'm not really a sociopath," I said, hiding behind the definition. "I have Conduct Disorder, which is much less developed. People my age almost never become serial killers."

"Almost never," he said, "but sometimes."

"I was in therapy to deal with it," I said. "I follow strict rules to help me avoid temptations. I've been completely open about my involvement in this case, and I've involved you at every step of the way. I'm trying to be the good guy here, so don't hold this one thing against me."

Forman stared at me for a while, for much longer than I expected, then grabbed a notepad and started scribbling something on it.

"Thanks for the tip about the killer's coat," he said, then tore off the note paper and handed it to me. It was a phone number. "If you remember anything else you don't need to bother coming in; just call."

He was sending me away, and I still hadn't learned much of anything about the new corpse. I thought about asking another question, but it was too dangerous—he was letting me go now without any further questions, which meant I might have convinced him I was innocent. There was no reason to rouse his suspicions again by asking questions about a corpse.

I took the note, nodded, and left.

"How could you do this!" Mom shouted, pacing back and forth in the living room. I was sitting on the couch, wishing I were somewhere else. "After everything we've done—after all the rules and the therapy and everything we do to help you fit in, now Agent Forman thinks you're a suspect."

"Technically, therapy was the main culprit here," I said.

"The main culprit was you," she said, stopping and staring at me sternly. "If you'd never gotten involved with this to begin with, the FBI wouldn't even know who you were."

"I was trying to help," I said, for what seemed like the millionth time over the past five months. "Was I just supposed to sit there?"

"Yes!" she shouted. "Yes, you can just sit there—you don't have to right every wrong you see, just like you don't have to run out in the middle of the night so a killer can chase you home."

So that's what this was really about—she was afraid that I was going to chase another killer and get myself killed. How many fights had we had about this? I rolled my eyes and turned away.

"Don't you ignore me," she said. She walked around into my new field of view, her eyes wide and imploring. "I'm not asking you to never help—you know I want you to be a good person— I just want you to stay away from certain things. It's one of our rules, even: 'when you think about killing, think about something else.' Anything else. But don't run out and get right in the middle of it!" Her face fell and she grimaced. "I just—I can't believe you did this!"

"And I can't believe you're asking me to stand by while people get killed," I said.

"That is not what this is about!" she shouted. "This is about staying out of trouble—"

"Which is going to leave other people *in* trouble," I said. "I went outside that night to try to save our neighbors from a killer."

"And it was very brave, and it was very stupid. You don't

chase a killer for the same reason that you don't run into a burning building."

"You just stand outside and listen to the screams?"

"You call the police!" she said. "You call the fire department, you call the paramedics; you let the people who know what they're doing do their job."

"It was a monster, Mom, the police couldn't have—"

"John—"

"You saw it!" I screamed. "You saw it with your own eyes, so stop pretending it wasn't real! It was a monster, with fangs and claws and I stopped it, and instead of a hero you're treating me like I'm crazy!"

"We don't talk about that—"

"Yes we do!" I felt a sharp pain every time she denied it, like a knife in my chest. I could feel a hole inside of me growing wider, deeper, darker—the need to kill, unsated for so long, growing harder and harder to resist. "I can't pretend it wasn't real any more than I could sit here doing nothing while it killed everyone we know!"

"We don't know for sure—"

"You saw it!" I shouted again. My eyes felt hot. "You saw it! Please don't say you didn't; please don't do this to me."

She fell silent now, staring at me. Watching. Thinking.

The phone rang.

We stared at it. It rang again.

Mom picked it up. "Hello?" She listened for a moment, shaking her head. "Just a minute," she said, then covered the mouthpiece and looked at me. "This discussion is not over," she said. "I'll be right back so we can finish talking about this."

She uncovered the phone and walked into her bedroom. "Just a moment, ma'am," she said, and closed the door.

I left immediately, struggling to sneak out quietly when all I really wanted to do was smash something. I ran to my car and started the engine, pulling out in a wide curve to head back out of our one-way street. Mom was watching through the curtains, shouting something through the glass but not coming after me. Did she think I was running away, or did she know the real reason?

That I was leaving to stop myself from hurting her?

The roar of the engine was dark and hungry, like a beast breaking free of a cage. Mr. Monster wanted to ram every car he passed; to run over every person he saw; to wrap the engine around every pole on every corner in town. I fought him back as I drove, keeping my hands steady and the speed low.

There were times when I needed to be alone, but more important than those were the times when I wanted to be alone but knew it was a bad idea. Alone—on the shores of Freak Lake, lighting fires at the warehouse, hiding outside of someone's window—I couldn't trust myself. Not tonight. I needed other people, and I needed the ones who wouldn't judge or threaten or condemn. What I needed was Dr. Neblin, but he was gone forever.

Brooke? Her presence would probably calm me down, but how long would it take, and how much would she see in the meantime? I couldn't risk horrifying her, not when she was finally starting to like me. I could visit Max, and sit back while he droned on about himself, or his comics. But he was sure to eventually start talking about his dad, and I didn't want to deal with that tonight. Unfortunately, that was pretty much everyone I knew.

Except for Margaret. I turned and headed toward her neighborhood, taking deep breaths and driving slowly. I didn't want to risk an accident, and I didn't want to let reckless speed become a temptation to slam the car into a target of opportunity. Margaret was the happy one in the family; the simple one, the rational one. We could all talk to Margaret because she never took sides and never started fights. She was our refuge.

When I pulled up in front of her apartment I could see her through the window, talking on the phone. It was probably Mom, warning her that crazy old John was out causing problems again. I swore and pulled away again. Why wouldn't she leave me alone?

There was one place I was sure to get away from her: Lauren lived just a few blocks away, in an apartment of her own. She and Mom hadn't spoken since Mother's Day, and only barely spoke before that. There's no way Mom would call her, and if she did Lauren wouldn't answer.

I paused in front to look for Curt's truck, but he wasn't there, and I let out a breath I didn't know I was holding. This was not the night to seek him out; I needed to stay calm and forget all about the bodies and the investigation and everything. I parked and walked into the complex, trying to remember which apartment was hers. I'd only been here once before. The stairs were crumbling concrete slabs embedded in a rusty metal frame, and the brick walls burned red in the early evening sun. It was either the third door or the fourth . . . the third door had a rolled-up newspaper thrown against it, wrapped in dirty plastic. I skipped it and knocked on the fourth.

Lauren opened the door, and her mouth smiled almost as soon as her eyes widened in surprise—almost as soon, though not quite.

"John! What are you doing here?"

"Just driving around," I said, concentrating on breathing slowly and evenly.

"Well come in," she said, standing back and gesturing inside. "Make yourself at home."

I stepped through the door and into the room, unfocused and uncertain. I wasn't here for anything specific, just because I needed to be somewhere, and this was the only place to do it. Now that I was here, I didn't know what to do.

"You thirsty?" asked Lauren, closing the door.

"Sure," I mumbled.

Her apartment was clean and bare, like a well-kept shell. The kitchen table was scratched, with the veneer peeled back in places to expose the plywood beneath, but it was washed and spotless, and all the chairs matched. The glasses in her cupboard were few and mismatched, and the water from the tap sputtered erratically when she turned it on. She handed me the glass with a smile.

"Sorry there's no ice."

"It's fine," I said. I didn't really want the drink, but I took a sip to be polite.

"So what you up to?" Lauren asked, moving to the living room and flopping down on a couch.

I followed her slowly, feeling the tension that swirled inside of me slowly beginning to seep away. I sat down mechanically. "Nothing," I said. "School." I wanted to talk, but it felt better simply to sit here, saying nothing.

Lauren watched me for a moment, her energy visibly draining away as she studied my face. She spoke knowingly. "Mom?"

I sighed and rubbed my eyes. "It's nothing."

"I know," she said, pulling her feet up onto the couch and resting her cheek on her knees. "It's always nothing."

I sipped the water again. There was nowhere to put the glass, so I took another sip.

"Is she still mad?" asked Lauren.

"Not at you."

"I know," she said, gazing at the wall. "She's not mad at you either. She's mad at herself. She's mad at the world for not being perfect."

Lauren was blond, like Dad, while Mom and I had jet-black hair. I'd always seen the two women as polar opposites, both in looks and personality, but in this light she looked more like Mom than I'd ever noticed before. It might have been the shadows in her eyes, or the way her mouth turned down at the corners. I closed my eyes and leaned back.

There was a knock on the door, and my insides twisted instantly back into a tight knot.

"That's probably Curt," said Lauren, jumping up. I heard the door open behind me, followed by Curt's voice.

"Hey sexy—oh, Jim's here."

"John," said Lauren.

"John. Sorry man, I'm crap for names."

He walked around my chair and sat on the couch, pulling Lauren with him. I wanted to get up and leave, right on the spot, but something stopped me. I took a sip of water and stared straight ahead.

"Still quiet?" asked Curt. "You realize I've never heard him actually talk? Say something, dude, I don't even know what your voice sounds like."

There were so many things I wanted to say to him, so many insults and put-downs and threats I'd come up with since the last time I saw him. None of them came out now. I wasn't afraid of anyone—I'd mouthed off to the bullies at school, I'd challenged an FBI agent right to his face, and I'd gone toe to toe with a demon, but for some reason I was completely cowed by Curt. Something inside of me went completely inert around him. Why?

"He gets a drink and I don't?" asked Curt. "What, no love for the boyfriend?"

Lauren slapped him playfully on the shoulder and stood up to get him a glass of water.

"And put some ice in it this time." Curt grinned at me. "Your sister's like the lava queen—she's probably going to put it in the microwave." Lauren turned on the tap and Curt turned to yell into the kitchen. "Not water, babe, soda."

"I'm all out," said Lauren. "Shopping's this weekend."

"Whatever," Curt called, then turned back to me. "She's always forgetting something. Women, eh kid?"

That's what it was—the thing that kept me down. It was all around him, in his words, his attitude, and even the way he smiled.

He was exactly like my dad.

It was the way he treated people, gregarious and cheerful but completely removed. Aloof. He was so excited about himself that there wasn't room for anyone else—we were an audience for his jokes, and a mirror to reflect his actions, but we were not friends and we were not a family.

And if we made our own actions instead of reflecting his, would Curt explode like Dad did? Did he yell at Lauren? Did he hit her?

"You still haven't said anything," said Curt, taking the glass from Lauren's hand and settling back into the couch. Lauren snuggled up under his arm.

"I was just leaving," I said, standing up. I couldn't stay with him any longer. I stood there a moment, as if waiting for his permission, then forced myself to turn away and walk into the kitchen.

"You just got here!" said Lauren, jumping back up. "Don't go yet."

"Don't let me scare you off," said Curt.

I set my glass down on the table, then thought better of it and moved it to the counter. It had left a moisture ring on the table, and I wiped it away with my hand.

"We could watch a movie," said Lauren. "I don't have very many, but there's . . . there's that cheesy kid one Dad sent me for Christmas. *The Apple Dumpling Gang*." She laughed, and Curt groaned.

"Please no!" he said.

"It's okay," I said. "I have to go."

"Now your movie's scared him off," said Curt, still lounging on the couch. "Hey Lauren, you want to get a pizza?"

"Bye Lauren," I said, and hurried outside.

"Bye John," she called, her voice higher than normal. She was worried. "Come back soon."

Mr. Monster promised, silently, that he'd come back to visit Curt as soon as he could.

9

The night school ended, I stood in the bathroom and stared at the mirror, gripping the sink. Another teenager might have been looking at himself, I guess, or combing his hair or dabbing on some Clearasil or making his collar perfectly straight. It was the night of my date with Brooke, after all, and I needed to get ready, but that meant something very different for me than for anybody else. I wasn't trying to look good; I was trying to *be* good.

"I will not hurt animals," I said, ignoring the rule sheet and staring straight into my own eyes. "I will not hurt people. When I think bad thoughts about someone, I will push the thoughts away and say something nice about that person. I will not call people 'it.' I will not threaten people. If people threaten me, I will leave the situation."

I peered deeper into the mirror, searching. Who was staring back? He looked like me, he talked like me, his body moved when I did. I swayed to the right, then left, then back to center; the person in the mirror did the same. This was the thing that terrified me the most—more than the victim, more than the demon, more even than the dark thoughts. It was the fact that the dark thoughts were mine. That I couldn't separate myself from evil, because most of the evil in my life came from inside my own head.

How long could I live like this? I was trying to be two people—a killer on the inside, and a normal person on the outside. I made such a show of being a good, quiet kid, who never caused problems and never got into trouble, but now the monster was out, and I was actually using him—I was actively seeking out another killer. I'd given in. I was trying to be John and Mr. Monster at the same time.

Was I fooling myself, thinking that I could split my life like this? Was it possible to be two people, one good and one bad, or was I forced to be a mix of both—a good person forever tainted by evil?

My throat grew cold, and I threw up in the sink. I shouldn't be going out with Brooke—it was dangerous. She was the one thing that Mr. Monster and I both wanted, and that made her the gap in my armor. She was the link between us, and anything that strengthened that link would make Mr. Monster stronger. I could only hope that it would make me stronger as well. I was starting a battle that only one of us could win.

But was Brooke the prize? Or was she the battlefield?

"Hey John!"

Brooke opened her front door quickly; she must have been

waiting for my knock. She was dressed in shorts, as usual, even though we were going to be out late. It was supposed to be pretty warm tonight, so she'd probably be fine, but if she got too cold we could hang out by the bonfire. Win-win. Despite the shorts she did have a jacket, though I stopped myself from looking at her shirt, to avoid looking at her chest.

What kind of crazy date would this be, if I didn't even know what kind of shirt my date was wearing? Was this really as insane as I thought it was? How long would it be before she realized I was crazy? The only thing to do was the thing I always did—fake it.

"Hey Brooke," I said. "Nice shirt."

"Thanks," she said, smiling and glancing down at it. "I figured it was appropriate, since this is kind of a school thing." I kept my eyes on her hair, which she wore long and loose like a blond waterfall. She looked like a shampoo commercial. I imagined myself washing it, brushing it gently, gently, while she lay still on the table.

I forced the thought out and smiled. "This should be fun. You ready to go?"

"Sure," she said, and started to pull the door closed, but someone called her from down the hall.

"Brooke?" It was her dad.

"Yeah Dad," she called back. "John's here."

Mr. Watson stepped into the doorway and smiled. "Headed for the bonfire tonight?"

"Yeah," I said.

"Well, you be careful out there," he said. "A bunch of kids get together in the middle of the night, you never know when one of them's going to do something stupid and hurt somebody. But then I suppose my baby's in good hands with you, right?"

It was frightening how much most people didn't know about me.

"We'll be fine," said Brooke, smiling at me. "Besides," she said, looking back at her dad, "there's teachers there too—it's like a real school activity."

"I'm sure everything will go fine," said Mr. Watson. He stepped onto the porch and put a hand on my shoulder, guiding me a few steps to the side. I glanced at Brooke, and she rolled her eyes. "I always imagined what I'd do the first time my daughter went on a date," he said.

Brooke groaned behind us. "Dad . . ."

"I always kind of imagined myself threatening the boy that took her out, you know? 'I have a gun and a shovel,' kind of thing. But I don't imagine that would really be all that scary to you, after what you've been through."

He didn't know the half of it.

"The thing is," he said, facing me directly, "the things you've been through recommend you pretty highly for the job. Every time I imagined this in my head, she was hopping on the back of some gangbanger's Harley and ignoring me as I waved good-bye."

"Oh my gosh," said Brooke, turning red and covering her face.

Mr. Watson kept going. "I guess what I'm saying is, given the options, I'm glad she chose the local hero instead."

What?

"Hero?" I asked.

"And humble to boot," he said, slapping me on the shoulder.

"Well, I won't take up any more of your time—you asked her out, not me. Brooke, you remember the rules?"

"Yes," she said, turning to go.

"And?"

She rolled her eyes again. "No drinking, no driving fast, home by midnight."

"And you have your phone?" he asked her.

"Yes."

"And you will call home if . . . ?"

"If we get lost or stuck somewhere."

"And you will call the police if . . . ?"

"If we see drugs, or if someone starts a fight."

"Or if he tries to kiss you," he said. Brooke turned bright red, and Mr. Watson laughed and winked at me. "Hero or not, you're still out with my baby."

"Holy crap," Brooke muttered, grabbing my arm and dragging me toward the car, "let's get out of here. Bye Dad!"

"Bye Bubba!" he shouted.

"He calls you Bubba?" I asked. Brooke was thin as a rail.

"Baby nickname," she said, shaking her head, though I could see that she was smiling. We crossed around the car to the passenger side and stood by her door.

And stood by it a while longer.

I realized abruptly that she was waiting for me to open it for her. I glanced at her quickly, then stared at the door. This was *her* door. One of things I never touched. I glanced at her again, just long enough to see that her eyebrows were scrunching down a bit—she was confused. If I delayed any longer, or if I made her do it, what would she think? She'd seen me look at the door, then back at her—I couldn't feign ignorance or bad manners at this point, unless I wanted to look like a complete jerk. I reached out my hand and opened the door, imagining as I did all the times her hand had touched the same door, her fingertips pressed against the same handle. When it was unlatched I let go and grabbed the top of the door instead, pulling it open that way.

"Is there something wrong with the handle?" she asked.

"There was a wasp in there earlier," I said, thinking quickly. "I think it was trying to build a nest."

"That seems like a weird place," she said.

"That's because you're not a wasp," I said, holding it open as she sat. "It's all the rage for wasps these days."

"And you're up to date on wasp trends?" she asked, smiling mischievously.

"I read one of their magazines," I said. "Not mine, of course, I saw it at the barbershop. It was that or *Moose Illustrated*, and I had to read something."

Brooke laughed, and I closed her door. How long could I keep this up? It was six o'clock now, and her dad wanted her back by midnight. Six hours?

Trying to look normal when I was one in a crowd was easy. Trying to look normal one-on-one was going to be very hard work.

I went to my door and climbed into the car.

"It's going to be weird seeing a big fire that you didn't start," said Brooke.

I froze. What did she know? What had she seen? Her voice had sounded so casual, but . . . maybe there was some hidden cue underneath that I hadn't picked up on. Was she accusing me? Was she threatening me?

"What do you mean?" I asked, staring ahead.

"Oh, you know, like the big fires the Crowleys used to have in their backyard, like for neighborhood parties and stuff. You're always the one who tends those."

I sighed in relief—literally a sigh, as if I'd been holding my breath without knowing it. *She doesn't know anything. She's just making small talk.*

"Are you okay?" she asked.

I started the car and smiled. "I'm great." *I need an excuse quick. What would a normal person say in this situation? Normal people have empathy; they would react to the people in the story, not the fire.* "I was just thinking about the Crowleys," I said. "I wonder if Mrs. Crowley's still going to have those parties." I pulled away from the curb and drove toward town.

"Oh!" said Brooke, "I am so sorry; I didn't mean to bring that up like that. I know you were really close to Mr. Crowley."

"It's okay," I said. I had to force myself to continue— talking to her had been against my rules for so long, it was hard to just speak freely. "Now that he's gone, I look back and I think I didn't really know him at all." *Nobody did. Not even his wife.*

"I feel the same way," said Brooke. "I've lived here for most of my life, and he lived right there, two doors down, and I didn't really know him at all. We'd see him at those parties, of course, and trick-or-treating and stuff, but I feel like I should have . . . I don't know, talked to him more. You know? Like, where was he from, and what was he like as a kid, and stuff like that."

"I would love to know where he came from," I said. *And if there are more like him.*

"I love talking to people and hearing their stories," said Brooke. "Everyone's got their own story to tell, and when you sit down with someone and really talk to them, you can learn so much."

"Yeah," I said, "but that's really kind of strange too." I was starting to fall into a rhythm, where words came more easily.

"Strange?"

"Well—it's strange to look at people and think that they have a past," I said. How could I explain what I was trying to say? "I mean, obviously everybody comes from somewhere, but . . ." I pointed to a guy on the side of the street as we passed. "Look at that guy. He's just some guy, and we see him once, and then he's gone."

"Oh, that's Jake Symons," said Brooke. "He works with my dad at the wood mill."

"That's what I'm talking about," I said. "To us he's like . . . like scenery, in the background of our lives, but for him, he's the main character. He has a life and a job and a whole story. He's a real person. And to him, *we're* the background scenery. And that guy," I pointed at another person on the street, "he's not even looking. He might not notice us at all. We're the center of our own universes, but we don't even exist in his."

"That's Bryce Parker," said Brooke, "from the library."

"Do you know everybody in Clayton," I asked, "or am I just picking bad examples?"

Brooke laughed. "I go to the library like every week, of course I'm going to know him!"

"So how about that guy?" I pointed at a man mowing his lawn about a hundred feet ahead.

"No, I don't know him," said Brooke, staring closely. We

drove past him and he turned at the last minute, giving us a clear view of his face, and Brooke laughed out loud. "Okay, okay, I do know him—he's the guy from Graumman's Hardware, uh . . . Lance!"

"Lance what?"

"Lance Graumman, I assume," said Brooke. "It's a family business."

"You know a lot more about the hardware store than I would have guessed," I said.

Brooke laughed again. "We remodeled our upstairs bathroom last summer, and I don't think we ever bought the right size stuff on the first try. I was in there a lot."

"That would explain it." It felt odd talking to her, chatting so freely about nothing. I'd fantasized about her for so long, and forbidden myself to communicate with her in any depth, that even this simple small talk felt powerfully intimate. Intimate and empty at the same time. How could such meaningless drivel feel as if it meant so much?

I turned out of town, on the road toward the lake, and fell into line behind a couple of other cars full of high school kids. I studied the backs of their heads, hoping I could recognize them and show Brooke that I knew other people too, but even though I knew I'd seen them before, I couldn't think of their names. They were a few years older than us, so I'd never really interacted with them.

"Hey!" said Brooke, "That's Jessie Beesley! That's not her boyfriend, though, I wonder what happened there."

The sun was still high, and I adjusted my shade flap thingy to block it. "You know every single person in town," I said, "and I don't even know what this thing is called."

"It's the . . ." Brooke grimaced. "The thing that blocks the sun?" She laughed. "What is that thing called? It's a . . . shade. It's a blocker. It's a very small awning."

"It's a flat umbrella."

"You could put lace on it and call it a parasol," said Brooke. "It would be *precious*."

I glanced over and saw she was smirking. I'm pretty good at reading people, for a sociopath, but sarcasm is so hard to identify.

Looking at her, my mind drifted back to her dad's words, and the trust he had placed in me to take care of her. He'd called me a hero—me, the crazy, death-obsessed sociopath who worked in a mortuary and wrote all his class papers on serial killers. A hero. It stirred up thoughts I'd almost forgotten—I'd been so focused on *how* to kill the demon, and on the psychological aftermath of actually doing it, that I'd almost forgotten *why*. I focused so much on "killing the bad guy" that "saving the good guys" had been pushed aside and forgotten.

But nobody knew I'd killed a demon. Even Mom did her best to forget what little she understood about the real story behind that night in January. All Mr. Watson knew was that I had been outside that night, that I'd moved Dr. Neblin's body, and that I'd called the police. Was that enough?

"I wonder what food they've got," said Brooke, and I realized suddenly that my thoughts had left a void of silence in the car. "I assume it'll be hot dogs; I don't know what else you'd eat at a bonfire."

Crap. It hadn't occurred to me that the food would probably be meat. *What was I going to eat?*

Just say something, I told myself. "They might have s'mores."

It was all I could think of. "Those are good bonfire food. Also squirrels, with very poor senses of direction or self-preservation."

Brooke laughed again. "That would have to be a really mixed-up squirrel to just wander into a bonfire."

"Or a really cold one."

"They could just build the fire on top of a gopher hole," said Brooke, "and then they could pop out pre-cooked, like a vending machine."

Wow. Did she *really just make that joke?*

"Sorry," said Brooke, "that was kind of gross."

I looked at her with new eyes, watching her as she talked. She glanced over at me and smiled. Did she think I was a hero?

Did she think I was good?

We pulled off the road at the end of a long line of cars—there was a field up ahead, of sorts, where big groups could park for parties by the lake, but the Bonfire always drew a massive crowd, and the sparse parking was overflowing by nearly half a mile. As we walked toward the party I looked at each person we passed—other students that I'd known for years—as if seeing them for the first time. Did this one think I was a hero? Did that one? It was the first time in my life that I'd assumed people were thinking good things about me, rather than bad ones, and I wasn't sure what to think.

But I liked it.

"I love this smell," said Brooke, walking with her hands in her jacket pockets. "That cool breeze off the lake, mixed with the smoke from the fire and the green from the trees."

"The green?" I asked.

"Yeah," she said, "I love that green smell."

"Green isn't a smell," I said, "it's a color."

"Well, yeah, but . . . don't you know that smell? Trees and reeds and grass sometimes just smell . . . green."

"I can't say that I'm familiar with the smell of green," I said.

"There's Marci," she said, "let's ask her."

I looked where Brooke was pointing and immediately looked away; Marci was wearing a low cut tank top that practically screamed 'look at these!' I watched Brooke's feet as she hurried to meet her, keeping my gaze down—just because I was breaking a few of my rules to be with Brooke didn't mean I was going to throw caution to the wind and break them all. Looking at a girl's chest was strictly prohibited.

"Brooke!" shouted Marci. "Lookin' hot! I love the shirt."

Man, I really wanted to know what her shirt looked like.

"Good to see you," said Brooke.

"And John," said Marci. "I didn't expect to see you here, that's awesome."

"Thanks," I said, staring at her feet. Then, because I didn't want to seem like a freak, I glanced up—first at Brooke's face, then at Marci's. Her line of cleavage was prominent in my peripheral vision, and I looked out across the lake. "Nice night."

"You gotta answer this question," said Brooke. "Do trees smell green?"

"What?" asked Marci, laughing.

"Green!" said Brooke. "The trees here smell green."

"You are insane," said Marci.

"Who's insane?" asked Rachel Morris, joining the group. I smiled at her politely, grateful that she was dressed more modestly than her friend.

"Brooke says the trees smell green," said Marci, struggling not to laugh out loud.

"Totally," said Rachel, nodding her head. "This whole place smells green—and a little brown, because of the smoke."

"Exactly!" cried Brooke.

"Can you believe these two?" asked Marci, looking at me. I focused on her ear, trying not to look at anything else.

"Must be a shared delusion," I said, then stopped myself before getting any deeper into a psychological hypothesis. That was probably not the kind of small talk that would go over well in this crowd.

It felt strange to be talking to Marci—partly because of the way she was dressed, but mostly because of the simple fact that we didn't know each other well. Just like the people in the car ahead of us, Marci was someone that I "knew," in theory, but in practice we had never really talked or interacted. I glanced around quickly at the mass of teenagers, all people I had grown up with, but with whom I'd had virtually no direct contact—no shared experience. It seemed unbelievable that we could have been born and raised in the same small town, going to the same schools in the same grade year after year, and yet we'd never really had a conversation. Max would have been delighted to talk to Marci—and to ogle her—but I was more bothered than anything else. My life had been just fine without all of these extra people in it.

"Can you smell other colors?" asked Marci, folding her arms for a mock interrogation of Brooke and Rachel.

"It's not the color," said Brooke, "it's the trees. Green's just a good word to describe what a tree smells like when it turns green."

"It's like spring," said Rachel, "except 'springy' sounds dumb."

"And 'green' sounds totally normal," said Marci. "Uh huh."

The breeze off the lake was cool, and I could see goose bumps on Marci's arms. Before I could stop them, my eyes wandered to Brooke's legs; they had goose bumps too.

"Why don't we head toward the fire?" I asked. Brooke nodded, and Marci and Rachel followed us through the loose crowd of people. The bonfire itself was visible through the trees ahead, a rough parabola of orange flame, though the sky was still too light for the fire to really stand out. The forest here was sparse and patchy, with more scrub than trees, and the fire itself had been made in a large, round clearing just a few dozen feet off the road. As we drew near I could see that the party organizers, whoever they were, had spared no expense on the fire—there were huge logs in its heart, and stacks of cordwood and split logs waited in the background, piled high against the trees. In the fire wood cracked and split, sap popping and hissing at the center, and behind it all was the dull static roar of oxygen being sucked into the center of the greedy flames. It was talking to me.

"Hello," I whispered, answering back. I stepped closer, holding out my hands to probe the heat. Just right in some places, but too cool in others and too hot at the peak. The structure at the base was more open than it needed to be; the fire would be hot and powerful, but it would burn itself out too quickly. Logs like that could last all night if you set them carefully and tended them just so with the other pieces of wood.

There didn't seem to be anybody in particular in charge of the fire. There was a five-foot branch with a blackened tip laying just to the side, which I assumed had been used to poke and position the wood, so I picked it up and adjusted the blaze; knock this piece down, stand that piece up. A fire could tell you what it needed, if you knew how to listen. I felt the heat; I listened to the growl of the air; I watched the lines of brilliant white heat on the surface of the wood, shining out as if something radiant and perfect were stretching out from within, ready to be born into a dull and lifeless world. Another tweak, another push.

Perfect.

A split log sailed past me in a tight arc, crashing into the fire and making it flare up with a roar.

"Yeah!" Someone screamed beside me, a thick senior with close-cropped hair and a meaty red face. "Let's get this fire going!"

"You'll get a better flame if you . . ." I tried to talk to him, but he turned and shouted to someone.

"Clayton Crusaders!"

Several voices hollered back, and he shook his fists triumphantly in the sky before heading back for more wood.

"It works better if you plan it out," I said, mostly to myself. I turned back to the fire and poked it again, trying to repair some of the damage, when a second log crashed into the middle, then a third.

"Clayton Crusaders!"

"You know," said Marci, standing next to me, "some things you just can't plan." I looked at her quickly, surprised, and she smiled. "You know?"

Where had she come from? I'd been so caught up in the fire I'd lost track of the girls completely.

"No hot dogs yet," said Brooke, walking over from somewhere. "They're not breaking out the food til around 6:30. Wanna hit the lake?"

"Well I'm definitely not going in," said Marci, "but I wouldn't mind taking a look." The three girls started walking away, then stopped and looked back.

"Are you coming?" asked Brooke.

But . . . there's a fire.

I looked back at the bonfire, still strong and powerful despite the chaos from the new logs. I didn't need the fire; I was here for Brooke.

"Sure," I said. "We'll be back at 6:30 anyway, right?" I put down the branch and walked toward them.

"Thanks," said Rachel. "We need our brave protector."

"No kidding," said Marci. "With all these dead women they're finding, even a huge group like this gives me the creeps."

There it is again: John the brave. How many people see me as some kind of hero? And how did I go so long without noticing?

"We used to come out here to go fishing," said Brooke, watching the clear line of water emerge through the thinning trees. The sky was still light, but muted, and the lake reflected the clear blue of the sky like the bottom half of a giant, lacquered shell. We stopped on a low ridge where the trees parted and the ground turned down sharply to the glassy lake beyond. Brooke stepped up onto a sharp rock to get a better view, teetered for a moment, then put her hand on my shoulder for stability. It felt electric, like a sudden surge of energy flowing in at the point of contact. I pretended to stare out at the water, but my whole being seemed focused on Brooke's hand.

"It's beautiful," said Rachel.

A couple of guys splashed by in wet shorts and T-shirts, hip-deep in the water.

"Come on in!" they shouted at us, though I had a feeling they were thinking more about the girls than about me. The girls ignored them, so I did the same. The guys saw another group up the shore and slogged toward them through the reeds, leaving us alone again.

Brooke sighed. "What are you guys gonna do?"

"Just hang around, I guess," said Marci. "See who shows up; see who's with who."

"Did you see Jessie Beesley?" asked Rachel. "I wonder what happened to Mark."

"Not that," said Brooke, "I mean, what are you gonna do with your lives? With the future?"

Marci laughed. "You're very cute when you're deep, Brooke."

"What, you don't have dreams?" asked Brooke.

"Oh, I've got dreams," said Marci, "believe me. And they have nothing to do with Clayton County."

"I'm getting out of here so fast," said Rachel. "A town with only one movie theater barely counts as civilization."

I stared at the lake, remembering the dead body the demon had sunk below the ice in November.

"Are you going anywhere specific?" I asked. "Or just running away from here?"

"College," said Brooke. "Travel. The world."

"Nobody wants to stay here," said Rachel.

"I don't mind the summers," said Marci. "But sometimes I wonder how we got here in the first place."

"The logging industry," I said.

"Yeah, but why *us*?" asked Marci. "Why are we here and not somewhere else?"

"It's not that bad," said Brooke.

"It's worse," said Rachel.

"Who were the first ones?" asked Marci, staring at the lake.

"Are we all just children of children of mill workers, who grew up and lost their dreams and got stuck forever? Somebody came here *first*, when there was nothing else, and they built a city in the middle of nowhere and made money out of nothing and they *did it*." She looked up at the sky. "I guess I just don't understand, if that's the kind of people we come from, why we all just sit here doing nothing."

Rachel opened her mouth to answer, but a shriek cut her off—loud and piercing, and just up the shore. We spun around to look, Brooke tightening her grip on my shoulder, and saw the two guys from before splashing frantically out of the water. The group of girls they'd been flirting with was backing up in terror, and now all of them were screaming. Brooke jumped down and ran toward them, and I followed close behind.

"She's dead!" someone shouted. "She's dead!"

More people were coming now, from all around through the trees. It looked like the group by the shore was backing away from a wild animal, like they were afraid of being bitten, but as we drew closer I could see what they'd been screaming about— there was a rotted log half in and half out of the water, sur- rounded with reeds, and poking out from beneath it was a human arm and hand.

"Call the police!"

"She's dead!"

"I'm going to be sick!"

As soon as we saw the hand Brooke stopped, hanging back, but I kept moving forward. When I reached the line of retreat- ing students I paused, wary, then made up my mind and broke through to the inner circle. It was just me and the hand.

It was a woman's hand, her body floating just below the surface and hidden in the reeds. Somehow they'd jostled the log and dislodged her, and the arm had popped out into the air. Her hand was poking up, twisted like a claw; her chipped, broken nails were painted bright red.

It's the new killer, I thought.

There was a voice behind me, deep—a man's voice. It seemed to echo through a vast, empty room.

"What do we do?"

I had to see it; I had to know if it was covered with the same little wounds as the others. "She might be alive," I said, splashing into the lake. "We've got to check." The exposed hand was soggy and covered with flecks of mud and rotten wood; there was no way she was alive. "We've got to pull her out."

There was another splash behind me, faint and distant. It was hard to hear with my own heartbeat suddenly roaring in my ears.

I grabbed the arm and pulled; it shifted, but it was heavier than I expected. Another pair of hands, rough and old, reached in next to me and we pulled again. The body shifted and the arm rose further out of the water, stiff and pale.

"It's been weighted down," I said.

"She's pinned under the tree."

"No," I said, "the body slides too easily to be pinned. Don't try to pull up, just drag it sideways toward the shore." We pulled together, dragging the body into shallow water where it could float closer to the surface. It was indeed a woman's body, stark white and naked except for a few bright nylon cords. The nakedness didn't bother me—dead bodies never did. I pulled on one of the cords, lightly at first, then harder as I tested the resistance. It was very heavy. With two hands I heaved it up and found a cinder block tied to the other end.

I looked at the person helping me. It was Mr. Verner, the social studies teacher.

"Someone weighted it down," I said again. The shore behind him was lined with students and other teachers, many of them turned away from the dead woman bobbing in the water. Beyond them I could see the bonfire raging, distant and bright.

"What do we do?" asked Mr. Verner again. Of course he was asking me; I knew more about this situation than anyone here. Did they know that? Was I revealing something secret?

"Call the police," I said. "Call Agent Forman of the FBI; he has an office in the police department."

I looked again at the body, twisted like a sculpture. Her limbs were stiff and crooked. "This is rigor mortis," I said. "It means it's only been dead a few hours, maybe a couple of days at the most." There were red marks on the wrists, and cuts and blisters on the chest and back, just like what we'd heard about the other bodies. "Did you call Agent Forman?"

Mr. Verner shouted to the shore. "Who has a phone?"

Rachel waved her hand and pointed at Marci, standing next to her with her cell phone to her ear. "She's on the phone with her dad," said Rachel. Marci's dad was a policeman. I looked at them, more directly now than I had all night, then looked back at the dead body, bobbing obscenely in the wavelets coming off the lake. It shouldn't be easier to look at it than at the girls, but it was.

In my peripheral vision teachers were herding the students away, and someone was bringing a blanket. Mr. Verner waded over to get it, then brought it back and draped it over the body.

"Come in to shore," he said, putting a hand on my arm.

I stumbled in, leaving the body in the water. The party had become a loose web of chaos, with some students pulling back, others dumbstruck and motionless, and still others crowding forward for a better view. Teachers were trying uncertainly to herd them in a knot of different directions.

Brooke met me at the top of the ridge, white as a corpse. "Who is it?" she asked.

"Do you have your phone?"

She nodded mutely and fished it out of her pocket. I dialed Agent Forman's cell number and sat stiffly on the ground, breathing slowly.

"This is Forman," said the voice on the other end, crisp and direct. There were sirens in the background.

"You're already on your way," I said.

"Dammit John, are you tied up in this?"

"Rigor mortis," I told him, "fully rigid. That means at least twelve hours, maybe more. The lake's pretty cool and that might have slowed it down."

"What are you doing, John?" Forman asked. "You're not a cop; you're not an investigator." He paused. "And yet you're always the one who finds the bodies first."

"Someone else found it," I said, closing my eyes. I could see the contorted body in my mind, stippled with angry red blisters. Had she been burned? "I'm just here by coincidence, Forman. The entire school is here, and everyone in town has known for weeks that we would be. If he left the body here recently, right here by the bonfire, he knew we'd find it. I think he wanted us to find it."

"Who's 'he'?" asked Forman.

"The guy who killed it," I said. *Was it a man or a demon?* "There's no missing body parts," I said, staggering to my feet, "and no major lacerations that I could see. I'm going to look again."

"No, John, leave it—"

Before he could finish something hit me from behind, slamming me between the shoulders, and I tumbled to the ground. I rolled onto my back and looked up: it was Rob Anders.

"What is wrong with you?" he said. "You dive in there like it's Christmas morning, you haul her right out where everyone can see her, you know the damn FBI agent's phone number by memory—"

"What?" I asked, shaking my head.

"Nobody innocent acts the way you act," he said. "Nobody normal knows the things you know. What's all that crap about rigor mortis?"

He was shouting, red-faced, waving his arms. He was far angrier than I would have expected. *Why is he so upset? Think, John, think like a person with empathy. Maybe he has a connection to the victim.*

"Did you know her?" I asked.

"What kind of a sick question is that, you freak?"

"Leave him alone, Rob," said Brooke, stepping in to help me to my feet. Rob shoved her away, knocking her to the ground—

—and I snapped.

I leapt up at Rob, taking him by surprise and knocking him down, pinning him under me. I'd never been in a fight—not with anyone who could fight back, at least—but I'd knocked the wind out of him, which gave me a moment to raise my fists and slam them clumsily into the top of his head. He swung a punch that hit me right in the eye and knocked me off the side. I staggered to my feet, ready for another swing, but Mr. Verner and another teacher were already there, pulling us apart.

"It's okay," said Brooke, pulling me back, "he's just a jerk, just ignore him."

I turned to face her, realizing what I'd done: she'd been threatened, and instead of trying to help her I had attacked the assailant. Just like I did with the demon. I didn't even help her stand up.

What's the right answer? I thought. *When do you help the good guys, and when do you stop the bad guys? I don't know what to do.*

I don't know which one I am.

I felt light-headed and sat down, finding Brooke's phone on the ground where it had been knocked out of my hand.

"He's a part of this," Rob was saying, arguing with Mr. Verner as he pulled him away. "He's a sick freak. He might even be the killer!"

I held the phone to my ear; Forman had already hung up.

"Call your dad," I said, handing Brooke the phone. "Tell him you'll be home late. This is going to take a while."

10

I spent all night trying to talk to Forman, but instead we were shuttled from cop to cop, giving our testimony over again for each one. At last I was given a sheaf of carbon copy papers and asked to fill out an official witness report. I spread it flat on the trunk of a police car and filled it out as thoroughly as I could, being sure to include the times and locations of my own actions as far back as school that day. Any more would have looked like I was trying too hard to look innocent. When I was done I turned it in and sat down by the dying bonfire, waiting to be excused. It was 11:30.

They wouldn't let us anywhere near the body, so I studied my memory of it as closely as I could. The wrists had been scratched and red—more ropes, maybe? But the ropes around its body hadn't left the same marks, so the ropes on its wrists must have been there longer, probably before it died. Someone—the killer, I assumed—had kept it bound. How long?

And the rest of the marks: red welts and blisters on pale white skin. There may have been deeper cuts as well, slices and stab wounds, though the water had long since washed the blood away. There were none of the huge, feral gashes that marked the Clayton Killer's victims. Could it be a new demon? One whose fingers turned to flame instead of claws, who left its victims scarred and mutilated but whole? Did demons work that way? Did they follow any rules at all?

I had seen one demon, or whatever it was, but that didn't mean that everything was connected to them. Humans were more than capable of murder all on their own. It was stupid to try to make this a demon when I knew so little. I needed to be patient—I needed to get her in the mortuary, where I could examine the wounds in detail, and read everything they knew about her in the file from the coroner. If only I could get to Forman, find out what he knew—

"I'm all done," said Brooke. "They said we're free to go."

I looked up and saw her standing above me, her arms folded tightly around her stomach, wrapping herself in her thin jacket. Her long legs were stippled with goose bumps, and she was shivering.

"That's it?" I asked. "They don't want to talk to us anymore?"

"It's almost midnight," said Brooke. "We've been talking to them for hours."

"But they haven't told us anything yet."

"I don't think they're going to," said Brooke. She picked up the fire-tending branch and poked the coals, sending up sparks and exposing the bright red heat beneath.

"Don't put it out," I said, stopping her. It was something Mr.

Crowley had said once: "I never kill a fire, I just let them go out by themselves." He'd killed ten people, maybe countless people in his life, but he wouldn't kill a fire. What was he, really?

"Are you ready to go?" asked Brooke.

I stared at the blackened firepit, a bank of half-dead coals in a six-foot circle of burned-out wreckage. It had been great once, massive and hot and glorious, but it had burned itself out early, and now it would linger for hours—most of a fire's life, maybe 80 percent, was just this: a long, slow death.

"Can we watch it a little longer?" I asked.

She stood, silent, limned with soft orange light. After a moment she set down the branch and took a seat next to me, crosslegged on the ground.

We watched for another hour, until the cops cleared the scene, put out the fire, and sent us home.

They announced the dead woman's name on TV the next morning: Janella Willis. She'd gone missing eight months before, somewhere on the east coast, but no one had any theories about how she ended up dead in Freak Lake. My guess on time of death turned out to be pretty accurate—she'd died almost exactly 24 hours before she was found, and had spent most of that time in the lake, under the log. The police and the news came to the same conclusion I had—that the body had been left there specifically for us to find—but I began to suspect something more. It seemed increasingly likely that the body had been left specifically for me.

The first two bodies had been left in spots that were easy to find—the second was even in a spot directly connected to the previous killings. So we knew the killer wanted them to be found, and we knew he was trying to say something. Now we had found a third body, carefully placed in a location that, on that one specific night, had a greater concentration of people than anywhere else in town. It was obvious he wanted it found. But more than that, it was a place full of teenagers—a place and time where *I* was guaranteed to be. If the bodies were messages from one killer to another, this last one had practically been left on my doorstep.

Messages on a door. . . . I felt my skin grow cold as soon as I thought of it. I'd left Mr. Crowley a long series of messages, trying to scare him and put him off guard. To draw him out and let him know he was being hunted. These bodies were exactly the same thing: the first corpse said "Here I am;" the second corpse, found at the scene of an earlier slaying, said "I am a part of what happened here." The third, left where I was certain to find it, said very clearly, "I know who you are."

I was being hunted.

School was out now, so I had nowhere to go, and I spent the entire day in my room poring over what little evidence I had. If I was being hunted, I needed to know who it was, and what they wanted. I didn't have much to go on, but you could learn a lot from even a single corpse—if you knew what to look for.

The central question of criminal profiling is: what did the killer do that he didn't have to do? This killer had tied up the victim, before death and after death. Were the two facts related— some kind of psychological need to bind people? That would be a control issue, which pointed, at least simplistically, to a serial killer. Or were the two tyings simply pragmatic—a way to keep her imprisoned before death, and weighted down after it? She'd been missing for eight months before she died, so the imprison-ment theory had merit. So why put weights on her when it would have been so much easier to just leave the body in the mud on the shore? If you want your victim to be found, why go through the pretense of hiding it in the first place?

Don't just ask, I told myself, *look for an answer*. What would have happened if he'd left it out, just lying there? A couple of kids in student government would have found it when they showed up to prepare for the Bonfire, and they would have called the police, and the Bonfire would have been cancelled or moved to the football field or something. Hiding it poorly meant that it would still be found, but not until later when there were plenty of witnesses.

What else? What did the killer do to the body that he didn't have to? He burned it. He cut it. Had he done anything else? The body might have broken bones, bruises, and who knows what other kinds of internal damage that I couldn't discover without a close examination. Speculation wouldn't help me—I needed real details. What was I forgetting?

Her nails! Her fingernails were chipped: did he do that, or had she chipped them herself by fighting back? Was she trying to dig her way out of something? They still had nail polish on them, after as many as eight months of imprisonment. Did nail polish last that long? If it did, it would mean nothing, but if it didn't, it would mean that she had been imprisoned relatively recently—or that the killer had given his prisoner luxury items, like nail polish, while she was still locked up. Why? That might say something very important about the killer's mindset, and his attitude toward his victims. I had to find out.

No one had mentioned the chipped nail polish on the news,

so Mom didn't know about it, and I could ask her without arousing suspicion—well, not the dead body kind of suspicion. She might have plenty of weird questions about why her son was asking about nail polish. It would be best to find out some other way, like looking it up online.

I opened the door to my room and heard the TV; that meant the computer would be free. I slipped into Mom's room to use it but she was there, a manila folder spread across the desk, working. She looked up when I came in.

"Hey John, do you need something?"

"I just wanted the computer," I said. "I thought you were watching TV?"

"That's Margaret," she said. "I'm just paying bills. I'll be finished up in a bit."

"Okay." I wandered in to the living room, where Margaret was watching some travel show.

"Hey John," she said, shifting on the couch to make room. I sat down and stared at the TV.

"Hey."

"I heard you had a big night a few days ago."

"Yeah, I guess."

"That's wonderful," she said. "Took a lot of guts, but I bet you're glad you did it."

I looked at her. "I just looked at it—I wasn't even the one who pulled it out of the water."

"I'm not talking about the body," she said, "I'm talking about the date. You finally asked Brooke out."

The date. I'd been so excited beforehand, but now it seemed like a lifetime ago. The body felt so much more important. So much bigger.

"It's too bad it got interrupted," she said. "You gonna ask her out again?"

"I guess so. I haven't really thought about it."

"What have you been thinking about?" Margaret stared at me a moment, then shook her head. "I don't know what kind of teenage boy would let a dead body distract him from a babe like Brooke. Haven't we had enough death for a while?"

"Do we have to talk about this?" I asked. The last thing I wanted was another lecture.

"You're sixteen," she said. "You should be thinking about live girls, not dead ones."

There was one quick way to turn this conversation around.

"Why didn't you ever get married?" I asked.

"Whoa," she said, taken aback. "Where did that come from?"

"You're talking about how I should be dating," I said, "but you're single and happy. Can't I be too?"

She raised one eyebrow. "You are a devious little bugger, aren't you?"

"You started it."

Margaret sighed, looked at the ceiling, then back at me. "What if you don't like my answer?"

I nodded. "Aha. That means it was my dad."

Margaret smiled grimly. "You're entirely too clever for a boy your age. Yes, it was your dad. What you probably don't realize is that I used to have a crush on him."

"You're kidding."

"Why wouldn't I? He was handsome, he was polite, and he and your mom and I were the only morticians in town. I think we both fell in love with him the day he showed up."

Margaret looked out the window as she spoke, and I wondered what she was seeing in her head. "You father could charm the oil off a snake," she said. "Our business was struggling until he got here, probably because no one took twenty-two-year-old twin sister morticians seriously. I don't even take us seriously, looking back. We interned with Jack Knutsen, and when Knut died we took over his business, but it wasn't until your father got here that things really took off."

"How could the only mortician in town not get any business?" I asked. "Either people died or they didn't—when they did, they'd have to come to you."

"Embalming is hardly a requirement," said Margaret, "and even today we only do about half the funerals here—the rest are in the local churches. No, we needed your father because he convinced Clayton County that they needed us. So he saved us, first of all, but it was more than that. He was . . . exciting. He was debonair. It was too good to believe that such a wonderful man had just dropped right into our laps, and the day I realized he loved your mother instead of me I could have died. And I would have, and gladly, if he'd looked at me the way he looked at her."

Her mind was somewhere else now—I could see it in the way her eyes focused so intently on something invisible and lost. When her eyes refocused on me and she smiled wanly, it was almost as if I could see her consciousness flow back into her body like a ghost.

"Of course," she said, "it didn't take long to realize I'd dodged a bullet. The sister who got left behind quickly became the pillar of support for the sister who thought she'd gotten everything she wanted. That was the only good thing to come of it, I guess—if your dad had been as good a person as we all thought he was, I probably would have stormed off and never forgiven April for stealing him." She looked at me a moment, mulling something over, then shook her head. "I shouldn't talk bad about your father in front of you," she said.

"What?" I asked. "You think I didn't notice what a jerk he was?"

"I know you did," she sighed. "I just wish it could have turned out differently."

"So are you telling me to date Brooke because you believe in the dreaminess of young love, or because you want to live vicariously through the relationships of others?"

Margaret raised her eyebrows, then laughed. "This is why your mother's going crazy," she said. "How can she live with someone who deserves a slap and a hug at the same time?"

"I'm a precious snowflake," I said.

"Computer's free," said Mom, coming into the room. "What are you guys talking about?"

"Nothing," said Margaret, turning back to the TV. I excused myself and went into the other room.

I didn't find anything specific, but I learned enough to know that an application of nail polish didn't stand a chance of lasting eight months. Assuming that Janella Willis had been a prisoner ever since she disappeared eight months ago, bound at the wrists and ankles, the killer had for some reason seen fit to give her nail polish. What was going on in this guy's head?

I needed to see that body. I cleared the Internet cache and locked myself in my room, staring at the wall and studying my memories of the body one more time. A killer was hunting me, sending me signals, but what did he want? If he knew who I was, why not just come and get me? Maybe he actually didn't know who I was, and this was his way of testing me to see how I reacted, to draw me out. Maybe he was waiting for a response.

John would never respond, but Mr. Monster would, and that's who this killer was really looking for. Mr. Monster is the one who'd killed the demon, and the one who dreamed about the new victims every night. He was the one who longed to send a message back to this new killer, though thus far I'd been able to stop him.

When this new killer finally did make his move, who would he find? John, or Mr. Monster?

11

I was in a dungeon, nailing someone to a thick wooden board, when the phone rang. I opened my eyes and sat up in my bedroom, listening to Mom's footsteps as she walked to her cell phone. It was five a.m. I'd been asleep for almost two hours.

"Hello?" she said. Her voice was muffled, but there was only one plausible reason for a phone call at this hour. The coroner was bringing the body, and they needed it worked on quickly. They were probably flying it back to the family this afternoon. I got out of bed and pulled on a shirt.

"Bye." I heard the soft snap as Mom closed her phone, and the creak of the floor as she began to move. Faint footsteps told me she was walking into the hall, and a moment later she opened my door. "Wake up, John, the . . . oh. Do you ever sleep?"

"Was that Ron?" I asked, pulling on socks.

"Yeah, they're bringing the . . . how do you do that?"

"I'm a genius," I said. "You probably ought to call Margaret if they're in this much of a hurry."

She stared at me a moment, then flipped open her phone. "Get something to eat," she said, walking back to her room. "And stop knowing everything."

Within half an hour Ron pulled up in the coroner's van, along with a couple of policemen. I stayed upstairs, watching through the window, as they met Mom by the back door and carried the body in.

Margaret pulled up as the van was leaving, and we all met downstairs to pull on our masks and aprons. Mom was leafing through the papers.

"No body parts reported missing," she said. We'd learned to check that before we got started, after a bad experience last fall. "They performed a full autopsy, bagged the organs, and sewed her back up." She set down the papers. "I hate these."

"Dibs on the cavity embalming," said Margaret, pushing open the door. The cavity embalming was where we used the trocar to suck all the gunk out of the organs and replace them with embalming fluid; with an autopsy case like this, where the organs had been removed, she could do that off to the side of the room while Mom and I did an arterial embalming on the rest of the body. The trouble was, an arterial embalming for a body with no organs was like trying to carry water in a sieve— there were too many holes, and the fluid leaked everywhere. We'd have to embalm it in at least four sections, possibly more.

The body was laid on the metal table, still in the body bag. I washed my hands quickly and pulled on a pair of disposable gloves, then zipped the bag open. The coroner had wrapped her in towels for modesty, and to soak up any blood that leaked out during transit, but there wasn't much blood left at this point. The body was white and empty, like a doll.

"Grab her head," Mom said, putting one hand under the small of the woman's back, and another under her legs. I supported the head and shoulders, and on three we lifted the body up while Margaret pulled the body bag out from underneath. We set the corpse back on the table and Mom started peeling away the towels. "Close your eyes," she said, and I did, waiting patiently while she stowed the transport towels in a biohazard bag and draped new ones over the chest and groin. I kept my eyes closed until she said, "all done."

The body's chest was cut in a Y-incision: two cuts from shoulder to breastbone, and one long cut from breastbone to groin. The top half had been stitched back up, but the bottom was still loose and a bright orange bag peeked through. Margaret carefully pulled the abdomen open and extracted the heavy bag, setting it on a metal cart and then wheeling it to the side counter by the trocar. Mom handed me a warm rag and a bottle of Dis-Spray, and we went to work cleaning the outside of the corpse.

Embalming usually relaxed me, but this time little details kept jumping out and spoiling the calm. First it was her wrists— no longer red, for there was very little blood left in the tissue, but obviously worn and tattered. They'd been bound for some time, and very tightly; portions of the skin were worn away completely to expose the muscle underneath. I imagined the body alive—a living, breathing woman, struggling desperately to escape her bonds. She twisted and turned, fighting back the pain as the ropes bit into her skin and tore it away. She couldn't escape.

I thought about the lake, calm and desolate, and pushed the

thoughts of struggle away. *I'm just cleaning—nothing more, nothing less. Let me spray some more on this part, and scrub it gently. Everything is quiet. Everything is fine.*

The skin was smooth for the most part, but marked here and there with cuts, scabs, and blisters. Now that the body was cleaned, far more of these blemishes were evident than I'd seen at the lake—they speckled the body like bits of confetti, random and horrifying. What could do this? The blisters were obviously from burns—ominous patches where the skin had bubbled and swollen like a hot dog on a grill. I touched one softly, feeling the bumps and valleys. The center of the blistered patch was tough, like a callus, or like it had burned hotter than the rest. Someone had placed something on this person, intentionally burning it, over and over in different places.

Someone had tortured it.

The cuts and scratches on the body that had looked so strange before made better sense now—she hadn't scratched herself by running through a forest or tumbling through the brush to escape, she had been deliberately stabbed and sliced numerous times. From the scabs that covered some of the wounds it was obvious that this had been going on for some time; I looked closer, searching for healed-over scars, and found some, thin and white, scattered all over her skin. How would someone make such small lacerations? A straight razor would make a long slash, unless it was used very carefully; these, on the other hand, were short, almost puncture-like wounds. I set down the Dis-Spray and examined one of the recent wounds in greater detail, stretching it apart with my fingers. It wasn't deep. I looked at another one, a tiny hole in the muscle of her thigh, and this time it was deep—long and narrow, like a nail hole. I flashed back to my dream this morning, hearing a girl scream, and imagined what I would use to make these kinds of wounds: a nail here, a screwdriver there, a pair of scissors somewhere else. It looked chaotic, but there was a pattern to it as well—a mind guiding the procedure, trying different tools to see what each one would do, and what reaction each one would get. Did a nail in the thigh provoke the same kind of scream as a nail in the shoulder? A nail in the abdomen? Which did the victim fear more when you came back the second time—a wound that pierced muscle, organ, or bone?

"John?"

I looked up. Mom was staring at me.

"Huh?"

"Are you okay?" It was hard to read her through the surgical mask, but her eyes were dark and narrow, and the skin around them was wrinkled. She was concerned.

"I'm fine," I said, picking up the Dis-Spray and getting back to work. "I'm just tired."

"You just woke up."

"I'm still waking up," I said. "I'm just groggy, I'm fine."

"Okay," said Mom, and went back to work on the body's hair.

Except I wasn't fine. Everything I saw, I imagined myself doing—every wound on the body I saw myself inflicting. This was not the serene death of an old woman who had passed away in her sleep; this was a brutal, violent death—a dehumanizing series of tortures and humiliations. This didn't pacify Mr. Monster, it excited him. He was a shark who smelled blood in the water. He was a tiger who smelled fresh meat.

I was a killer who sensed a victim—not this body, but the

thing that had attacked it. I was a killer of killers, and a new one in town meant it was time to kill again.

I slammed down the Dis-Spray, harder than I'd meant to, and left for the bathroom. I couldn't be in there anymore. I peeled off my gloves and tossed them in the trash, turning on the sink and scooping handfuls of cold water into my mouth. I swallowed, wiping my face on my sleeve, then paused. After a moment I drank again.

I would not allow myself to think those thoughts. *I am not a killer*, I thought, *Mr. Monster is the killer. I'm the one who stops him*. I was scared.

But I had to get back in there. I had to know everything I could about the body, because that would tell me more about the person who'd killed it. But why did I need to know? Agent Forman's words came back to me: "You're not a cop. You're not an investigator." I didn't need to study this body at all. I could ignore it completely.

I walked back in to the embalming room without thinking, as if my feet were moving by themselves. I turned to walk out but instead pulled two more gloves from the box on the counter.

"Everything okay?" Mom asked.

"Everything's fine," I said. I walked back to the table and picked up my rag, using it as an excuse to look closer at the cuts in the corpse's arms.

"We're all done with the top," said Mom, "help me sit her up so we can do the back." I took one shoulder, Mom took the other, and we pulled; rigor mortis had come and gone, and the body moved easily.

"Uh oh," said Mom, freezing in place. The body was halfway

sitting, but it was light and hollow and easy to hold up. I looked at Mom's hand and saw her pressing against the skin of the body's back. It moved strangely. "Tissue gas," she said.

Margaret turned and looked warily at Mom. "You're kidding."

"Check it out," said Mom, and moved her hand again. I peered closer and saw it—the skin moved over the top of the muscle freely, as if it were disconnected. That was bad.

"The skin is slipping," said Mom. "The autopsy cleansers must have masked the smell." She leaned in close to the back, sniffed, then pulled down her mask and sniffed again. She reeled back in disgust. "Oh, that's horrible. Lay her back down, John."

We laid the body down, minds racing. Tissue gas was an embalmer's worst nightmare—a highly infectious bacteria that thrived on dead tissue and released a noxious gas inside the body. Smell was usually the easiest way to detect it, but some-times—as with this body—the smell was buried under other chemicals, and the only way to identify it was the "skin-slip" Mom had found on the back, where interior gas bubbles sepa-rated the skin from the muscle. The gas itself was bad enough, because the stink would soon become so foul it would be all but impossible to cover up. That didn't reflect well on us when people showed up for the viewing. Even worse than the gas, though, were the bacteria that made it—once they got into your workspace, you might never get them out again. If we didn't put a stop to this right now, every body we embalmed would catch the same bacteria from our tools and table. It could destroy the entire business.

"Everybody stop and think," said Mom. "What have we touched?"

"Rubber gloves," said Margaret. "A scalpel to cut open the hazmat bag; the trocar."

"Just one?" asked Mom.

"It was already attached to the vaccum," said Margaret. "I didn't even open the drawer with the others."

"I touched the Dis-Spray bottle, three rags, the comb, and the shampoo," said Mom. "John touched a bottle and a rag."

"And the doorknob," I said, "and the bathroom doorknob."

"You didn't take your gloves off first?"

"No."

"John . . . ," said Mom, annoyed. "Okay, anything else?"

"I touched the cart," said Margaret, "and we should disinfect the counters as well, just in case."

"And the table, obviously," said Mom. "Let's designate an infection zone by Margaret, and put all of our used tools there; we'll keep the rest of it clean, and when we're done embalming we can clean the room til it screams in protest."

"And we need to call the police," I said.

Mom and Margaret both looked up in surprise. "Why?" asked Mom.

"This might be important to the investigation."

"You don't think they already know?" asked Mom. "They've been studying this body for four days."

"Was it in the paperwork?" I asked.

Mom thought, then glanced at Margaret. "He's right. Ron would have told us if he knew. The bacteria might not have developed yet."

"Plus Ron's got to disinfect his whole lab," said Margaret. "It won't do us any good to keep clean if every body he sends us is already infected." She rolled her eyes. "I have half a mind to go clean it myself—I don't know if I trust Ron to do it right."

Mom peeled off her gloves, threw them in the trash, then washed her hands with hot water and soap in the sink. She turned off the water, thought a moment, then turned it back on and washed the water handles and soap dispenser as well. When she was certain everything was clean she motioned for me to open the door, so she wouldn't have to touch anything else in the room, and went to the office to call.

"Smart thinking, John," said Margaret. "If they don't know about the tissue gas, one of the wounds might be a lot older than they think it is. You've got a knack for this stuff." She turned back to her pile of organs, and I went back to the body. Tissue gas was most common in bedsores—big, nasty ones on hospital patients, or on old people who never moved for weeks or months at a time. Gangrene was another possible source of the bacteria, and usually showed up in the same types of cases. It was possible that this body could have developed tissue gas in one of those ways if she'd been held in one place for months on end, without being allowed to move, but there was no evidence of that here—besides, both of those causes would leave massive exterior wounds. Most of hers were small, and any obvious infections had been cleaned away during the autopsy.

There was one other way to get the right kind of bacteria, that didn't require a big wound. I put my hands under the body's shoulders and lifted, feeling the skin slide sickly under my fingers. The back was covered with cuts and punctures and burns, just like the rest of the body, but some, as I'd noticed before, were bigger. More misshapen. The coroner had cleaned the body so well that there were no visible infections, but the shape of the wounds was enough if you knew what you were looking for: a series of wounds similar to the others, but irregular and distorted as if they'd been stretched out of shape. Just like a bedsore, but smaller. There were only a few ways that kind of thing would happen to an ordinary wound, and only one of them would result in tissue gas. Somehow, by accident or by design, these wounds had been infected with human waste.

I peered more closely at the wounds. She might have been kept for days in a cell with no toilet, or some feces might have been forced into the wounds manually by her attacker. Either way, the cruel, devastating dehumanization hit me like a wave, pulling me back down into the waking nightmare I'd been in ever since we started on the body.

I was in the embalming room, but I was also in a basement somewhere; I was with Janella Willis the corpse, but I was also with Janella Willis the crying, screaming victim—not just once but a dozen times, a hundred times, all at once, different realities lacing in and out of each other as they howled around me. I was stabbing her, I was burning her, I was breaking her bones. Sometimes I laughed, sometimes I cursed and raged, and other times I was simply there, blank and hollow. Part of my mind was enjoying the thrill of it, while another part was trying to analyze the possibilities; I tried to shut them both off, desperate to think about anything else, but it was too much. Instead I focused on the analytical side, trying to force myself to turn this into something helpful, hoping there was some way I could learn something or discover something by living through the scenario in my mind. Instead I found myself playing out the same scenarios with Brooke instead, simultaneously thrilled and repulsed by each piercing scream.

No! I refused to let myself sink to that. My eyes were open, but dark daydreams clouded my view and melded with the reality around me. The woman on the table was Brooke, her abdomen sliced wide open. *No! Never Brooke!* I tried again to push the thoughts away entirely, but again I was too weak. The best I could do was to twist them, to change them into something less intense.

Marci.

Marci was physically beautiful, but she was nothing to me—and that made her easier to bear thinking about. Fantasizing about Brooke felt wrong, like I was betraying her directly, but if I did the same for Marci . . . I had no attachment to Marci. There was nothing to betray. I latched on to the thought—Marci's shape and her color, the dark brown of her hair—and then there she was on the table. I could breathe easier now.

With my mind under stronger control I realized that I was gripping the table with one hand, steadying myself against it. I needed to get out of there. The door opened and Mom came through, sighing, and I put another hand on the table, taking another step toward the door.

I can do this, I thought. *I'm leaving a bad situation. I can barely control my own thoughts, but I'm still in command of my actions.* Mom said something to Margaret, something about Ron and the phone. I ignored them. I needed to leave.

One more step. I was doing it.

And then the door opened again, and Lauren was standing there—her face bruised, her eyes puffy from damage and tears.

"What happened?" Mom cried.

Lauren was whimpering, a lost kitten in a vast and deadly

wilderness. Her words were a wrenching knot of terror and confusion: "He hit me."

And then the world shattered, and Mr. Monster roared so loud that Mom and Margaret and Lauren could all hear it. They looked at me in shock, and I ran from the room.

Death! Death!

Confusion became rage, and the deep, driving need to kill exploded in a torrent of red-hot emotion. *No more waiting—it has to be now!* I stumbled through the halls, lost in my own home, until at last I found my way outside and sucked in the fresh air like a drowning man.

Kill him! Make him scream!

NO!

It was still early, but the sun was rising and the town was infused with ghostly half-light. I paused for balance, holding the wall, then walked to my car and turned it on. I had to do something. The tires squealed as I pulled away, and in my mind Curt answered with a squeal of terror. At the corner I forced myself to turn in the opposite direction from his house, my driving wild and erratic, as if my own hands were fighting with me.

I will not kill!

Then what?

I pushed my foot down hard, pressing the pedal all the way to the floor, letting the pure animal thrill of speed wipe the fog away from my mind. When it cleared I slowed down and answered myself.

Fire.

I could feel the need boiling inside of me, a knot of angry tension that shook and struggled like a living thing. Fire would calm it. Fire.

I drove wildly to the old warehouse, sliding to a stop in the gravel outside. I climbed out of the car and slammed the door, loving the wrenching crash as the force of it shook the car. There was no one else there, and I stormed inside looking for fuel; I didn't have my gas can, but there in the middle of the floor were the cans of alcohol-based paint. I picked up one of these and splashed the contents across the mattress and a pile of wood I'd built the other day. I picked up another and threw the whole thing; it bounced off a wall and hit the ground with a thud, spraying its flammable liquid all across the warehouse. I kicked a barrel to knock it over, but it stayed up and I kicked it again, then again and again, feeling a rush of adrenaline as the barrel resisted, resisted, and at last tipped over.

Then I thought of Curt beating Lauren, and I yelled again. It echoed madly in the warehouse, inarticulate and inhuman.

I fumbled in my pocket for a book of matches—the one thing a pyromaniac was never without—and pried a match out of it with trembling hands. I folded the matchbook over backwards, trapping the chemical head between the strike pad and the cardboard, then ripping it out violently. The head popped to life and the match lit, and with it I lit the entire book. I felt a thrill as it flared up, my breath growing fast and urgent, and dropped the ball of flame onto the fuel-soaked mattress. Fire rippled across it instantly, flashing brightly and then dying down as the initial fuel was consumed. Soon the mattress itself was on fire, not just the paint, and I stepped closer. It was beautiful.

The fire spread to other things—the pallets I'd stacked it on, the wooden planks nearby, the splash of paint on the floor. I watched it move from one object to the next, sometimes running, sometimes leaping, always moving and growing and crackling with joy. Was the cat here? I didn't care—let it burn. I stayed until it wasn't safe anymore, relishing the release. This was what I wanted! This was power! With fire itself doing my bidding, I was practically a god.

I backed out slowly, watching the flames dance behind the windows. As I stood in the doorway a flash of movement caught my eye, and I saw the white cat streaking out from a hiding place toward the open door. I timed its approach and slammed my foot into the door frame right as it passed, hearing it hiss and cry as my kick pinned it to the wall. I grabbed its tail in my hands and yanked it up angrily, pulling it across and slamming it into the wall. It cried again, desperate, and I windmilled it back into the wall on the other side of the door. It hit with a sickening crunch.

"Is this what you wanted?" I was screaming. "Is this what you wanted?" I leaned back and then whipped it forward, hurling the cat into the middle of the jubilant orange flames. It arced through the air and slammed sickeningly into a stack of wood. I heard it mewl again, weak and wretched, and then the heat was too much and I backed out of the building completely.

12

"You saw what he did to her. Are you sure there's nothing you can do?"

It had been two days since Curt had hit Lauren, but Lauren refused to press charges, and there was nothing the law could do. Mom had spent the first day yelling—usually over the phone, though we all got our share of her attention—but now she was tired and worn. She continued to call, begging for someone to intervene and save her daughter, but her protests were weak and fatalistic: everyone who could possibly help had already said no.

"Yes, ma'am, I do understand the law. I sued my husband with that law, so I know it very . . ." Pause. "No, they were not married. Why should that have anything to do with it? Is assault not a crime anymore unless you're married?"

I'd spent the entire time hiding in my room, desperate to get out of the house but scared of being arrested. The entire warehouse had burned to the ground, and the flames had somehow spread to the surrounding trees; it had taken the fire department all day and most of the night to put it out. I'd left the scene before anyone got there, of course, but arson was suspected almost immediately. I was safer inside.

More than the fire, what scared me the most was the cat. I'd killed a cat. I'd never done that before, and it terrified me. I'd broken several of my rules in the past year, but it had always been for a reason: I decided very rationally that I should stalk Mr. Crowley, specifically to help me find a way to stop him from killing. I attacked his wife as part of a careful plan, because it was the only way to trap him, and I eventually killed him because it was the only way to save the town. These were all delicate, painful decisions, and I'd weighed each one carefully before taking that step and breaking that rule. But the cat—the cat was different. The cat was an impulse, an emotional urge, a heat-of-the-moment decision that I was barely aware of until it was over. In all of my previous decisions, I'd chosen to grant Mr. Monster power. That day in the warehouse, Mr. Monster had taken power for himself.

And if he'd done it once, he could do it again. I was terrified to think of where and when it could happen, and what I could possibly do to stop it.

"Please . . . my daughter was attacked. She was brutally beaten by a citizen of your community, who's still out there right now. No, I'm not being unreasonable! May I please speak with your superior?"

I sat on the floor of my room, the door locked tight, my body squeezed into the gap between my bed and the wall. I had a pillow pulled down over my head, but I could still hear the shouting.

"Hello, Agent Forman? This is April Cle—" Pause. "Yes, I know, and I'm sorry to call you again, but—" Pause. "But I've already talked to them, and there's nothing they can do." Pause. "No, I've talked to her too—" Pause. "But there has to be something you can—"

There had been a lot of bugs in that warehouse, I thought. I probably killed them all. Were bugs against the rules? I bet I've killed plenty of bugs in my life—there were some dead ones on the windshield of my car, for crying out loud. Was I supposed to feel guilty about all of them? I turned the thought over in my mind, examining it. *Bugs were probably fine. They didn't feel anything, and they didn't care what you did to them, and nobody else cared either, so I might as well do something. That's practically why they're here in the first place, right? They're not doing anything else for us. I should go outside and find one—just one. I wouldn't even kill it, just pull off a wing or a leg. Just something small. No one would ever notice.*

"Hi, is this the domestic abuse hotline? My name is April, and I live in Clayton. . . ." Pause. "Yes, Clayton County." Pause. "I know you don't have an office here, I called long distance to reach you. . . ." Pause. "I've already called the police, and they won't . . . yes, I'll hold."

I stood up to go outside. I only needed one bug—a tiny one, like a ladybug. There was usually a big pile of ants by one of the cracks in the sidewalk, and I could mush a whole footprint-full if I wanted, but that wouldn't help. There'd be no satisfaction in a quick stomp. I wanted one bug I could spend some time on, and watch what happened as each leg came off. I wanted it to know that it was being hurt by me, by a purposeful mind, and not by some change in the weather. I unlocked my door and started down the hall, hoping I could get out without Mom stopping me.

I was just three steps from the apartment door when somebody knocked.

Mom looked up from the phonebook, red-eyed and gaunt. She stared at the door with a blank, uncomprehending gaze, as if she wasn't sure what it was. The knock came again.

"Well, see who it is," Mom snapped.

I opened the door and felt my stomach lurch; it was Lauren, her eye black and her face streaked with dry tears. She looked at me with a broken smile and reached for my face where Rob Anders had punched me.

"We're twins," she said softly. She rested her fingertips on my cheekbone, right below the thin scab where Rob's punch had split the skin.

"Please tell me you've come to your senses," said Mom, standing up. "You can stay here if you need to—"

"No, Mother, I'm here to tell you to stop," said Lauren. "I tried to call you, but I can't even get through because you won't get off it. Stop calling the police!"

"But you need to report this!"

"No I don't!" said Lauren. "Listen, I was just scared that day when I came here, and I didn't know what I was thinking, but now I do. I know you don't understand—"

"You think I don't understand?" Mom asked, stepping forward. "You know what we lived through here! You know what your father did to me!"

"Stop trying to bring Dad into this!" cried Lauren. "It has

nothing to do with him, because Curt is not Dad and I am not you. Curt really loves me, and we've talked about it, and we know that it's never going to happen again, and—"

"Don't be such an idiot, Lauren!" Mom shouted. "How can you possibly—"

"I didn't come here to get yelled at, Mother!"

"No, you've got someone at home to do that for you!"

I turned to walk back into my room, but Mom grabbed my arm.

"Don't walk away from this," she told me, "you're as much a part of it as any of us. Tell her she needs to call the police."

"Don't drag John into this. . . ." said Lauren.

"Tell her!" said Mom.

I didn't know what to say, so I stared back helplessly and tried to think peaceful thoughts: Freak Lake in winter, alone and calm; our street at night when nothing moved; a body on the embalming table, perfectly still and silent.

"You can't live like this," Mom told her, then looked back at me. "Tell her she can't live like this."

"I don't want to get involved," I said quietly.

"You don't want to get involved!" Mom shouted. "All you ever do is overreact to problems, and now you're not reacting at all?"

"I don't want to get involved," I repeated.

"You're already involved!" Mom shouted. "Am I the only sane person left alive? Am I the only person left in the entire world who thinks that my daughter getting beaten up is a big deal? That it's something worth fighting back about? I mean . . . Lauren, baby . . . don't you love yourself at all?"

"I don't know why I came here," said Lauren, turning to

leave. "It's like talking to the most hostile brick wall in the world."

"You came here because you know that I can help you," said Mom harshly, following her onto the stairway. "I've lived through this, and I know what you're going through."

"Just because you ruined your own relationship doesn't mean you get to ruin mine," said Lauren, her voice distant. She was halfway down the stairs.

Mom laughed—the kind of dry, brittle laugh that wanted to be a scream and a cry, and compromised somewhere in the middle. "You think I ruined my relationship? You think my black eyes and my broken ankle and the whole divorce were all my fault?" Her voice grew even more raspy and desperate. "Do you think your black eye is your fault? Is that what this is all about?"

The door opened downstairs, but instead of Lauren's footsteps storming away I heard Brooke's voice.

"Um, hi," she said brightly. "It's Lauren, right?"

"Yeah," said Lauren slowly. She apparently didn't recognize Brooke. "Are you here for John?"

"Hi Brooke," said Mom at the top of the stairs, hastily wiping her eyes. "Come on up, sweetie."

"I don't want to interrupt anything," said Brooke.

"No, no, it's fine," said Mom, gesturing toward the living room. "Everything's fine. Come on in."

"What happened to your eye?" Brooke asked.

"John's got one just like it," said Lauren, avoiding the question. "They run in the family."

Mom glowered.

"I hope you're okay," said Brooke.

"I was just leaving," said Lauren, and called out to me. "Bye John!"

I didn't say anything for a moment, then shouted "Bye Lauren!" when I heard the door hinges squeak open louder. Footsteps creaked up the stairs, and Mom stepped aside to let Brooke in. She was dressed the way she typically was, in bright summer colors, and I slouched down in my black, rumpled pajamas; I hadn't even bothered to get dressed yet.

"Hey John," she said, her eyes lighting up. She laughed. "Wow, I wish I was still in pajamas."

"Yeah," I said. Mom was scowling behind her, eyeing the stairs, obviously wanting to chase Lauren outside and continue their fight.

"No!" said Brooke, suddenly embarrassed, "I don't mean to . . . I'm not trying to make fun. Dangit." She squeezed her eyes shut. There was an awkward pause, then Brooke smiled again. "Pretty crazy night the other night, huh?"

"Yeah," I said. Outside, Lauren's door slammed, and a moment later her engine roared to life.

"So anyway," said Brooke, "I um . . . this is stupid, but . . . I wrote you a poem."

I stared back. "You did?"

"I know it's kind of cheesy," she said, "but it was my mom's idea. I mean, the poem was my mom's idea, but the thing the poem's about was my idea, I don't want you to think that . . ." She rolled her eyes, embarrassed, and then grinned cheerfully. "I am really screwing this up, aren't I?"

Mom was crying silently behind her.

I waited a moment longer. "So, did you bring it?"

"Oh!" said Brooke. "Sorry, I'm just kind of nervous. Yes;

here." She handed me a piece of paper. "It's just a short poem, I don't want you to get all excited about getting a big sonnet and then it's just a little . . . so anyway, here you go."

She grinned again, looking at me, not moving. "I was going to recite it for you," she said, "but then I'd have to crawl into a hole and die of embarrassment, so you're on your own. Sorry."

I looked down at the paper. It was four lines, written in a curvy, slightly ornate handwriting that said she'd written it somewhere else and transferred the finished product here to make it look nice.

We went out to the Bonfire on a dark and stormy night.
We thought it would be lots of fun; instead we got a fright.
I still want to go out with you, so we should try again.
Come pick me up tomorrow night, if you're not busy then.

She wanted to go out with me again—after everything that had happened, after every horrible thing I'd done in the last week, she still wanted a date. And I didn't know if I trusted myself anymore.

"I know it's a dumb poem," she said, looking down. "But I thought it would be fun, since we didn't really get to finish our last date . . . I mean, we barely started, really, and anyway . . ."

I couldn't rely on the mortuary to let out pressure anymore, and the fire hadn't worked at all—it had made me more anxious, not less. Brooke might be the best way to forget everything and feel normal.

She pursed her lips, and her face started turning red. I suddenly realized I hadn't said anything yet.

"Yeah," I said quickly. "That sounds great." Her face brightened immediately. "Tomorrow night?"

"Yeah," she said. "Around five?"

"Sure." I paused. "What do you want to do?"

"Just let me take care of it all," she said. "You just bring you. And your car." She laughed.

"Okay," I said. "I'll come get you at five."

"Cool," she said. "Great!" She turned around, smiled at my mom, then waved at me and clattered happily down the stairs. "See you tomorrow!"

"That figures," said Mom, stepping in from the landing and closing the door. "The only member of this family with a normal relationship is a sociopath." She laughed thinly and sat on the couch.

In the back of my head, a tiny voice told me that this was a bad idea.

That's weird, I thought. *Usually the voice tells me to follow Brooke, and I tell it to stay away. Huh.*

13

In the trees behind my house I made a pile of crickets, small and black, wings fluttering wildly, and next to them a pile of tiny cricket legs like thin plastic shavings. Without their legs the crickets wiggled helplessly, abdomens curling like stubby fingers, wings flailing against air and dirt and gravity. They couldn't take off from the ground, it seemed—they needed legs to leap up and catch the air. It was fascinating to watch.

I thought perhaps their leg stumps would bleed, either blood or whatever was inside a cricket, but the joints popped apart like petals from a flower, separate and whole. There were no wounds.

I buried the squirming pile and brushed off my hands. I needed to get ready for tonight.

Brooke was in absolutely no danger from me—and for a lot of reasons. First were my rules: they stopped me from doing anything I shouldn't do, and I'd been following them strictly for days without a slip. The second reason, related to the first, was the simple fact that Mom had been out of the house all day. She'd gone to Margaret's, then to Lauren's, to try once again to persuade her to file a report of domestic abuse. I had pushed them all from my mind, filling it instead with pleasant thoughts and calming mantras: 1, 1, 2, 3, 5, 8, 13, 21. I was at peace. Brooke had nothing to fear from a mind at peace.

The third reason, of course, were the crickets; any violent or dangerous tendencies I might have had were sated and still, buried with them in the dirt. Mr. Monster was happy, I was happy, the world was happy.

I paused in the woods behind my house. Brooke's house was just a little ways off on the left; I could see the roof from here. During the winter I'd spent many hours in these woods, high up in a tree behind Brooke's house, watching through her window. It was dangerous, but I was careful, and no one ever saw me. She never closed the curtains, probably because she never expected anyone to be back there—our street was right on the edge of Clayton, and there was nothing behind any of our houses but a mile or two of forest.

I'd stopped, of course—it was dangerous to spend that much time thinking about Brooke, which was why I'd started avoiding her in the first place. But things were different now. I was spending more time with her—and she wanted me to spend more time with her. I could think about her without feeling guilty. And I still had my rules, so nothing was going to happen.

There was at least one rule, though, that I really ought to change. It felt stupid, on our last date, that I hadn't allowed myself to look at her shirt. It's not like I was staring at her breasts or anything—I just wanted to know what kind of shirt she was wearing. There was nothing wrong with that.

I was standing behind her house now, still buried fifty yards or more in the cover of the trees. I could see her window from here, but it was too bright outside to see inside—and I wasn't there for that, anyway, I was just passing by. Though if I could see in, I'd be able to know what she was wearing, and I could dress to match. I still had no idea what we were doing: something classy? Something messy? Something in between? I might dress completely wrong for whatever we were doing, which could ruin the whole date.

Don't do it.

I caught a flash of movement in one of the lower windows. Maybe just a quick peek—I didn't want to stalk her, like before, but a quick peek wasn't stalking. I just happened to be in the area, and if I happened to see what she was wearing, there was no harm done. It would actually be a good thing. Considering how devastated she'd feel if I showed up in the wrong clothes, or in clothes that clashed with hers, I practically owed it to her to take a peek. She invited me on this date, after all—the least I could do was dress appropriately.

I crept closer, my eyes darting back and forth between the two rear windows. They had a sliding glass door in their kitchen, leading onto a low deck, and I could see someone moving around inside. Was it Brooke or her mom? The door opened abruptly and I stepped behind a tree as a small form dashed out. Brooke's little brother, Ethan. What if I was found? Would she call off the date? I ducked down and began to walk backwards, crouching below the line of brush, when suddenly a voice rang out from the house, clear and beautiful.

Brooke.

I rose up slowly from my crouch, moving my head slightly to the side to peer through the trees. She was standing in the doorway, calling Ethan back inside. She was wearing jean shorts, as always, and a pink top with white flowers. She was gorgeous. Ethan ran back in, and Brooke slid the door closed again.

See? No harm in that at all. It was good to drop that rule and let myself look at Brooke freely.

This date was going to be perfect.

Back at home I picked out some clothes—nice, but casual enough to match what Brooke had been wearing—and then showered carefully, washing my hands five times to be sure the smell of dirt and crickets was gone. I'd been in the woods most of the day, and it was almost time to pick her up.

I dressed quickly and grabbed my wallet and keys from their spot on my dresser. Next to it was an old pocketknife, from my days in Cub Scouts; I'd started sharpening it over the last few days, just to fill the time. Should I take it tonight? I wasn't likely to need it, of course, but you never know. What if I'd had it at the lake, for example, when we found the body in the reeds? I could have cut it out of the ropes. And after all, I still didn't know what Brooke was planning for our date—we might very well come upon a loose screw, or one that was too tight; we might need to open a bottle or puncture a can. Brooke was dressed pretty casually, after all, and she'd said last time that she loved fishing at the lake, so for all I knew we were headed out there, and I might have to scale and gut a fish.

Don't take it.

Nonsense; the knife was honed and sharp, perfect for sliding into the meat of a fish and slicing it clean from end to end.

Brooke would love it. I patted the knife in my pocket and smiled. Time to go get her.

I arrived at Brooke's house early and knocked on her door. There was a shout from inside, followed by the clomp of hurried footsteps on the stairs. When Brooke opened the door, smiling widely, she was in a different shirt: blue and white and black in jagged stripes. I frowned and stepped back.

"Hey John!" she said.

Why had she changed?

"You okay?" she asked.

"Yeah." I smiled falsely. I thousand reasons ran through my mind: she knew I'd been watching, and changed her shirt as revenge; she guessed I'd been watching, and changed her shirt to gauge my surprise and learn the truth. It didn't matter why— it was different, and it felt wrong. An afternoon full of imagined scenarios crumbled away, false and sickening in the face of this new, unseen, unplanned-for shirt.

"Are you sure you're okay?" she asked. "You look kind of sick."

She was worried about me. Which meant she cared about me. Which meant that I was stupid to get so worked up. It wasn't the shirt that bothered me, really, it was the change—the shocking difference between my vivid fantasies and the dull, brittle truth. And the new shirt was nice—it was fitted but loose, and complemented her figure without showing too much. I needed to get over it.

I smiled again and stepped forward. "I'm fine; the shirt's fine."

"The shirt?" She looked puzzled. I thought quickly.

"My collar was a little itchy earlier," I said. "It's fine now. Ready to go?"

"Yup." She grabbed a canvas bag from inside the door and stepped out onto the porch. She wore pants now instead of shorts, and her long blond hair was loose and wavy. She looked wonderful, and I allowed my gaze to roll over her appreciatively as she shouldered her bag and closed the door. She was thinner than Marci, less curvy, but more elegant somehow; the difference between the two girls was stark in my mind—Brooke was on a higher plane, elevated and graceful. I followed her to the car.

"You're lucky today," she said, smiling. "Dad said he'd already grilled you once, and you did fine last time, so he didn't need to do it again."

"I did fine?" I asked.

"Everyone else freaked when they saw the body, but you were the only one brave enough to do anything about it."

"That's because dead bodies aren't scary," I said. "When you think about it, dead bodies are the least scary kind of bodies, right? I mean, there's nothing they can do to you, unless I guess you don't wash your hands or something."

Brooke laughed and stood by her door. I opened it smoothly this time, anticipating it, relishing the forbidden touch of the door handle. She hadn't ridden in my car since the end of school, but the door still felt special; it had been hers for so long that it could never go back. I got in on my side and pulled out my keys.

"Where are we going?" I asked.

"First things first," she said, holding her finger up in mock reprimand. "You're not dressed yet."

I looked down at myself. "I'm not?" It was exactly what I'd been worried about—and despite all my efforts, I'd still done it wrong. She was much dressier than I was; I must look like a disgusting jerk next to her.

"Well, John and Brooke are dressed, I guess," she said with a smile, "but we're not John and Brooke anymore—we're tourists."

What? That wasn't what I'd been expecting at all. "Where are we going?"

"We're going to the exotic town of Clayton," she said, digging in her bag and pulling out a handful of clothes. She handed me a bright Hawaiian shirt. "Put this on."

My expectations for the evening crumbled further—I'd been expecting an activity like fishing, or a trip to the movie theater, but this was completely different. I'd played the evening out in my head a dozen times or more, and it had never gone like this.

Brooke was pulling more clothes out of the bag—a loud Hawaiian shirt for herself, and a big black camera on a multi-colored strap. I didn't go on a lot of dates; this was my second ever, in fact. I'd never seen kids around town dressed as tourists, though; this couldn't be a common dating scenario.

"Do you do any good accents?" Brooke asked.

"I'm afraid not."

"I do a really stupid Russian accent," she said, putting on a wide-brimmed sun hat. "I guess that will have to do."

I wasn't sure what to do, but it felt so good to be with Brooke—to look at her, to talk to her. Whatever I had to do to stay with her, it was worth it. I picked up the Hawaiian shirt and looked at it, trying to think of something funny to say.

"You mean your Russian accent's stupid," I asked, "or your accent sounds like a stupid Russian?" Wow, I needed to do a lot better than that.

"Don't make fun of accent," she said thickly, sounding for all the world like a villain in a Bond movie. She must practice a lot. "You are Boris and I am called Natasha. Put on shirt."

I watched her pull her Hawaiian shirt on over her clothes. Being with her this way, being able to look with no restrictions, gave the same forbidden thrill I'd gotten from opening her door. She pulled her hair up and out of her oversize costume, and it flowed down her back in golden waves. It was an odd visual dissonance: she was still Brooke, the untouchable fantasy, but she was someone else, too. Someone real and, yes, very touchable.

Just stick to the rules.

"You know," I said, "you're really kind of strange once people get to know you."

Brooke arched an eyebrow melodramatically. "You don't like plan?"

"Are you kidding?" I asked, pulling the tourist shirt on over my own. It gave me the dizzying sensation of being somebody else, as if I'd stepped outside of John Cleaver altogether. I was Boris now, and Boris didn't have any of the problems John did. "I think this sounds awesome."

"Good," she said, putting on a pair of gaudy plastic sunglasses. "Travel brochure say good things about Clayton. We start with local cuisine: Friendly Burger."

"You sure you want to eat at Friendly Burger?" I asked. "There's nicer places to go."

"You do not know this," she said sternly, wagging her finger. "Boris has never been to Clayton."

I sat back and stared at her—she was really going to play this role, and be strict about the ridiculous rules of her scenario. Well, little did she know, I was an expert at ridiculous rules.

"If I've never been here," I said, "then I don't know where anything is."

Brooke smiled triumphantly and pulled a sheaf of papers from her bag.

"Is okay," she said, "I download maps from Internet."

I laughed and started the car, and she started reading me driving directions. We followed them to the letter, feigning complete ignorance about the town, and arrived at Friendly Burger only slightly later than we would have otherwise. As soon as we parked Brooke jumped out and grabbed a woman on the street, pressing a camera into her hands.

"My friend and I visit from out of town," she said, her Bond villain accent as thick as ever. "You take picture?" The woman stared at her in shock, then nodded her head uncertainly. Brooke and I stood in front of the weather-beaten Friendly Burger sign, pointing at it stupidly, and the woman took a picture. Brooke thanked her, took back the camera, and did the same inside with other people, getting pictures of us by the counter, the menu, and even the rickety old model train that ran around the borders of the ceiling. I watched her flow easily from one conversation to another, leaving each person confused but cheerful. Finally she ordered two 'cheesy burgers with fries from France,' and we sat down to eat. I bit into the burger, feeling the flesh in my teeth, and smiled.

"I like this place," she said, biting a fry in half. "Is good American food. Make us fat, like Americans."

The muscles in her neck moved slightly as she chewed, in and out, in and out, rippling sensuously beneath her skin.

"What's next?" I asked.

"We go other places," she said. "Places tourists would go if they came here. County Courthouse. Shoe Museum."

"Ooh, a Shoe Museum," I said, grinning at the idea. The shoe museum was pretty much just some crazy guy's house, which he'd filled with shelf after shelf of shoes and other shoe-related junk he'd accumulated throughout his life. One of those classic "American Heartland" kind of places that survived on kitsch value alone. It was a laughingstock among the local kids, but it was the only real tourist location in Clayton, and going with Brooke might actually be fun. I imagined her breathlessly taking pictures of the shoe displays, pretending to be amazed at everything she saw, and I smiled.

"We are tourists," she said innocently. "Billboard on highway says visit shoe museum, we visit shoe museum."

"Awesome," I said. "Or whatever we say in Russia when we mean awesome. Sputnik."

She laughed. "Sputnik?"

"It's Russian for 'awesome,'" I said. "The name of the satellite was an accident, really: they built it, looked at it, and said 'Sputnik!' The name stuck. They've been embarrassed about it ever since."

Brooke laughed again, then shook her head. "You mean *we've* been embarrassed about it ever since," she said. "We are, after all, native-born Russians." She fell back into her accent. "This is first time out of country."

I smiled. It was fun to think of myself as someone else—it was liberating, as if all my baggage, all my fears, all my tension had disappeared. There were no worries.

There were no consequences.

I ate a fry and leaned forward. "So who are Boris and Natasha?" I asked. "How do we know each other?"

She looked back, meeting my eyes, studying me through her cheap plastic sunglasses.

"We grew up in same small town outside of Moscow," she said. "Claytonograd."

"So we've known each other our whole lives."

"Most of our lives, yes," she said. "We are old friends."

"We must be pretty good friends if we're on a trip together," I said. "I mean, Boris doesn't go to America with just anybody."

A tiny smile touched the corner of her lips. "Neither does Natasha."

I wanted to reach out to her—to touch her, to feel her skin under my fingers. I'd never allowed myself even to think about touching her, though that had never stopped the dreams, night after night, of her body on the embalming table. I washed and brushed her hair; I cleaned her pale, precious skin; I massaged her rigor mortis-stiffened muscles until they were loose and warm in my hands. There were other dreams, darker dreams, but I pushed them from my mind now just as I always had before. I would not think about violence. 1, 1, 2, 3, 5, 8, 13.

"I think," I said, "that this trip to America is going really well. Thanks for inviting me."

"Thanks for coming."

The entire world seemed coiled and tight, focused on this moment. I wanted—I needed—to touch her hand. I would never have dared before, because of the thoughts it brought, but that was the old John. That was the John who wasn't even allowed to look at her—for him, touching was completely illicit. But not for Boris. Boris could look. Boris had no rules; he had no fear. There was no danger in touching a hand—it was just a hand, a thing on the end of her arm. Her hand had touched the table, the bench, the food—why couldn't it touch me? I reached out, steady and even, and put my hand on hers. Her fingers were smooth and soft, just as they were in my dreams. I held it a moment, feeling the texture of her skin, the lines of her knuckles, the sharp crystals of salt from her fries. She squeezed back, trembling and thrilling and alive.

She smiled. "Sputnik."

We stared at each other, stared into each other, feeling a hum through our fingers that made the entire world brighter—the colors deeper, the edges crisper, the sounds rich and resonant. We ate our food one-handed, grinning like idiots, neither acknowledging our clasped hands nor daring to let go. There was a connection between us, vibrant and charged and . . .

. . . Something wasn't right.

I pushed the thought away, but once my mind became aware of it the feeling was impossible to ignore. As wonderful as this was, there was something . . . missing. Something that should have been there but wasn't, like a dark hole in a beautiful jigsaw puzzle. Was it my expectations again, angry that they had only been met halfway? But no. I had imagined this moment, or one like it, a hundred times—a thousand times—and there was nothing missing. I felt excited; I was in control of myself and of the situation; Brooke was beautiful and just as eager as I was. What could possibly be missing?

But something was missing, and it ate at me like a canker.

I looked around the room, searching for something amiss. There was no one I knew—no one laughing or crying or yelling at me. I saw the TV droning in the corner; I saw the drink machine dripping slowly, drop by drop; I saw the napkins and the straws and the plastic knives, stark white in their dispensers.

And then I knew what it was.

My eyes fixed on the plastic knives and I knew, like a bolt of lightning through my mind, that the connection I felt to Brooke was just a shadow of the earth-shaking connection I had felt once before, in the kitchen of my house, holding a knife while my mother cowered in terror. We hadn't been two people then, we'd been one, united in body and mind by an overwhelming emotion: fear. We had moved together, felt together, and together we thought two sides of the same thought. It had been a pure, unbridled rush of emotion, the kind of connection that sociopaths were never supposed to have, but I had felt it all, and it had been more real and more powerful than anything I'd ever experienced.

This should have been the same—it should have been even better—but it wasn't. And that was the hole. In all my dreams of Brooke we had felt that same intense connection, and now that the moment was finally here the connection was not. Why not? Had I done something wrong? Had Brooke? I looked at her now and saw her staring back, no longer cheerful but concerned. The lapse of emotion made me flare with anger, enraged that she would break the already-tenuous link, but I calmed myself. She was just sensing the same hole that I had. But now that I knew what was missing, I could plan for it next time—I could force it out like a knot from a tangle of hair.

Holding hands wasn't enough, it seemed. I needed more.

"I can't believe it," said Brooke, her voice flat. "I can't believe it."

Was she talking about me? But no, she wasn't looking at me at all—it was the TV. Everyone in the restaurant was staring at the TV, silent and pale as corpses.

I turned to watch, already guessing what I would see.

"Police say the body is far more disfigured than the first three," the reporter said, "but it was bound in a similar way. The police have not released any further details at this time, but they do urge everyone in the area to report any leads or information that they may have. You, the people of Clayton County, are the only ones who can stop this killer."

14

"We're two for two," said Brooke, standing on her porch. Two dates, and a dead body found during each of them. "Thanks again for coming, though. You want to risk a third?" She smiled sickly.

"Sure," I said, trying not to think of her body floating in the lake. "It's just a coincidence."

"It's a pretty terrible one," she said. We stood silent for a moment. "Anyway, I'll see you tomorrow."

"See you tomorrow."

She unlocked her door and went in, bag of tourist paraphernalia in tow, and I walked back to my car unsteadily. Another victim. Another message from the killer. What was he saying with this one? I needed to know more.

Forman had been on the scene—I'd seen him on TV. He would know more, but could I convince him to tell me? He'd asked for my help before; he might accept it now, in return for information. Even just hanging around the police station I could probably glean something. There was one way to find out, and I had to find out. I felt like my mind was eating me alive.

I climbed in my car and turned it around, heading back into town. Forman was probably still at the scene, but he would have to come back to the station with reports to file and evidence to register. I could wait all night.

From the outside the police station was dim and lonely, though I noticed with interest that Forman's office was lit. The front was lit as well, and I could see Stephanie the receptionist inside, juggling phones with a tired, harried look on her face. I went in and waited for a break in her calls, but she quickly made eye contact and pointed toward Forman's office. I hesitated, not sure what she meant, then she pointed again, mouthing "go in." I waved a silent thanks and walked to Forman's office; the door was unlatched, and I pushed it open.

"Hello?" Forman looked up from his desk, his face just as lined and harried as Stephanie's. His notepad was full of intense doodles, dark and pressed deep into the paper. Mom did the same thing when she didn't have an outlet for her stress. I figured the new body must have really bothered him.

"John," he said tensely. "What are you doing here?"

"What are you doing here?" I countered. "Are you done with the crime scene already?"

"No, no," he said, shaking his head. "The whole department's still over there; probably be there all night. Did you need me for something?"

"Um, yeah," I said, "I just didn't expect to find you here."

"Then why did you come?"

I looked at him oddly; this was not the way Agent Forman usually acted.

"I need you to tell me about the body," I said, sitting down.

"Why?" he asked, furrowing his brow, "and why would I tell you? You're not a cop." He was still agitated, but as he spoke I could see the panic melt tangibly away: he sat up straighter, he looked more stern, and his voice seemed deeper. Within seconds he was sharp and assertive. "Maybe you can help," he said, leaning back and eyeing me carefully. He seemed calmer now. Clearer. "Think about something for me; it will help us both stay sharp. Why did the Clayton Killer kill?"

"You think this is the Clayton Killer?" I asked. "Nothing matches."

"Not at all," said Forman, looking down at his paper, "but I do think they're related. So tell me: why did the Clayton Killer kill?"

This was easy, freshman-level profiling. "How detailed do you want me to get?" I asked. "On the basic level, serial killers kill because they have a need, and killing fills that need."

"Okay," said Forman, still staring at his paper. "What did the Clayton Killer need?"

"Why are you asking me this?"

"To keep us sharp," he said, "I already told you that."

"Why 'us?' " I asked. "Why do you keep saying 'keep *us* sharp?' "

"Don't you want to be?" He turned to look at the window, as if peering straight through the slats of his blinds. "You're a very smart young man," he said. "You can figure this out."

Forman seemed completely different every time I saw him—suspicious, or laid back, or nervous, and now . . . what? Sharp? What did that even mean?

"The Clayton Killer took body parts," I said. "So I suppose, on a basic level, we could just say that he needed body parts. But there's usually more to it than that."

"Indeed," Forman mumbled. He was still facing the window, but he closed his eyes like he was meditating.

"The classic serial killer need is control," I continued, watching Forman carefully. I wasn't even sure he was listening. "Killing people and stealing their body parts may have been a way of exerting control over them. That's why a lot of serial killers keep souvenirs—it gives them a measure of control over the person even after they die."

"And you think the Clayton Killer was trying to control people," he said.

It was hard to know how to answer, because I couldn't let Forman know how much I really knew. I had to think like Forman, which meant I had to think only of the things he knew, and set aside all the things he didn't. He didn't know the killer was Mr. Crowley; he didn't know Crowley was a demon; he didn't know the demon was dead. As far as anyone else knew, the Clayton Killer was still out there.

Except, I realized, that Forman was talking about the killer in the past tense.

"You think the Clayton Killer's dead," I said.

Forman stood up and walked to the map, running his finger along certain roads and stopping now and then to tap a thumbtack or a pencil mark. He was ignoring me completely.

"You think the Clayton Killer's gone for good," I said

louder. "You're talking about him as if he's dead, with no question. What do you know?"

"You're doing fine," he said, still studying the map. "Keep your mind focused."

"Why do you think these victims are related if you're so sure the killer's already dead?" He ignored me. "Is there a copycat killer? Is there a . . . similar . . . killer out there?"

Forman paused and looked at me. "A 'similar' killer?"

I was talking about another demon, but I couldn't very well say that. "An organ snatcher," I said. "But nothing was taken from the first three bodies. Was something gone from the fourth?"

"Too many questions, John," he said, turning back to his map. He tapped it one more time, near the wood plant—the approximate location, based on what I'd seen on the news, of the latest body. He sat down and pulled out a file. "Stop asking questions and start answering them; you're only confusing things."

"I'm asking because I don't know the answers," I said. "You're not giving me anything."

"And don't get frustrated," he said. He thumbed through the file.

"Are you just doing this to distract me?" I asked. "I'm here because I'm trying to help, I don't want to get brushed off like a kid."

"You are a kid," he said, looking straight at me, "and the only person you're here to help is yourself. You're obsessed with death and you can't wait 'til this corpse shows up in the mortuary so you want me to spill it all now; that's why you're here. Don't pretend with me."

I tried to think of a response, but he cut me off. "You can

still help though, whether you realize it or not—I just need you to stay focused. Here's a second question to keep you going: why did the Clayton Killer stop?"

He was playing me somehow, but for what? He couldn't possibly want my opinion of the Clayton Killer—he was a professional serial killer investigator with all the resources of the FBI. My opinion was nothing he couldn't come up with on his own. But then why so many questions? Where was he leading me?

I'd gotten his attention once; maybe if I kept talking I could get him back, and find out more.

"There were two possible reasons for him to stop," I said, ignoring what I knew—that I had killed the killer—and spouting pure theory. "Either his need was filled, or he died. But serial killers' needs are almost never filled—they just build up, and build up, until they're completely uncontrollable and . . . the killer can't stop himself." I thought about the burning warehouse, and the cat.

"Good," said Forman, paging through the file intently. "Keep going."

"There are a lot of serial killers who go in cycles," I said, "killing actively for a few months and then disappearing for months or even years. BTK came back like that, long after everyone assumed he was gone. Edmund Kemper just turned himself in one day because he decided he was done."

"He did," Forman mumbled.

"But you don't think this one stopped on his own," I said, leaning in and watching his eyes for a reaction. Maybe I could prompt a better response if I addressed him directly. "You're pretty certain, though I'm guessing not 100 percent certain, that the Clayton Killer is gone. Dead. But none of the evidence suggests it, so you must know something else."

Forman looked up. "What makes you so sure you know what evidence I have?"

His eyes were dark, but somehow bright and alive. He wanted to stay "sharp"—is this what he meant? I felt like I was dueling with him, mind to mind, and every time I thought I had the upper hand he was right there to block me, just as quick as I was.

Just as sharp.

I had his attention now; it was time to press the attack. "I was right in the middle of the final crime scene," I said. "I saw everything, and there was nothing to suggest that he was done with killing—if anything, the fact that he never stole anything from Dr. Neblin suggests that he felt unfinished. He'd kill again just to get a sense of closure."

Forman's black eyes bored into me, and I stared straight back as I plowed ahead. "You said the new victims were connected, but why? Why would you assume a connection?"

"I'm sorry to break it you," said Forman, "but you live in a very small town. It's extremely unlikely that you'd have two completely unrelated serial killers, right on top of each other, in a place like this." His focus had shifted from whatever had occupied him before, and it was now completely centered on me. Apparently my antagonism had rubbed off, and now it was his turn to press the attack.

This was what I'd been building toward—he was interested now, and he was talking. Just as he'd done to me, I gave him a question to direct his thoughts. "And what could that relationship possibly be?"

"The only logical one," he said. "They crossed paths. One killer met the other, they saw themselves reflected, and only one survived—maybe it was territorial, maybe it was coincidental, maybe it was something else. My job is to find out."

A chill ran through me; he was describing me, though indirectly enough that he might not recognize it. He was closer to my secret than I'd thought. Suddenly my obsession with the new victims had turned into a desperate need to protect myself. I had to know what he knew, and what he suspected, about this killer.

"Is there any evidence to support your theory?" I asked, "or are you just shooting in the dark? Serial killers follow close patterns, and it seems pretty unlikely that the guy who killed the large, male Clayton Killer has gone on to focus on small women."

"A serial killer's first kill is usually accidental," said Forman. "It's likely that the presence of the first killer triggered a preexisting psychosis in the second, catalyzing it, throwing both people into conflict. When the dust cleared the first killer was dead, but a second was created, and all of his subsequent kills were planned and carried out much more carefully. Those later victims would, naturally, be more in line with the new killer's awakened psychosis."

He was so close to connecting me to this—that profile was almost, but not quite, a perfect description of me. Why hadn't he made the final link? Because there were four new bodies, and I had nothing to do with them. But he'd been investigating for months, and the new bodies only showed up to confuse him a few weeks ago. There had to be something more—something that happened months ago to throw him off my trail.

Of course. "You found a fifth body," I said. "Or a first one, I guess. Months ago, maybe all the way back in January, you found another body from the same killer." It made perfect sense—they'd been tracking this new killer longer than I thought because they'd known about him longer than I had. "Somehow you hid it from everyone," I said. "You kept the whole thing a secret."

Agent Forman smiled.

"I suppose you feel very clever," said Forman, "guessing at the existence of another victim." He pulled open the drawer of a filing cabinet. "You put all the pieces together, and you came up with that. Very interesting. Anyone else would have come to a very different conclusion." He pulled a gun from the open drawer and laid it, very gently, on the table. "We've already established that the Clayton Killer is dead, so most people in your situation would have guessed that the other body we found was the Clayton Killer's corpse—but that didn't occur to you at all. Why is that, John?"

Think fast. Point this anywhere but at me.

"Because if you'd found the Clayton Killer you'd have told the whole world," I said, keeping my breathing slow and steady. "He was national news—the whole country was holding its breath waiting for you to catch him. If you'd found his body, you could never have kept it this quiet."

"The thing about sociopaths," said Forman, "is that even though they're missing a lot of emotions—guilt especially— one of the ones they do very well is fear. They don't just cause it—they feel it intently. It guides their lives. Tell me, John: just now when I told you I was on the trail of a second killer, why did you feel fear?"

How did he know what I was feeling? Even my mom couldn't read me that well. "Anyone would be scared," I said. "The last killer nearly got me—it makes sense that I'd get a little worried about a new one."

"But you weren't scared when we talked about the *existence* of a new one," said Forman, speaking evenly. "You were scared when we talked about *catching* the new one. More specifically, you were scared when we talked about the new one killing the old one. Is there anything you want to tell me?"

My mind churned through the possibilities, trying to figure this out. There was no way he could have read me that accurately. I'd built my life around learning how to read people—how to deduce their emotions from visual signals, since I couldn't connect with them directly—and even I would have trouble picking up on the faint sense of fear from a practiced, un-emotive sociopath. And yet he had.

He'd flushed me into a trap, and I could feel it drawing closed; he didn't have any proof that I'd killed the Clayton Killer, but he'd caught the scent, and he was ready to follow it like a bloodhound. I hadn't expected a trap from Forman—he was too open, too direct. He'd had the last two bodies on the news almost as soon as they were found; he'd even told the reporter that he thought they were connected to the Clayton Killer, long before he could have performed any kind of meaningful study. Those were not the actions of a subtle man. And yet here he was, sitting with a gun while I tried to struggle out of a trap I hadn't even seen.

I forced myself to calm down and think this through, staring at him while he stared back at me, his hand on his gun. It made no sense that there was subtlety in some of his plans and not in others—it should be all or nothing. So why would he reveal something that might drive the killer into hiding?

Unless he thought it would flush the killer out.

"You used the bodies as bait," I said.

His dark eyes grew more intense. "Bait?"

"You told the reporter that the new bodies were connected to the old, knowing that the new killer would get rattled by the suggestion and possibly expose himself. This entire investigation has been a trap."

"One that caught you, apparently," he said. "I just didn't expect you to come right into my office."

"If your only case against me is that I came to see you at a bad time, you're going to have a very hard time proving it in court."

He raised the nose of the gun, just slightly, from where it rested on the table. "Do I look like I need to prove this in court?"

"Are you threatening to shoot me in a police station?"

"No need to rush," he said icily, "I can shoot you anywhere."

His hands were steady, his eyes barely blinked, and his face was as hard as granite. This was new territory for me—I'd spent months in the vicinity of a killer, but never, not until the very end, did he know who I was. I had always been safe. That Forman was watching me now, threatening my life face to face, was a completely different situation. Even if he didn't shoot me, he was convinced I was guilty, and I might spend the rest of my life in court or in jail because of it.

Or on the run. If I could get out the building without being shot, I could run and never come back.

But no, he was too close; he was too ready with the pistol.

He had completely control over the situation, and I was help-less. And feeling helpless made me feel incredibly angry.

"You must be the worst FBI Agent in the entire world," I said. "The entire world. You're just going to shoot every kid who comes in here and mouths off to you? No solving crimes, no due process, you don't even ask good questions—you just haul out the gun whenever your magical fear detector goes off and you start threatening people. That's some fine detective work, sparky."

Forman raised the gun and aimed it straight into my face; the barrel was no more than two feet away from my nose. "Listen, you little mental case: this is not about the FBI, and this is not about a serial killer, and this is not even about two serial killers. I am looking for something very important, and you are popping up often enough that I figure you've got to know more about it than you're telling me. So why don't you cut the tough guy crap and tell me what you know."

"*I'm* the one doing a tough guy act?" I asked. "Did you forget the part where you pulled a gun on an unarmed sixteen-year-old?"

"What do you know?" he demanded.

"I know that I've been threatened by much scarier things than you," I said. "If you think this 'loose cannon' stuff is going to terrify me—"

"What do you mean 'things'?" he asked.

"What things?"

"You just said 'things,'" he said, "you've been threatened by much scarier 'things' than me. Not 'people.'"

"You think 'people' is as far as it goes?" I asked. "Do you have any idea what else is out there? There are things that would shake you to your . . ."

His eyes were wide—in surprise, yes, but not in shock. Not in confusion. It was not the look of a man who had found a monster under his bed—there was too much control. Too much recognition. Agent Forman had the face of a man who expected to find a monster under the bed, and found it in his closet instead.

I was trying to shock him with talk of the demon, but somehow Agent Forman knew exactly what I was talking about.

I could see him thinking: the way he pursed his lips; the way his eyes flicked rapidly from point to point, searching for something. I did the same, straining for a mental foothold. Did he really know about the demon? How?

He'd said he was searching for something very important— something unrelated to the FBI. His entire life might be a cover, pretending to search for serial killers while secretly trying to track down a demon. Or demons—he might hunt them professionally for all I knew. Whatever he was, he knew about the demon—and from the stunned look on his face, he knew that I knew. Should I run? Should I play dumb? What was he going to do next?

We watched each other, frozen in place, each one almost daring the other to make the first move. His gun never wavered. After a very long moment he opened his mouth to speak.

"Mkhai?"

It was a heavy, ancient word, thick with dust and age and unfathomable sadness. I stared back, blank and wary.

His eyes grew dark, and his face hardened. "Then he is

dead," said Forman. The words were final, like a doctor's pronouncement, made not to a person but to the entire world. Let it be known to the ends of the earth that a man is dead. He stared intently at nothing, not at me or behind me but beyond me, as if existence had ceased to exist. After an eternity of waiting, his eyes focused back on me again. "We were afraid of this," he said, "but I didn't believe it. You will tell me everything."

But then he smiled, and I could think of nothing that would look more out of place.

It made no sense, but I could see it in his face—he was happy. His face was brighter now, his eyes wider, his mouth turned up in an open smile. His entire body was loose and relaxed. It was like a switch had been flipped—one moment he was somber, with the weight of a world I could barely imagine resting fully on his shoulders, and the next moment he was bright and cheerful.

"Are you . . . happy?" I asked.

"Happy as hell, John," he said, breaking into a wide grin. "I hate it when this happens."

"You hate being happy?"

"Happy, sad, whatever," he said. He stood up and walked past me to the door. "It's not the feeling, it's the imposition. I don't have time for this right now." He opened the door and called out. "Stephanie?"

"Yes, Mr. Forman?"

"Is anyone back yet?"

"Just the three of us," she said. "Listen, I've got great news—"

"I thought you might," he said, cutting her off. "Why don't you come on in and share it with us?"

"Great!" she shouted, and I heard her chair shift, followed by the clatter of heels across the floor. She stepped into the room, smiling from ear to ear, words pouring out in a jubilant flood. "I just talked to my boyfriend on the phone, and he—"

Agent Forman swung his gun like a club, slamming her square in the face with a sickening crunch that must have shattered her nose. She staggered back against the open door, her cry cut off by a gurgle of blood in her throat, and Forman hit her again, this time in the side of the head. Her eyes were wide, too surprised to be scared.

"Do you like that?" he demanded, watching her reel to the side, trying to keep her balance. "Some people are trying to *work* in here," he hit her again, "and we can't *do* it," another hit, "with cheerful little Stephanie out there so damn *happy* all the time." He hit her again, on the back of the head, knocking her to the floor. I stared at her in shock, then looked up at him.

"That's a very brave defense you put up," he said to me, walking back to his desk. "Stephanie is eternally grateful for the way you stopped me from beating her unconscious."

"Who are you?" I asked.

"That's right," he said, picking up his coffee cup. "Puzzle it out. Stay sharp." He carried the cup to Stephanie's body, rolled her over with his foot, and probed the carpet for blood. Her nose was bleeding, and there was blood in her hair from what was probably a cut from the gun barrel. She was breathing, but unconscious. Forman wiped a spot of blood from the carpet with his shirtsleeve, then poured the coffee out all over the spot on the floor.

"That's lesson number one," he said. "In a small-town dump like this you're not going to have a CSI team going through the place with a fine-toothed comb. They see spilled coffee, they'll think spilled coffee, and I'll be back to clean it up tomorrow. Now pick her up."

"Why?"

"Because we're going home," said Forman. "Consider it a trade: I'll introduce you to my toys, and you tell me how you killed a god."

15

"I found him," said Forman, holding his cell phone to his ear while he drove. I was in the passenger seat; Stephanie, still unconscious, was lying in the back. "No, not him," Forman said, "the person who killed him. I know, I know—you were right. Well, that's the part you're not going to believe: he's just a kid. Human. No, I have no idea, but I'm going to find out. I'll call you."

Forman clicked off his phone and dropped it in his shirt pocket. His gun was in the pocket of his suit coat, on the far side away from me. We were almost to the edge of town, and I didn't know where we were going after that; I was terrified, but more than that I was confused.

Did he say Crowley was a god?

I could have run, back when we first reached the car, but I had to know what he knew. Forman had all the answers I'd been looking for, and I'd do whatever it took to get them.

"Who was that?" I asked.

"Nobody," said Forman, and laughed. "Now, where to start? I really have no idea. I suppose the first question is, how'd you do it?"

"How did I do what?"

"Don't play stupid," he said. "You killed him. Bloody—I don't even know who he was. Who was he?"

"Who was . . . who?" I didn't want to play dumb, but I didn't know what else to say. He was accusing me of killing Mr. Crowley, that much seemed clear, and he seemed to know that Crowley was some kind of supernatural being. After that I started to get lost. And who was he talking to on the phone?

"Mkhai," he said, pounding emphatically on the steering wheel. "The god you killed—the Clayton Killer. You know about him and you're not dead—that means he's dead, and that means you're probably the one who killed him."

"It was attacking me," I said. "It was trying to kill me. I didn't—"

"Whose body did he take?" Forman demanded. "You probably thought he was someone from your community—maybe even someone you knew. He might have even been in Bill Crowley's body by the time you saw him."

Aha. Forman knew less of the story than I thought. He thought the demon had jumped into Crowley at the end, after killing Neblin, which meant his story was incomplete. I held onto his lack of knowledge like a lifeline: if I knew something he didn't, that gave me power—not much, but it was something. There was no sense telling him any more than I had to.

"It was a demon," I said. "It had big claws, and really sharp teeth—a lot of them, more than even make sense—and huge eyes, like plates, that glowed in the dark." I didn't say anything about Mr. Crowley.

We passed under a streetlight, and I saw Forman smile before the light fell behind us and the car plunged into darkness again. We were outside of Clayton now, on the one-lane road into the forest, and as my eyes adjusted to the dark I saw his face lit by eerie red lights from the dashboard, his smile dark and feral.

"Mkhai . . ." he said.

"You said he was . . . a god?"

"Compared to you, without question," said Forman. "When your ancestors crawled out of the muck and howled at the darkness it was he who answered them, great and terrible."

I watched him silently, seeing in the dim red light Forman's eyes light up with a terrifying zeal.

"We were all gods then," he continued, "or at least that's what people called us. Mkhai was the god of death to some, vengeance to others; even the god of faces to a kingdom on the banks of the Nile. But time moves on, and glory fades. That's what killed us in the end: time."

He said "us." I'd assumed he was some kind of hunter, or maybe a worshiper, but . . . was he another demon, like Crowley?

"You're scared again," he said, glancing at me quickly. "So is Stephanie, but not of me. Not directly. A reflection of me, perhaps, somewhere in the back of her mind. The nightmare me that she sees while she sleeps. I assure you," he said, looking at me again, "the reality is far worse."

He turned back to face the road, gripped the wheel tighter, and slammed on the gas, and all of a sudden we were accelerating

insanely as the engine screamed in protest. Glowing in the headlights, the trees on the side of the road blurred to a wall of white,
and I gripped the armrest tightly.

Forman whooped with exhilaration.

"I never get to do this!" he shouted. We took a turn too fast,
the car skidding to the side and almost careening off the road.
"Most of the people who ride in my car think I'm an agent
with the government, so I can't very well do this to them. And,
of course, all the other people who ride in my car are unconscious, like her." He laughed and took another turn, pulling
hard to the left this time, and I could feel the wheels catch and
whine as they lost and regained their grip on the asphalt. There
was no way we could survive this—or at least no way that I
could. Forman, if he really was another demon, might regenerate and walk away like it was nothing.

He shouted again, half a laugh and half a scream. "I love it!
I love it!"

"You're going to get us killed!" I shouted, holding on tightly
with both hands.

"Yes I am!" he cried, almost a squeal. He seemed as scared as
I was now, but he didn't slow down. The road was a narrow
strip of white, each curve and rise coming into the headlights
just seconds before we rocketed past it and into the blurred un-
known.

"We're almost home now," he said, gritting his teeth as we
hurtled through the trees. "We're almost home. My toys will
hear us coming, and they will rattle in their chains. Here they
are."

He turned another corner, the car flying wildly to the side as
he slammed on the brakes and an old house came into view,

tucked into a clearing in the trees. The car slid through dirt and gravel, nearly tipping over, and slammed into a pair of garbage cans with an angry metal crash. Stephanie's body flew off the seat and hit the back of ours before thudding to the floor; the airbags in the front exploded with the sound of a gunshot, catching me on the side of my head with the force of a solid punch. We hit one of the garbage cans again, crushing it against the side of the house, and just as suddenly everything was still.

Forman was cackling like a maniac, loud guffaws that degenerated quickly into sobs of terror. I felt like I could barely think—my brain was scrambled from the crash, making it hard to know where I was or what was happening, but even the things I saw clearly were nightmarish and impossible. Why was he laughing? Why was he crying? Why didn't anything he said make sense? My breathing was fast and shallow, and I was desperate to leave. I fumbled with the door and finally opened it, breathing deep gulps of air while I wrestled with my seat belt. It seemed in that moment like an unknowable, impossible object, as if I'd never used a seatbelt before. Forman's body twitched, doubled over and wracked with tears. Finally I found the button and opened the latch, falling out of the car before the belt could even retract. It clung to me like a spider's web, and I shook it off madly.

I was free. The car was parallel to the house, shining its headlights out across the road and into the trees on the far side. I didn't know how far we'd driven—how far we were from Clayton or any other living thing—but I knew which direction we'd come from. The air was cold and sharp, pricking my sweaty skin like needles of ice. I steeled myself and ran through the gravel driveway, just a few stumbling steps before the ground in front of my feet leapt up in a black tuft, and I heard the loud crack of a gun behind me. I kept running, and it happened again—an explosion of dirt, a bright spark on the asphalt of the road, and the sound of a shot behind me.

"Stop running!"

I was at the near edge of the road, far from cover with nowhere to run. At this distance he probably couldn't hit me with any great accuracy, but he'd have time for four or five good shots before I reached the trees, which put the odds in his favor. I stopped and raised my hands.

"Don't raise your hands, this isn't a stickup."

I lowered my arms and turned around slowly. Forman was standing by the open passenger door, aiming his gun at me.

"Get back here and help me carry her inside," he said.

He was back in control again, somehow. What was going on? My curiosity overpowered my fear, and I walked back slowly. I had to find out what he was, and what it all meant. When I reached the car I opened the rear door and leaned in to look at Stephanie, putting a hand near her face, like we did with the corpses; her puffs of breath were faint but warm. She was still alive.

"Just grab her feet and haul her out," Forman said curtly; I went more slowly, grabbing her under the arms and pulling her to a sitting position before stepping back and pulling her out of the car. Forman turned off the engine and headlights and led me around to the front door. There was no porch, just a narrow wooden step. He opened the door and I followed him in, laying Stephanie's body gently on an old, threadbare couch.

Forman lit a lamp and sat in a sunken chair, calm and satisfied. "What do you want to do with her?" he asked.

"You're the one that brought her here," I said. Her nose was probably broken, and her mouth and neck were covered with a brown smear of drying blood.

"Don't be an idiot," said Forman. "You've got a pretty girl in the middle of nowhere—show a little imagination. Consider it my gift to you."

The house was sparsely decorated, if at all; it looked like he'd bought the place on sale, half-furnished, and never bothered to add anything else.

"How long have you lived here?" I asked.

"Three months," he said, shaking his head. "But don't change the subject."

"I'm not going to hurt her," I said.

"But you want to," said Forman, leaning forward. "You want to hurt everybody else—why should she be different?"

"I'm not going to hurt her because you want me to."

"But you did hurt my friend," he said. "You killed him—a being practically made of power, and you killed him. How did you do it?"

I looked back, still wary of revealing what had happened. You never know what kind of knowledge will be useful, and when.

"You're another one, aren't you?" I asked.

Forman smiled thinly. "Another god?"

"I called him a demon," I said. "I guess I have a dimmer view of him than you do."

"We've been called demons before," said Forman. "Shades, wraiths, werewolves, boogeymen. Even serial killers, though only by reputation. People like us can be anything we want to be—just like her." He pointed at Stephanie, lying inert on the couch.

"Is she one of you too?"

"Of course not," he said, standing up and walking toward her. "On her own she has no power at all—no more than any of you—but with our help, ahhhh . . . she can be anything you want her to be. You want a slave? You want a lover? You want a beast of prey to hunt out back? She can be it."

He leaned in and pulled up a strand of her hair—not gently, but casually, as if he were shopping. "Never underestimate the power of torture," he said, "it's a truly amazing tool. Not for getting the truth, of course—when you want information you have to use other means, which is why I'm not currently torturing you. But what you get with torture that you can't get anywhere else is complete and utter malleability. So come on, what do you want her to be?"

He *was* a demon, though so far I hadn't seen any demonic transformation. I might as well ask.

"Do you steal bodies too?"

"I stole two tonight," he said. "Counting you."

"No, I mean like the one I killed. You said he could take bodies, and look like someone I knew. Can you do that too?"

He eyed me. "It would be a very boring world if every god were the same. Sure, you could pray to all of us when you wanted to steal a body, but then who would you turn to when you wanted something else?"

"I don't believe there's ever actually been a patron god of body-snatching," I said.

"You're ignoring my questions, so I'm being indirect with yours."

"I won't tell you anything unless I get something in return."

"But I'm giving you exactly what you've always wanted!" he said. "Your very own victim, unconscious and ready to play whatever games you want. She's no Barbie, I'll grant you that, but as dolls go she's definitely attractive, and there's more than one man in this town who'd give his left eye to have her here in this situation."

I said nothing.

"Perhaps your tastes run elsewhere," he said, eyeing me carefully. "What is it you want, I wonder? We could clear the kitchen table and lay her across it, and perform our very own embalming, right here. How about it, John?"

I wanted to—you can't know how badly I wanted to. He was going to kill me anyway, I assumed, but if I played along would that delay it? Could I buy time to escape by torturing Stephanie? In many ways I was in a situation with no repercussions: I was either dead or an eternal prisoner, so nothing I did in this house would ever leave it.

And Stephanie was beautiful—long blond hair and pale skin, like Brooke. I could live out so many dreams.

I wanted to, but I wouldn't. Whatever Forman was, I was stronger. Whatever his plans were, I would block them. If he wanted me to hurt this girl, for whatever twisted reason, I'd make it my mission to keep her safe.

"I'm not going to do anything," I said. "I'm not like you."

"No you're not," he said, "but you'd be surprised at how much I'm like you."

"What are you going to do with me?" I asked.

"I'm not sure," said Forman. "Do you agree to answer my questions?"

"About the demon I killed?" I said. "Not a word."

"Then you'll do fine in here, for now," he said, walking to a closet. The door was fitted with a padlock, and he opened it and gestured inside. I didn't move, and he gestured again more sternly. "Don't try my patience, John. You killed someone very important to me, and I'm not exactly pleased with you. But I happen to find you interesting, and I suggest you do everything you can not to jeopardize that."

I hesitated a moment longer, just long enough for him to raise his gun, and then I walked into the closet. Forman smiled and closed the door, and I listened as he snapped the heavy padlock into place on the other side.

"I'll see you in the morning," he said, tapping on the door. "For now, since you didn't want her, I get Stephanie all to myself."

I heard footsteps, followed by a grunt or two; I assumed he was lifting her body. Then more footsteps, slower and heavier this time, walking past me and into another room—first soft steps on the carpet, then strident snaps on something hard, like linoleum, then soft again when he reached another carpet. There was a loud thump which I felt through the floor, then a distant thud.

I tested the door, but there was no interior handle, and the padlock on the outside held firm. I probed the edges with my fingers, searching for a gap or a hole or . . . I don't know. Something. I was trapped in a house with a madman—a mad demon—who'd just tucked me into bed with a story about how much fun torture was. This was not a place where I wanted to stay, but the door gave me nothing to work with. I was here for the night, at least.

I ran my hands around the edges of the closet and found deep gashes in the plaster walls, some of them small and finger-sized, like someone had tried to tear their way out, while others

were large and irregular, as if someone had picked it apart trying to escape. The wall behind the sheetrock was reinforced
with wood, as if he'd refinished the walls to make them stur-
dier. I picked at another wall that didn't have any big holes, but
when I got through and found more wood beyond I gave up. It
was like he had specifically redesigned the house to stop people
from escaping.

I could probably just break the wood panels down—or the
door, for that matter—but that would be noisy, and destruc-
tive, and Forman was not likely to appreciate it. For obvious
reasons, I didn't feel like antagonizing him at the moment.

But what were my alternatives? Waiting here for him to
come back? What would he do? Even if I escaped, where would
I go? He knew where I lived, and he was obviously willing to
break the law when it suited him. And I still didn't know what
kind of demonic power he might have.

That's when I heard the first scream.

They were muffled by distance and walls and doors, but I
could hear them well enough. One sounded like "why are you
doing this?," another like "I didn't do anything!," and then the
rest were mostly inarticulate cries.

Part of me wanted to turn away—to plug my ears and pretend I couldn't hear it—but I didn't. I listened carefully, straining to catch each word, imagining the scenario in my head. I
could only assume that the tortured body I'd seen in the mortuary was one of Forman's "toys," that he was the second killer
from our earlier conversation. That meant that I'd seen his
work before, and I knew what he was doing to Stephanie. The
high screams were probably fire; the low grunts probably came
from punches and stabs. I knew what each sound meant, and I

could have tried to block them out, but it was easier simply to stop caring. Like so many nights in my room as a child, I curled up in the dark and turned myself off.

After a while a second voice joined in the screaming—a man's voice. Forman's. It was a horrifying sound: he was screaming at her, but he was also screaming with her at some shared terror. The two voices built together in a crescendo of fear until at last a distant door slammed open and a screaming, crying voice fled down the hallway and past me to the front door. The steps were hard and fast, desperate to leave the house. I heard the outside lock rattle, then again, then a pounding on the front door, then a rattle that finally opened it with a crash. The footsteps ran outside, and Forman's voice howled a scream so primal that I felt my skin grow cold at the sound. It lasted several seconds and went dead, with no noise but the wind in the trees and the door clapping erratically into the wall.

The footsteps returned, slowly, but this time they steered not into the back room but straight at my closet. I heard a groan, and felt the door creak into place as Forman leaned against it.

"Help me John," he said, his voice strained. The door rattled as his body shook against it. "Help me. Help me."

"What do you—" I didn't know what to say. "What happened?"

"It's too much," he said. "Too much pain. Terror. I can't take it; I can't take it."

Forman was a monster—a demon, by his own confession. What could possibly scare him this much? "I can't help you in here," I said. Could I use this to escape? "Let me out and tell me what you're afraid of."

Something heavy struck the door. His fist, pounding against it.

"Forman? Can you hear me?"

I heard a gasp, then another, like a drowning man finally breaking the surface and desperate for air.

"Forman? Let me out. I can help you."

"You already have," he said. His voice was steady now. The door tightened against the frame as he leaned against it, then it went loose again as he stood up. I heard the floor creak as he stepped away.

"What are you talking about?" I shouted. "Forman!"

"You're a breath of fresh air, John. I'll see you in the morning."

He left, and the house fell silent, and then slowly the silence came alive with sounds: muffled whispers, distant sobs, and staccato screams that choked off almost as soon as they appeared. The boards creaked—in the roof, in the walls, in the floor—and behind it all was a low static of clinks and scrapes and shuffles from some dark space below the floor. The house cried; the house groaned; the house breathed and feared and hated.

I closed my eyes and dreamed of death.

16

I came awake to the sound of water running; a shower. Rays of light crept under the closet door, faint, but nearly blinding to my tired eyes. It was morning. The shower was short, followed by a smattering of footsteps. The creak of bed springs. The metallic swish as hangers scraped across a closet bar. The entire house seemed to hold its breath, listening. Soon more footsteps sounded, growing louder as they came closer and then softer as they passed and went on. The front door opened and closed. A ring of keys rattled, muffled by wood and distance. Locks turned and bolts slid into place.

A car door slammed, an engine rumbled, and gravel crunched as the car pulled away. The sound of the engine revved, then faded slowly to nothing.

We were alone.

I forced myself to wait as long as I could before trying to open the door, just to be sure Forman didn't come back—or that he'd even left at all, and wasn't just tricking me and hiding in the room beyond. I felt paranoid and sick. The minutes ticked by with agonizing slowness. When I finally convinced myself it was safe, I braced my back against the rear wall of the closet and pushed my feet against the door as hard as I could. It didn't budge.

I repositioned my body, braced my left foot against the door frame, and lined up a kick with my right. There was a faint line of light outlining the door, and I gauged my kick to land just to the side of it. Thud. Nothing. I kicked again, then again, harder and harder. The door must have been reinforced, just like the walls.

"Who's doing that?"

I jumped in shock, not expecting the noise, but the voice was soft and distant. It was a woman.

I called back. "Stephanie?"

"Who's Stephanie? And who are you?" The speaker was somewhere in the house, but in a far corner of it, probably with the door closed. She sounded . . . angry.

"My name is John," I shouted. "Forman brought me here last night."

"Are you the one he was playing with?"

Playing with. He'd said something about his "toys;" I guess this confirmed that they were people. "No," I said. "That was Stephanie. She's the receptionist at the police station."

"It doesn't matter who she is," said the voice. "Why are you breaking something?" The angry tone was stronger now.

"I'm locked in a closet," I said. "I'm trying to get out."

"You think I don't know that?" she asked. "You're going to piss him off, and I can guarantee you don't want him pissed off."

I paused, remembering the sounds of Stephanie's screams last night. Why would this woman be so mad at me for trying to escape? "Are you another prisoner here?" I called.

"What the hell else would I be?"

"I can escape," I said. "I can get out, and I can get help."

"No!" she shouted. The anger was still there, but joined by something else. Desperation. "What did you say your name was?"

"John."

"John, listen: I know you think you can get out of here, but you can't. We've all tried. You think we're just playing around down here? But no one has ever gotten away, and the closer anyone gets the more he hurts us."

I kicked the door again, hard. It splintered slightly on the edge.

"John!" the voice shouted, enraged. "John, stop it!"

I kicked again, further out from the frame, using it as leverage. The blow bent the wood.

"You're going to get someone killed!" she shouted. "You think he won't do it? He's killed four of us in the last few weeks."

"Janella Willis," I shouted, kicking the door again. It bent further. "And Victoria Chatham. I don't know the other names."

"How do you know those two?"

"He left them for us to find," I said. "He was trying to trap me." I kicked again and the door splintered outward, leaving a long crack and a hole. "But I don't intend to stay trapped."

"Dammit!" she shouted. I leaned forward and pushed out the broken piece of door with my hands. It was wide enough to crawl through, but it wouldn't be comfortable. "You think he's just going to let this slide? You think nothing's going to happen? He won't stop when he's done with you—he'll take it out on all of us!"

I bent my head close to the opening, avoiding the shards and splinters of broken door, and peered carefully around the room. It was duller in daylight—dirtier, and emptier. The furniture was old and sagging, and a yellowed roll of wallpaper sat against the side wall.

I reached one arm out, carefully, then used it to push back against the door so I could pull my head and shoulders through the hole. The splintered door scraped against me, raking across my back, but I forced my way past and extracted my other arm. It emerged raw and red through the shattered hole. With both arms free I pulled torso through, sucking in my breath to stay as small as possible. Once my hips cleared the hole my legs came easily, and I rolled to my feet with a grimace. My left arm and back were bleeding. The voice was still shouting at me, joined by a chorus of wails.

"How many of you are there?" I shouted.

"Four in the basement," said the voice, "plus whoever he was playing with last night."

"Are you sure there's no more?" I asked, walking to the front window and peering out. We were in the deep woods. The car was gone. "This is a pretty big house."

"We can hear when he brings people in," said the voice, "and we can tell when he kills one, because he screams about it for hours. It's not hard to keep a tally of who's alive and who's dead."

I paused, halfway to the kitchen. "Why does he scream?"

"Because he's a sick bastard," the voice growled. "Why do you care?"

"Because after I get out of here, he's going to come after me again," I said, entering the kitchen. It was filthy—dishes covered the counters and stove, and the walls were spattered with grease. A cupboard door was missing, and one of the two chairs at the table was barely more than a metal frame around a tattered, hollow cushion. "Next time he comes for me I want to be ready, so I need to know how he works."

"You're not going to get away," the woman's voice insisted.

Forman's house was like a shabby reflection of my darkest dreams. Everywhere I looked there were signs of imprisonment, torture, and death: bloodstains on the walls; a long, thick chain bolted to the corner of the floor; scratches and gashes in every surface. A smear of dried, brown blood crossed the floor and slid under the pantry door. A pot on the stove held something dark and murky, full of formless, floating shapes and smelling sickly of meat. The kitchen window was barred. In the hallway beyond I could hear raspy, labored breathing, and somewhere below my feet the basement hummed with the desperate voices of Forman's toys.

"John," the woman called, "Please listen to me: if you keep thinking about escaping it will only make it worse when you can't do it. You've got to believe me. I'm telling you this for you own—"

"I'm already out," I said. "How do I get to the basement?"

Silence. I left the yellow kitchen and probed deeper into the house, following the sound of breathing.

"Hello?" I said. "Can you hear me?"

Another woman screamed from the basement. "Help us!"

"Quiet!" the first woman shouted. They sounded much closer now. "What do you mean you're out?"

"I broke through the closet door and got out," I said. "Tell me how to find you."

"We're in the basement!" the second woman shouted. "It's the door in the kitchen!"

"Don't do this to yourselves!" the first woman said. "I want to get out of here just as much as you do, but we can't keep setting ourselves up for disappointment like this. I don't think I can take it anymore."

I went back in to the kitchen. There was only one door, which I had assumed was a pantry. I tugged on the handle, rattling it in the frame, but the handle was locked. I rattled it again. There was a soft noise from the other side, almost too quiet to hear. I leaned up against the door and heard a low sobbing:

"Please, please, please, please. . . ."

I leaned back and tried the door again. "Does he keep the key on him?"

"How am I supposed to know?" the woman shouted, obviously upset.

"Alright," I said, "just calm down. I'll look around."

"Hurry!" the second woman screamed.

I went back into the hall and into the back of the house, following the pained breathing. It led me to a closed door, but this time it wasn't locked; I opened it carefully, wary of some kind of trap, but nothing happened. It was a small bedroom, with an empty, coverless mattress on the floor in the corner. The flowered wallpaper was faded and slashed. I opened the door wider and stepped in, and gasped.

Stephanie was hanging against the wall, her wrists tied up with thick ropes that ran up to a pair of ragged holes in the ceiling. They pulled her arms up and to the sides, just high enough that she couldn't quite kneel; she hung, unconscious, like a crooked cross. She was still wearing her clothes from yesterday—the blouse and skirt she'd worn to work—but they were streaked now with sweat and blood, and a pool of blood and urine had soaked into the carpet around her feet, joining a much larger, much older circle of blood; she was not the first victim to hang in that spot. Her head hung forward limply, her dirty blond hair a long, stringy clump obscuring her face and chest. The room smelled like bitter smoke and singed meat.

I stepped into the room, my mouth open in awe. The scene was terrifying and repulsive and beautiful—here, in one room, was so much of my life distilled to solid form. All the dreams I'd lost sleep to avoid; all my darkest fantasies of what I wanted to do to people. How many times had I imagined this exact scene with my mother, to teach her never to control me again; how many times had I found Brooke here in my mind, desperate for me to save her, eager to do whatever she could to win my favor. I had spent my entire life—built all of my rules, severed all of my human contacts—to avoid this room, but that same focus had made it loom large in my mind, like a phantom triumph. It was simultaneously a personal hell and an unattainable ideal. It was everything I had always denied myself, which made it, inescapably, everything I had ever wanted.

Stephanie's breath was pained and wheezy; the unnatural angle of her arms was probably constricting her chest and cutting off air to her lungs. Even so, she was breathing, so I knew she was alive, and the fact that she still hadn't reacted to my entrance—or to my shouted conversation with the women in the basement—meant she was probably unconscious. I stepped closer, studying her closely. Her blouse was short-sleeved, and her arms were covered with red marks—shallow cuts and bright, angry burns. I leaned around the side, peering in at her face behind its web of hair. Purple welts and bruises covered her cheek and eye, and her nose was smashed from Forman's attack in the police station.

I closed my eyes and remembered her screams.

There was a dresser just a few steps away, covered with an array of tools—not the orderly array of clean torture implements you'd see in a spy movie, but a haphazard pile of kitchen knives and construction tools: screwdrivers, pliers, a vise grip, a hammer. There was a pincushion studded with needles. There was a book of matches, a set of candles, and, oddly, a box of firework sparklers. I picked up a pair of snubnose pliers; there was something black and ragged caught in the metal teeth. I set them back down and picked up a paring knife, its short blade covered with dried blood—layer after layer of it, as if it had cut a hundred victims and never been cleaned.

Stephanie hung motionless from the ropes on her wrists. Completely still, like a corpse. I held the knife toward the corpse, blade up, like an offering. So many dreams . . .

Gravel crunched in the driveway outside, and I looked up abruptly.

"John!" screamed the woman downstairs.

I dropped the knife and took a step toward the door, then stopped, went back, and grabbed the knife again; I didn't know what good it would be against a demon, but it was better than nothing. If I was lucky, I could get out without confronting him at all.

I ran further into the house, stepping lightly and hoping the floor didn't squeak. There had to be a back door. I found another bedroom, probably Forman's own, still largely unfurnished but with a closet full of good suits and clean white shirts. Beyond that was a bathroom, the tiles cracked and mildewed, and beyond that another bedroom, locked this time. There was no back door. I could hide in one of the other rooms and wait until he left again—but no, he'd know as soon as he came in the house that I'd escaped. The broken closet door was practically the first thing he'd see. He'd know I was out, and he'd be looking for me.

The front door opened, a distant jangle of locks and keys, and Forman called out:

"Did you honestly think you could escape, John?" He paused, then spoke again. "That was a new door, John. I'm going to have to get a metal one this time."

He'd started talking before he was even inside—he'd known I was out before he even saw the door. How?

"Confused, John? That's natural. Didn't the toys warn you that nobody ever gets away?"

I crept quietly back toward the room where Stephanie still hung unconscious. There was a window in there; I might be able to open it and get out before he came in.

"Ah," said Forman, "hope. I feel a lot of that at work, but it's been a long time since anybody felt it here." I could hear his footsteps, still several rooms away but coming closer. "If you have hope then you have a plan, but you're not nearly angry enough to attack me, which means you think you can get away. There's no back door, and the windows are obviously not an option. What could it be?"

I slipped through the door into Stephanie's room and glanced at the window—it was barred, just like the kitchen. Was the whole house barred shut?

"Desperation is mounting," said Forman, his voice drawing closer. "You're plan isn't working, or I'm scaring you—maybe both. Either way, you're out of options."

If I hadn't been so focused on Stephanie's torture the last time I was in here, I would have seen the bars on the windows— what else had I missed? I spun around, looking for anything I could use to get away or fight back. There was a small closet in the corner, but the door was missing, and the pile of boxes inside was too small to hide behind. I could go through the drawers of the dresser, but he was too close now—he'd hear everything I did. I was desperate now, searching for anything I could find: the mattress was old; the single light bulb was off; the rear wall was new sheetrock, still bare. There was a—

There were eyes in the wall.

Right about my own eye level, in the rear wall, there was a hole in the sheetrock with two eyes peeking through. I jumped back, startled, nearly tripping, but it wasn't Forman—it was someone else, someone dirty and motionless. I paused, waiting for the eyes to move, for the head to shake, for any sign of movement. The eyes blinked and glistened; they were crying.

It was another prisoner. Forman had built the new wall around someone, leaving only an eye hole aimed directly at his torture station across the room. The woman in the wall, mute and immobile, had been forced to watch everything Forman had done to Stephanie last night.

She'd seen everything I'd done in the room, too.

"Surprise," said Forman, standing in the doorway. His gun was drawn and pointed right at me. "Shock, really. And both things most likely to shock you are right here in this room. Really, John, you didn't even make it fun."

"Who is she?" I asked, pointing at the eyes.

"An experiment," said Forman. "An upgrade to the dungeon, so to speak. An intensifier."

"To intensify what?"

"Two victims for the price of one," said Forman. "I can get a similar effect downstairs, of course, but having one actually trapped in the wall adds a distinct touch of despair that I can't replicate any other way. I'm kind of a connoisseur, as you may imagine."

"Of torture?"

"Of emotions, John. Torture's a method, not an end."

Emotions. That was how he'd tracked me through the house, and how he'd read me so accurately the night before— because he wasn't actually reading me at all, he was literally feeling the same things I felt. That was why he'd been so scared in the car, because I was scared; that was why he'd been such a wreck after torturing Stephanie last night, because he felt all of her fear—and the woman in the wall's fear—at the same time.

"Understanding dawns," said Forman. "You're putting it all together now."

"You feel what we feel," I said.

Forman nodded, smiling.

"Could the other demon do that? Mahai, or whatever you called him?"

"Mkhai," said Forman. "And no, he couldn't—it's not likely you could ever have killed him if he did, because he'd have known you were coming before you ever got in place."

"You can read minds?"

"It's not reading, John, it's feeling—I feel exactly what you feel." He took a step forward, the gun level and menacing. "If I feel anticipation then I know that someone nearby is waiting for something. Someone's excited. Then I start to feel a little fear, and I know that whatever they're waiting for is dangerous, and then I feel something darker—hatred, or aggression, and I know that whoever's out there is planning to hurt someone because all of a sudden *I* feel like hurting someone. Which also means that if you ever get up the guts to use that thing," he pointed his gun at the paring knife in my hand, "I'll know it as soon as you do."

I looked at the knife in my hand, then set it down on the dresser.

"If you feel everybody's emotions," I asked, "why do you hurt people? Wouldn't you spend your time spreading happiness and joy and filling the world with good feelings?"

"Feelings aren't good or bad," he said, stepping closer. "They're just weak or strong. Love, for example, is weak: someone loves you, you love them back, you're happy for a while, and then it fades away. But if one of those lovers betrays the other, then you have a real emotion—then you have something powerful, something that leaves a mark you'll never be rid of. Betrayal is the most delicious of all, but it takes a while to set it up, and fear can be just as intense if you know what you're doing."

He advanced on me slowly, smiling slightly. "You know fear. When you faced Mkhai you must have felt a fear more intense than most people ever know. Fear, betrayal, anger, despair—lesser emotions pale in comparison."

I held my ground. "I'm a diagnosed sociopath, Forman," I

said. "Wringing intense emotions out of me is going to be a lot more trouble than it's worth."

"You're not here for fun," said Forman. "You're here to tell me about Mkhai."

"But you know more than I do," I said. "You've known him for hundreds of years."

"Thousands," he said. "But forty years ago he disappeared, and now he turns up dead. You know where he's been during that time, and you're going to tell me."

"And you're going to torture it out of me?"

"Nothing you tell me under torture would be of any value," said Forman. "You'll tell me when you're ready. For now, I think it's time I introduced you to the rest of the toys."

17

Forman tossed me a ring of keys from his pocket. "Unlock it. It's the little round one."

We were in the kitchen, and Forman was keeping his gun trained right on me. The gun interested me— Crowley/Mkhai never needed one, because he could turn his hands into claws. Could Forman do that? I had assumed that all demons were more or less the same, but apparently not; Crowley had been able to steal bodies, but this emotional thing was completely new. Did Forman also have a demon form lurking underneath his human one, or was his body structure more fixed than that?

I found the right key and opened the door. The smell from below was rank and bitter, like a sewer.

"What's down here?" I asked.

"The toys," said Forman. "Radha and Martha and . . . no, I think Martha's gone now. They all look the same to me, especially after they've been in the basement for a few months."

"Are you going to lock me down there too?" I asked.

"Well I can't very well have you running around upstairs anymore, can I? Doors are expensive." He shoved the gun into my back, a cold metal tube. "Now get down there."

The stairs were steep and narrow, and I had to hold the handrail to keep from falling. There was a small, dirty window at the top of the far wall, but the light from it was faint and my eyes hadn't adjusted to the darkness yet; I was completely blind until halfway down the stairs, when Forman flipped a switch behind me.

"Stop there," he said.

The room below lit up with a harsh, yellow light, and four filthy, emaciated figures curled in on themselves like shriveling weeds. They were women, dressed in rags; three of them were hiding their faces. The room was made of bare concrete, with a sewer pipe in the corner that the women had been chained to, and a series of hooks hanging from the ceiling. The floor looked like it was also concrete, covered with a layer of dirt, refuse, and blood. In the corner was a layer of wooden boards topped with a trio of squat metal barrels.

"These are my toys," Forman whispered in my ear. "These are the ones who survived the early tests. Our mutual friend Stephanie is not likely to join them."

"Why not?"

"She's too weak," said Forman. "I'll grow tired of her very, very quickly. This one, however, is my favorite." He pointed at the woman in the far corner—the only one of the women who dared to look back. She stared at us angrily. "Look at her," said

Forman, "practically chomping at the bit. I have to get back to the station, but . . . there's time. Take the keys and bring her to me."

"I'm not helping you."

Forman shoved me forward with the gun, knocking me off balance. I clutched at the handrail, barely catching myself, but he slammed the grip of his pistol down on my fingers and they opened involuntarily, letting go of the handrail. I fell down the stairs, cracking my head solidly against the wooden stairs and then knocking the wind from my chest as my spine hit the hard cement floor.

"You will not talk back to me again," said Forman evenly. "That is a lesson the other toys have learned well."

I raised myself to my knees, groaning, and sat there for a few seconds to let my head stop ringing. I grabbed the end of the handrail and climbed to my feet.

"Very good," said Forman. "Now bring her to me."

I walked across the room, stepping carefully to avoid piles of garbage and scattered cans of dog food. Each woman shrank back as I passed. They were dangerously skinny and caked with mud and dirt; their clothes were ripped and tattered, exposing scarred skin stretched tight over bony ribs.

There were four women here in the basement, and at least two more upstairs; the entire house was a pit of terror and loathing that was almost palpable, even to me. How could Forman stand it? From what he'd told me upstairs, his emotional mirroring wasn't something he could just turn off—it was always on, and he would always feel everyone around him. That was probably why he stayed on the stairs and sent me down for a victim; he'd be so scared down here that he'd be almost useless.

Could I use that against him?

The woman in the corner stared at me as I approached, like the cat in the warehouse. Her skin was dark, though I couldn't place her race exactly. She looked a little older than Lauren, but given her condition I couldn't be sure.

"It's you, isn't it," I whispered, kneeling down in front of her.

"Go to hell."

"Who's the woman in the wall?" I asked.

The woman looked at me warily. "Who?"

"Upstairs," I said softly, unlocking her slowly to draw out the conversation. "There's a woman trapped in the wall."

"Which wall?"

I paused. "In the torture room."

"I don't know what you're talking about."

"You have to have seen her."

"Who are you?" she demanded.

"I'm John Cleaver."

"Not anymore. You're one of us now. Or maybe something different." She narrowed her eyes. "We're just toys; you're a pet."

"Don't dawdle, John," called Forman.

"Listen," I said, "what's your name?"

"Radha."

"Radha?"

"It's Indian," she snarled.

"Fine," I said, "now listen—we don't have a lot of time. I think I can kill him, but I need your help."

"You'll fail," said Radha, "and he'll take it out on us."

"He'll take it out on me."

"Don't be an idiot," she hissed. "You broke down his closet door and who knows what else up there, and who's he punishing for it now?"

I shook my head. "He's not going to punish anyone," I said. "Now, how does he come to get you when I'm not here? How did he get the others?"

"Why do you care?"

"Just tell me—can he come down here?"

She snorted and looked behind me. "He's right there on the stairs. He can do anything he wants."

"Yes, he can, but *does* he?" I stared straight into her eyes, trying to get her to focus. "I need to know if he's ever come down here before, and what happened."

She looked over my shoulder. "He's getting impatient." Her fingers brushed a nasty set of scars on her chest.

"Answer me," I pleaded.

"Of course he comes down here," she said. "You think we just go up on our own?"

"Does he get scared when he comes down? Does he look jumpy, or does he tremble, or anything like that?"

"Why would he possibly be scared of us?" Radha asked. "He's got a gun, and we're all in chains. How does an idiot like you possibly expect to stop him?"

She was almost snarling with anger. *Aha.*

"It's you," I said, looking quickly around. "You're angry, and he focuses on that."

"I've got a lot to be angry about," she said.

That's why Radha was his favorite—she was strong-willed and angry, and he could use that thread of anger to keep himself going when anybody else's fear would make him run away.

That's why he ran away from Stephanie last night—she was all fear, so he was too. He'd come to me to calm down.

"You can't let yourself get mad," I said. "You've got to be terrified—so do I. It's the only way."

"He's coming," said Radha.

"He can focus in on one emotion and push the others away. That's how he found me in the house, even with all of you down here throwing out interfering signals. He can push those all away—"

"What are you talking about?" she asked.

"I'm saying that I think you're right," I said. "He *is* using me as a pet. He's using me to calm down after he hurts the rest of you."

She didn't seem to catch on. Did she not know that he absorbed emotions?

"What does that mean?" she demanded.

"It means my plan won't work," I said. "I need to find another weakness—"

Something hard and fast-moving hit me in the side of the head, and my vision exploded in a flare of white. I fell to the ground, clutching my head, and I heard Forman's voice above me, indistinct against the buzzing rush that filled my ears. I struggled to rise, but he kicked me hard in the stomach and I rolled over, doubled up in pain.

"Didn't she warn you not to plot against me?"

I coughed harshly, then rolled onto my side and threw up.

"One thing I'll thank you for, though," he said. "You actually made Radha hope, just for a second, and that made her subsequent disappointment much sweeter."

I coughed again, clutching my stomach with one hand and wrapping my other arm over my head.

"Get up," he said. I didn't move. "Get up!" he shouted, and fired his gun. The noise was deafening, and some of the women shrieked at the sound. I wasn't hit; it must have been a warning shot into the wall.

I heard the woman nearest me whimper, and I thought about all the fear that must be flowing into Forman. I looked up and saw him smiling, almost leering, his eyes wide. He looked drunk.

It was like a drug.

"Now get up," he said. I struggled to my knees and he kicked me again, softer this time—just enough to let me know who was in charge. I paused on my knees, gasping for breath, and raised myself to one foot, then the other. I stood for a moment bent over, my hands on my knees, trying to breathe deeply and ignore the pain.

Radha was silent, shrinking back against the wall. In spite of all her anger, apparently she'd still learned not to antagonize him directly.

"Pick this up," said Forman, dropping something on the ground before me. It was my pocketknife.

"Pick it up," he said again. I stooped and picked it up. "Since you and Radha have become such good friends," he said, "why don't you get to know each other a little better. Cut her."

"No," I said.

He kicked me in the back of the knee and I fell over again, dropping the knife to catch myself.

"I have already told you that you do not talk back to me," he said. "Now stand up."

I retrieved the knife and climbed back to me feet. Radha was staring at me ferociously, her dark eyes narrow and her teeth bared.

"I've read your psychological file," said Forman. "You're obsessed with death. I also happen to know, thanks to our conversation last night, that you've already killed one person, and I imagine the memory of it has been festering in your gut for months. You're probably desperate to hurt someone again."

Radha's face was hard and set, like a mask of death. Her hands were curled into fists.

"I've spent my life studying people like you, John, and I know exactly how you think." Forman was behind me, but his voice filled the room. "You dream about hurting people. You torture pets. You pull the wings off of flies. That's all she is, John—she's a fly; she's an insect. She's a nothing. Cut her."

She was staring me down, but her eyes were wider now; her gaze was less straight. She'd thought I was on her side, but doubt was creeping in. She was starting to fear me.

Somehow, the blade on the pocketknife had come unfolded in my hand. I held it up and watched the reflected light shine and run and drip off it like honey.

The knife felt so . . . right. Strip everything away and this is who I was: a man with a knife, feared and respected, free to do and say and be anything I wanted. Months ago I had been in this same situation—this exact pose—holding a knife to my mother, watching her squirm and knowing that I could do anything I wanted. I had been a god, just as Forman had been a god, and I had thrown it all away. Why? So I could force myself into an ill-fitting mold and live the rest of my life as a painful lie? So I could spend my days in isolation and my nights in a losing fight with my own nature? I'd wasted sixteen years trying to be somebody I wasn't, and all that time I'd been asking the wrong question.

Instead of 'how long could I keep this up?' I should have been asking 'why should I keep this up at all?'

Radha could see it now—some change in my eyes or my hands or my body that let her know I was going to do it. She was scared now. She knew how much I wanted to cut her, to open her up, to hear her screaming just for me.

For me? Or for Mr. Monster?

I hadn't thought about Mr. Monster for days. He used to fill my mind like an infection, duplicating and growing, but now I hadn't even thought about him since . . . since the night I killed the cat in the warehouse. Which meant he hadn't disappeared at all, he'd just blurred so fully into my own consciousness that I had become him completely. John had virtually disappeared.

I held up the pocketknife, staring at it intently. There were so many options, so many blades and tools: a can opener, a saw, a corkscrew. I wanted to try them all. I wanted to feel her muscles tense as I pressed the knife into her back, to hear a whimper of pain, soft and terrified. It's who I was.

But it wasn't who I wanted to be.

I put a finger on the back of the blade and slowly pushed it closed: up, over, and down. It snapped into place.

"John . . ." said Forman slowly. What was he feeling from me?

I held out the pocketknife, closing it tightly in my fist, looking straight into Radha's eyes. She was hard to see, as if my eyes were blurred. I was crying. I dropped the knife, and as it fell it tore a gash through my soul, cutting Mr. Monster away like a massive tumor. I was wounded—I was broken in half— but I was me again.

"You idiot," said Forman, and then he hit me again, a solid blow to the back of the head that dropped me like a sack of rocks. Radha caught me, dropping to her knees to slow my fall. Behind me Forman was swearing darkly, and I heard something loud and metallic.

"You idiot," said Forman, "you sick, stupid idiot. You think I can't do anything to you? Why don't you ask your new girl-friend there about how fun the pit is, huh?"

There was a loud screech, and Radha pulled me closer, away from Forman. Something heavy fell on my foot, clipping the edge, and I turned and saw that a thick plank of wood had fallen on it. The three barrels in the corner had been moved, and the boards beneath them shifted. Underneath was a wide hole in the concrete floor, with nothing but blackness beyond.

"Never give in," Radha whispered. "No matter how bad it gets, and no matter what he wants you to do. Never give in."

Something grabbed me from behind and yanked me back-ward, pulling me away from Radha and wrenching my foot out from under the plank.

"You'll love it in here," said Forman. "It's a great place for an idiot like you—nothing to do, nothing to see, nothing to think about except how much you hate yourself." He dragged me across the floor and I saw that the hole was full of brown, oily water. I tried to pull away but Forman's grip was too strong; he pulled me to the edge and tossed me in.

The water was shallower than I thought, maybe a foot deep, and I hit the bottom awkwardly with a painful, unexpected crash. The water was slick and cold. I pulled up, struggling to reorient myself, just in time to feel one of the heavy boards slamming down on my head. I fell face forward into the water and suddenly everything was quiet; sounds were distant and dull, fading away into nothing at all.

I wanted them to fade away forever.

18

"John!" It was a harsh whisper, loud and soft at the same time. "John, are you okay?" The sound was hushed and distant.

I was cold, and my head was throbbing like mad. I shifted slightly, and lances of pain shot through me. Dirty water lapped against my face.

"He moved," said the voice. "He's alive."

"Can you hear us?" said another.

The pain in my skull was centralized; I tried to reach my hand back to feel it, but I slipped under the water as soon as I moved. I put my arm back down and sputtered to the top. The water was deep enough that I couldn't lie down, so I had to prop myself up on my arms, but at the same time the planks above were so low that I couldn't sit up comfortably. I balanced more carefully and raised my hand to touch my head. It was hard to twist my body into the right shape, but my fingers brushed a big, throbbing bump. It was huge. I was lucky I hadn't drowned.

"John?" said a voice. Then softer, to the side, "he did say his name was John, right?"

I tried to answer, but my throat was raw and my voice was an unintelligible rasp. I coughed and swallowed and tried again.

"Radha?" I asked.

"He took her upstairs," said the voice. "She won't be back 'til tomorrow. I'm Carly."

I thought of Stephanie, hanging upstairs, and all the things Forman had done to her. He would do them to Radha now. Somewhere inside of me, Mr. Monster longed to be there when the women were tortured—longed to be a part of it. That was good; if I was aware of Mr. Monster, that meant we were separate again. I was back in control.

"There's another woman upstairs," I said. "Her name is Stephanie. He brought her in the same night he brought me."

"He'll bring her down here eventually, if she survives," said Carly. There was a pause, then another voice spoke.

"Where are we?"

I paused. "What do you mean?" I asked.

"I'm from Atlanta," the new voice said. "We're nowhere near there anymore, are we?"

Atlanta. Is that where Forman had lived before coming here? None of these women had come from Clayton, or we would have heard about the disappearances on the news. "No," I said, "we're nowhere near Atlanta. Are you all from there?"

"We're from all over," said another woman. That was all three, minus Radha. "What day is it?"

I thought back to the previous day, though it seemed so long ago. "Today is June twelfth."

"Three months," said one of the women.

"Four for me," said Carly.

"Almost five weeks," said the third.

Forman had been in Clayton for almost seven months, but he traveled often. Had he collected these women from all over the country?

"You, from Atlanta," I said. "He got you there three months ago?"

"No," she said, "Nebraska." After a moment she added, "my name's Jess."

"Jess," I said. "And you've been here since then?" My head was beginning to throb again, and I shifted carefully to ease up pressure on the bump.

"Not here," she said, "but prisoner, yeah."

"There was another house," said Carly. "Most of us came from the old house, but he wasn't there a lot. Someone came by once a week to feed us—we don't know who—but Forman still visited often enough to keep us terrified. About one month later he packed us all up in a moving van and came here. He got Jess at a truck stop."

"I was traveling," said Jess softly.

"He got me in Minnesota," said the third voice. She paused, then added, "I'm Melinda."

"So he came here about seven months ago to investigate the Clayton Killer, but he still took time to travel all over and kidnap you—plus the four he's already killed." It was like an addiction: he couldn't go for long without torturing somebody; he needed the emotional buzz just like a drug. Could I use that against him? There had to be some kind of way out of this. "Was the pit already here when you arrived?"

"Yes," said Carly, "and the chains, and the ropes through the rafters upstairs."

"The walls are reinforced, too," I said. "It took him a while, but he prepared everything so he'd have a working dungeon by the time you got here. That's a lot to move."

"He's moved it once before," said Jess, "at least once. Radha remembers a third house; she's been here the longest."

Of course she had. Radha was his favorite, because she was a fighter. Every day she chose between fighting and being his favorite victim, or giving up and being killed.

"How long has she been here?" I asked.

"A year," said Melinda.

A year. After enough time, most people would choose to die. Apparently not Radha.

And then her screaming began, drifting down from upstairs like a prophecy of doom. We all fell silent, and I slid down in the water until it covered my ears and drowned out the noise.

The water was rank and oily; it had probably held several prisoners, and had likely never been cleaned. When I started to feel the urge to pee I held it for as long as I could, but eventually there was nothing to do but let it go. The water grew warm, and I finally stopped shivering.

I drifted in and out of consciousness, always aware, even in sleep, of my head and arms and the surface of the water. I tried to twist my body at an angle, to press against the boards above me, but they were too heavy to budge. The barrels on top were probably full of dirt, or more water.

I ended up perpendicular to one of the walls, my head wedged up against the side and my arms crossed under my head; with my hands balled into fists, one on top of the other, they were just tall enough to keep my face above water. I held myself still, breathing slowly, barely conscious.

I'd had nothing to eat or drink since my date with Brooke. After hours lying in the pit, my hunger made me feel sick and weak, and I was so thirsty I could barely swallow. There was nothing to drink but the water I was laying in, so I sipped it gingerly and tried to sleep.

"Is he still in there?"

"Yeah. He never talks, but we hear the water every now and then, so we know he's alive."

"Sleeping, then." The voice was weak, but familiar. Radha was back.

"I'm awake," I said, pressing my head and arms more firmly against the wall. The water sloshed around me in tiny waves.

"Who are you?" Radha asked.

"My name is John Cleaver," I said.

"I know your name," said Radha, "but who are you? Why are you here?"

"Same reason the rest of you are here," I said.

"But he's never taken a guy before," said Carly.

"And he said you're a killer," said Radha.

"I . . ." I stopped. What could I possibly tell them? More importantly, what could I learn from them? They'd lived with

Forman far longer than I'd even known him—if he could transform into a demon, they might know about it. "Have you ever seen him Forman looking . . . different?"

"You mean in a disguise?" asked Radha. "I've never seen one."

"No," I said, "I mean have you ever seen him, I don't know, grow claws or something? Fangs? Does he ever look like an actual monster?"

Silence. After a moment I heard Radha speak softly.

"He's hallucinating."

"The pit does that," said Melinda.

"No," I said, "it's real. One of his friends was . . ." I stopped. I didn't know if Forman was listening in, and this was information I hadn't given him yet. That's the whole reason he had me here, supposedly—to find out what had happened to the demon Mkhai.

Regardless, their confusion had already answered my question—if they had seen him change forms they would have recognized my meaning immediately. There was no point giving away any more info.

"Never mind," I said.

"So did you really kill someone?" asked Radha.

"I did," I said. "A friend of his. But I didn't want to hurt anyone."

Silence again.

"Can you kill Forman?" asked Melinda.

I heard a gasp from the others, and a grumble of protest from Radha.

"Just stop," Radha said. "Do you have any idea how many women he's killed for trying to escape?"

"And what's the alternative?" Melinda demanded. "You just want to let him torture you until you end up dead, like the others?"

"I want to wait for the right moment," said Radha. "I've been here a year, Melinda—a whole damn year. I know how he thinks, and I know what I'm doing. He takes me upstairs sometimes to cook; he trusts me. And some day he's going to trust me enough to leave me an opening, and then I'm going to take it, and I'm going to get us all out of here. But we can't move before that happens or we'll lose everything!"

"And what happens in the meantime?" Melinda demanded. "You let him hook you up to a battery and stab you a few hundred times?"

They were getting too angry—he'd feel it, and he'd get suspicious.

"Quiet," I urged. "You're going to bring him down here."

"He can't hear us," said Radha.

"But he can feel you," I said. "Don't you know?"

"You said that before," said Carly. "What do you mean?"

"Forman is like . . . he's like an emotional vacuum. Anything you feel, he feels. That's why he gets so scared when he scares you, and that's how he always knows what's going on down here."

"Can you kill him if I get you out?" asked Melinda.

I hesitated. "I don't know. He might be stronger than we think—he might have some kind of power beyond the emotional thing. Fangs and claws, like I said." Gears turned in my head, connecting ideas, and I started to form a plan. "But we might be able to surprise him."

"How?" asked Jess.

"Can you actually get me out?" I asked.

"I can almost reach the barrels from here," said Melinda, and I heard her chain scrape the floor. "I can probably push one of them far enough out of place to let you move a board."

That would be enough; I could squeeze out and lie in wait for the next time he came down. But if he sensed anything out of the ordinary—hope, excitement, anticipation—he'd know we were planning something. I might be able to mask my own emotions, but the women needed to do the same.

"Everybody, think about your families," I said. "Think about how much you miss them, and how long it's been since you've seen them, and anything else that will make you sad. I know it sounds horrible, but you've got to be sad. Ignore Melinda, ignore me, just try as hard as you can to be sad."

"But what are you going to *do*?" asked Jess.

"Sadness first," I said. "You've got to trust me."

Silence.

"Please," I begged.

There was a long pause, and finally Radha spoke. "We'll do it," she said, "but when he catches on, I'll tell him everything. I'm not going to jeopardize the trust I've earned."

"Fine," I said. "Melinda, go for it—but don't think about what you're doing. Just be sad."

I heard her chain scrape again, and then noise above me—a light tapping, a soft scrape and shuffle, and then a low grating as the barrel scraped across the wood—not far, but it did move.

This will never work, I told myself, trying to dampen any emotion of hope. *I'll never see my family again. I'll never see Brooke again. She'll grow up, get a job in the wood plant, and marry Rob Anders—and he'll beat her every night.* I felt myself growing angry, and tried to tone it down. *She won't marry Rob, she'll die young: hit by a car in a freak accident. Young and innocent, splattered across the highway.*

The barrel above me moved again.

Lauren would die too, and Margaret, but not Mom—she'd live on for decades, old and alone. In fact, it was probably her fault that the other two died; she'd blame herself forever. I paused. It wasn't working. That should have been sad, but I wasn't feeling sad. Why not?

Because bad things that happened to others didn't bother me. I was a sociopath.

I heard one of the girls crying; I couldn't tell which. How close were we? How much longer would it take? The barrel scraped again, and a moment later light flooded into the pit through a gap in the boards. It wasn't a gap exposed by the moving barrel—it was a long line that stretched the entire length of the board. Someone had turned on a light.

Forman was here.

"How very interesting," said Forman, almost too quiet for me to hear. He was still far away, but his voice grew slowly louder and I guessed he was coming down the stairs. "A house full of scared, angry, desperate people grows suddenly sad— positively despondent, almost at the drop of a hat. Did you think I wouldn't notice something like that?"

The women were silent.

"And now I find that someone's been trying to open the pit," said Forman, much closer now. "And you all know, rather acutely if I recall, that you are not allowed to open the pit. Isn't that correct?"

Silence.

"So I figure if one of you was touching the pit, that means you want to be in it, right? Please allow me help you with that." There was a massive crash above me, then another, and another. The barrels were gone, and Forman kicked away the boards. Light flooded into the pit, blinding me, and I squeezed my eyes shut.

"Come on out, John," said Forman, "one of the toys has volunteered to take your spot—and I'm guessing she wants a little bit of the good stuff, too."

I forced my eyes open and saw him standing by the wall with a long extension cord. The plug had been cut off, and the two main wires had been stripped and separated, leaving two long tendrils tipped with three or four inches of bare wire. He tapped these together and they sparked.

"You already know how much fun this is on your chains," he said, facing the women. "Imagine how much fun it's going to be in the water."

I stood up slowly, grabbing the edge, my legs stiff and painful.

"So all I need to know," said Forman, "is which one of you was trying to open the pit?" He paused, waiting, and after a moment he sparked the wires together again. "Anybody?"

I looked at Radha; all of the women were looking at her. This was exactly what she'd warned us about, and it was her time to do exactly what she'd promised. This was her chance to gain Forman's trust. It was smart. It would take longer, but it would work eventually. She could be free.

Radha caught my gaze, her large eyes deep and clear. She held them a moment, then turned her head just slightly so that her dangling hair hid her face from Forman's view. I peered closer and she mouthed a phrase: *Never give in.*

She turned back to Forman. "I did it," she said.

"Excuse me?" said Forman.

"I'm sorry," she said. "I meant, 'I did it, you wart-brained bastard.'"

What was she doing?

"Get in the pit," said Forman, as cold as steel.

"Sure thing," said Radha, "I'll just pop out of these chains and saunter on over there. Good plan."

Was she an idiot? She was getting angry—angrier than usual—which was forcing him to get angry back. But why? It didn't make any sense.

"Out of the pit, John," he said, throwing down the wires and storming past me. Radha readied herself to fight but he hit her easily, a backhanded slap across the face that sent her sprawling to the floor. She looked thin and spindly, like a starved scarecrow. Forman pulled out his keys and unlocked her chain from around the sewer pipe, then used it to drag her over to the pit. "I said out of the pit, John!"

I stumbled backward, up and onto the filthy cement floor, sopping wet and shivering. Forman threw Radha into the hole and started stacking the boards back on top of her, keeping the long length of chain firmly under his foot.

"Get the barrels, John."

"No."

He pulled out his gun and fired at my feet, missing by inches. "I said get the barrels!"

The three barrels were small but heavy, probably filled with dirt. I rolled one onto the boards and righted it, then started back for another when a voice floated up from underneath, strained but defiant.

"Can't even do this to my face, you coward?"

Did she *want* him to kill her?

Forman stormed past me, picked up the extension cord, and brought it back to the pit. He touched the bare wires to Radha's chain and she screamed; the boards shook, and I imagined her body spasming against them from inside the pit. He pulled the wires away just half a second later; they had barely touched the chain.

"You might kill her," I said.

"No," said Forman, "you might kill her."

He held up the wires, gesturing for me to come. Radha choked and gasped for air, then started screaming insults at Forman.

"No," I said.

He shocked her again, and her sudden scream was cut off by a gargle as she fell below the surface of the water. The boards rattled, even the heavy barrel shook in place. Forman pulled the wires away.

"You can stop this whole thing, John," said Forman. "The shock you give her will be her last one, you have my word, but until then . . ." he shocked her again, and the boards above the pit jumped with her. "I'll just keep doing this."

What was I supposed to do? What was Radha's plan? She'd spent a year trying to earn his trust, and now she'd thrown it all away for . . . what? To save Melinda from a few shocks? It didn't seem worth it.

I could save her—I could walk right over and shock her, and Forman would let her go. But could I trust him? And even if I could, and he let her go, what had Radha's choice accomplished? Nothing, except to make me obey Forman. That couldn't be what she wanted; she'd told me to "never give in."

He shocked her again, and her scream was loud and primal. The other women were crying, shrinking into themselves, trying to hide from the world that had gone mad around them. Forman pulled back the wires and again offered them to me.

Was Radha's plan a trick? Had she known that Forman would ask me to help? Was this whole thing designed to give me a weapon—to get my hands on the wires so I could attack him? But she couldn't have known that would happen, could she? All she had known was what I had told her—that I was a killer, and that I didn't want to be.

Never give in.

I stood my ground. "I won't do it."

"You're sure?" he asked.

"I won't."

"Burn in hell, Forman," said Radha, her voice weak and raw.

"You first," said Forman, and touched the wires to the chain.

She screamed again, and the planks over the pit shook and jumped and rattled. Forman didn't pull the wires away this time; he held them there, watching the commotion. I rushed at him but he held up his gun with one hand, keeping the wires on the chain with his other. All three of the other women were screaming now, and I watched helplessly—we were scared out of our minds, but Forman's face was a snarl of rage. Radha was filling him with rage, and he was embracing it fully.

And then, abruptly, the boards stopped shaking and Radha's rage disappeared.

It was a visible, physical change—the muscles in Forman's face and body, so tense with anger, grew softer, then rigid with fear. Instead of hunching over the chain, leaning forward like a predator, he leaned back, eyes wide, horrified. His breathing quickened and he dropped the wires, clutching his chest and swallowing hard. He was sweating, and scooted back, then tried to stand and run but his legs gave way. He crawled toward the women as if seeking shelter, but this only scared them further and they shrank back. Forman howled, an animal scream of terror, and curled up in a fetal position on the floor. The gun lay discarded on the floor nearby. Forman was helpless.

This was Radha's plan. She'd told me before that he broke down whenever he killed one of them—the emotions from the other women, and from the victim herself at the moment of death, were simply too much for him to handle. They'd never been able to take advantage of it because they'd always been chained up, but I was free. She'd sacrificed herself to put him in this state, for this moment when I could take advantage of it and finish him off.

The wires were closer than the gun, just a few steps away. I picked them up quickly, careful to touch only the plastic, and walked toward Forman. His screaming dulled—he was feeling my clarity now, pushing away the women's fear and pulling himself together. I didn't have long. I ran the last few steps and jumped out with the wires, but his hands shot up and caught my wrists at the last second.

How could he be that fast?

I fought to bring the wires down, to touch him anywhere with the exposed metal, but he was too strong. Slowly he grew more focused, more determined, and began to bend my arms back. I expected him to push the wires toward me, but he pushed them out to the sides—he didn't want the wires to touch me because he was touching me, and I was soaking wet, and any current that passed through me would shock him as well. He didn't want that to happen, and that meant it would hurt him.

And if it would hurt him, I wanted to do it.

"Never give in," I said, and reversed the direction of my hands, pulling them towards me instead of away from him. I felt a white fire tear through me, every muscle in my body screaming and flexing and burning at once, and then everything went black.

19

My third date with Brooke was a continuation of our second: we dressed up in gaudy tourist clothes and went to the shoe museum, holding hands and laughing at the rooms and hallways stacked high with shoes. There were grayed felt spats from old military uniforms, and bright Velcro sneakers from the Eighties. There were adjustable wooden molds from England, high wooden sandals from Japan, and heavy wooden clogs from Denmark; there were boots of alligator skin, snake skin, and shark skin. There were novelty slippers with faces and tiny lights. There were running shoes with long metal cleats. There were snowshoes. There were stilts.

I could hear someone's voice down the hall, familiar but impossible to identify. I turned to ask Brooke if she recognized it, but she was gone. I heard the voice again, and it was Brooke's voice, and I followed it down a maze of shoes and shelves. The hallways were long, stretching out and converging on a single point; each corner revealed more rooms, more shoes, until at last I realized that the walls themselves were made of shoes, vast piles of them, like a cave hollowed out in an endless mountain of shoes. Brooke's voice called me on, urging me to wake up. My own shoes were gone now, and my feet were wet and cold. I reached for a pair on the wall and my hand touched bare cement.

I was in Forman's basement, awake and cold. I was handcuffed to a pipe in the corner. My feet were bare, and my mouth tasted like vomit. I touched my chest gingerly, my muscles sore, and felt two burns where the current had forced its way through my skin and into my body.

"John?"

I looked up and saw the other women looking at me. Stephanie had joined them, chained into the corner where Radha used to be. I didn't know the others by sight, only by sound, but outside of the pit it was hard to recognize their voices.

"What happened?" I asked, still groggy.

"You got shocked," said one of the women. She was younger than the other two, but maybe a little older than Stephanie. Jess, maybe? "It knocked you both out."

"He fell too far for any of us to reach," said another. "I think I dislocated my wrist trying to reach him." That had to be Melinda.

"To reach his keys?" I asked.

"Or to kill him," she said, shrugging coldly. Definitely Melinda.

"Wasn't the gun right here?" I asked.

"It got knocked over there," she said, gesturing toward the stairs. She spoke softly. "He took it when he left."

"So he woke up first," I said. Maybe he could regenerate, like Crowley had. "How long was he unconscious?"

"An hour, maybe two," said the last woman; I recognized her voice as Carly. "Same as you. You actually started to move first, but he woke up first and gave you some kind of a shot. We thought it was poison."

"It was a sedative," said Jess. "That's the same way he kidnapped me."

So my guess about the electrical shock had been right—he was just as susceptible to it as a normal human. Maybe he couldn't regenerate at all. If I could find a way to shock him without getting myself next time, I could stop him.

"Where is he now?" I asked. From the pit in my stomach I guessed that I'd been asleep for several hours; I'd been here for maybe 48 hours now, and hadn't eaten a thing.

"He left," said Jess. "He chained you up, then he brought her down, then he left." She pointed at Stephanie, and I looked at her closer. She was terrified and quiet, curled up in the corner with tears streaking her face.

"Are you okay?" I asked. She nodded dumbly. "What about the woman in the wall?"

She started to cry. "The eyes?"

"She's still there?"

Stephanie started sobbing uncontrollably.

I closed my eyes. I felt . . . not empathy. Not concern. I felt responsibility. Just like I had with Mr. Crowley, I swore that Forman wouldn't kill anyone else if I could help it. I'd kill him, and that's where the killing would end.

The three long-time prisoners stiffened abruptly, heads cocked and listening, eyes going wide. "He's back," said Carly.

I listened carefully, but I didn't hear anything until the front door opened. Footsteps crossed the floor above us, followed by a dull, heavy scrape. He was dragging something. Another prisoner?

We listened in silence as the footsteps moved into the kitchen, then the hall, and on into the back of the house. Several minutes later they came back, and we heard a burst of water in the kitchen sink. The pipe I was chained to rumbled with the noise of rushing water, and a moment later another pipe, thicker this time, trickled lightly as water ran down the drain. It was as if the whole house was an extension of Forman himself, moving and reacting with everything he did. He surrounded us. He controlled us completely.

The door above us opened, and light flooded in from the kitchen. Forman's silhouette came in, slowly coalescing into a real body as my eyes adjusted to the light.

"You're awake," he said. "Excellent." He came toward me quickly, neither menacing nor cautious. I was too weak to attack him, even if I wanted to—too groggy from the drugs and my two days of hunger. "There's something I think you should know," he said, dropping down on one knee to reach my handcuffs. "You're now officially wanted for the murder of Radha Behar."

"I didn't touch her," I said.

"Early forensic evidence suggests that you did," said Forman, "including your hair mixed with hers, and your shoes found nearby. But don't worry—I'm practically in charge of the investigation, and it would be very easy for me to steer it in another direction. Assuming, of course, that you meet with my requirements."

"You want to know about Mkhai."

"I've given you two chances," he said, undoing my handcuffs, "and you've thrown them away. This is your third. Up we go."

I rubbed my wrist and struggled to my feet. "What two chances?"

"Two chances to be yourself," he said. "To live the life you deserve. You're not one of them," he said, gesturing at the four terrified women. "You're not a toy; you're not a victim cowering in a corner. You're a warrior, like the legends of old. You killed a god, John. Don't you want to take his place?"

He took my by the arm and pulled me toward the stairs. I followed unsteadily, trying not to lean on him for balance. My legs didn't want to respond, and my head felt light.

"I'm not like you," I said.

"Nobody is," said Forman, shoving me forward onto the stairs. I grabbed the handrail and tried to climb. "There was nobody like Mkhai, either," he said, "and there's nobody like you. You're a precious snowflake. Now hurry up."

I climbed the stairs and paused in the kitchen, willing my legs to wake up while Forman locked the door behind us. I was free, but I was too weak to do anything—even when he was completely incapacitated, he'd been able to feel my intentions and protect himself. Did that mean I could only attack him unintentionally? Could I plan some kind of accident?

A cell phone rang, and Forman reached into his pocket. He glanced at the number, smiled, and answered. "Nobody," he said, "how nice of you to call." Pause. "No, still nothing. We're about to find out, though." He looked at me. "He's stronger than we thought, and weaker. I can't wait for you to meet him." Pause. "Yes, I told you, I'll call you as soon as I know. Be patient."

Pause. "Bye." He put the phone away and pointed toward the hall. "After you."

I started down the hall, keeping a hand on the wall to steady myself. I wondered if there were any more people in the walls, buried and sealed off forever.

"You had Radha in chains, and I gave you my knife, and you refused to hurt her. She liked it, you know—being hurt. She always had a sense of satisfaction when we finished."

"That's because she'd survived," I said.

"And you mortals appreciate the chance to survive," he said. "Your life is defined by death, and each time you face it you grow stronger. You learn more, and feel more. It sounds stupid to say it like this, but *not dying* makes you more alive."

"What defines you demons?" I asked.

"The things we lack."

We passed his bedroom, moving down the hall to the torture room. My legs were growing firmer again; blood was flowing more strongly, and my balance was better.

I wondered who was in the room—it had to be someone I knew. Who would he force me to torture? My mother? My sister? Brooke?

"Your second chance came when she was in the pit," said Forman, "and that should have been an easy one: you didn't have to hurt her directly or even see her face, just touch the wires to the chain. It would have been a kindness, in fact, because it would have saved her life. But still you did nothing."

"I don't want to hurt people," I insisted.

"That's what you keep saying," said Forman, "but it didn't stop you from hurting Mkhai, and it didn't stop you from attacking me in the basement. We all have our tastes, of course, and I just had to realize that I wasn't addressing yours properly. You didn't hurt Radha because she was innocent, and you only hurt the wicked. So, I brought you somebody wicked."

We turned into the torture room and there he was: Curt, my sister's attacker, bound and gagged and completely at my mercy.

He was awake; his eyes were wide, and his mouth was sealed tight with a thick wrap of duct tape. His feet were securely fastened to floor, where Forman had broken through the hardwood and run thick lengths of chain through the heavy floor supports. His hands were bound at the wrists by ropes that ran up and into the holes in the ceiling, but where Stephanie had been hanging loosely, Curt had somehow been pulled tight. He was spread-eagled, held firmly in place.

Curt stared at me, with wide, scared eyes that said he didn't know what to think. I'd been missing for almost two days, and he was sure to have heard about it, and I definitely looked like a prisoner—I was covered in dried muck from the pit, with burn marks on my shirt and vomit crusted on my clothes, and I could barely walk. It wasn't hard to guess that I was a prisoner and a victim. And yet I was here, unbound, and Forman was treating me so graciously. Like an equal. If Curt had heard any of what Forman had said in the hall, he'd be even more confused.

And more terrified.

"There he is," said Forman. "You learn a lot of things working in a police station—like how a certain Mrs. Cleaver calls every fifteen minutes to rant about her daughter's abusive boyfriend. 'Arrest him. Lock him up. Kill him.' But there's not a lot the law can do in a case like this, is there?" He walked over to the dresser and began sifting through the tools. "Women in abusive relationships are, by nature, accepting of abuse, and poor little Lauren was too browbeaten to accuse her browbeater formally. She actually told the paramedics she'd fallen out of bed, if you can you believe it." He held up a flathead screwdriver, examined the tip, and put it back down. "They didn't believe it either, but there wasn't anything they could do about it. If the victim says there was no abuse, the law says there was no abuse. The law is helpless." He turned and held up an old, dirty scalpel. "But you're not."

He stepped toward me and offered the scalpel. "This is what you want, right? You're a punishing angel. You won't hurt anyone, for any reason, unless they deserve it—and who deserves it more than Curt? You saw what he did to your sister. And don't think he stopped there—he got away with it, after all, so what's to stop him from doing it again? He can slap her and punch her and beat her until she falls unconscious, and he'll always get away with it. Nothing can stop him."

He placed the scalpel in my hand. "Nothing but you."

Curt was shaking his head wildly, tears filling his eyes, but I didn't see him as a victim—all I saw was Lauren's face, red and purple and black. She had a cut on her cheekbone, right where I did; I reached up and touched my face, feeling the scab. I deserved mine, but Lauren had been completely innocent. Curt had beaten her in cold blood.

I stepped toward him. Wasn't this the same decision I'd made with Mr. Crowley? To stop a bad man from hurting the innocent? I'd tried to tell the cops, and they'd ended up dead. Crowley had been a situation the law couldn't deal with; it was me or nobody. I'd stopped him because nobody else could, and now that was true again. The law was helpless—the only plan the police had was to sit and wait while he beat her more, again and again, until at last she finally decided to accuse him. Could I, in good conscience, allow that to happen? Not when I could stop it, forever, right here and now.

I stepped forward.

But no, this was different. Crowley was a killer—a supernatural killer—and killing him was the only way to stop him. He was killing more than once a week by the end—how many more people would be dead now, six months later, if I hadn't stepped in? But Curt was not a killer, and his punishment could not be death. It was too much. I couldn't do it. I stepped back.

But . . . I could hurt him. It didn't need to end in death. I'd hurt Mrs. Crowley, after all, and she was far more innocent than Curt was. I took two more steps forward, close enough to smell his sweat and hear his ragged breathing. He had caused pain, so his punishment should be pain. It made sense. It was fair. A bruise for a bruise.

But then what?

I turned suddenly and walked to the window; it was evening, and the sky through the thick pine trees was a deep, royal blue. What would happen after I hurt Curt—we couldn't just let him go, or he'd tell people what I'd done. We could keep him here, chained in the dungeon; he deserved prison, and we could give it to him. But forever?

I looked back at Curt. His eyes were closed; maybe he was praying, or maybe he was simply too afraid to look. He was a rude, arrogant monster; he bullied everyone he met, he insulted the woman who loved him, and when things came to a head he beat her—powerfully and mercilessly. He ruined lives, as surely as Crowley did; was I a hypocrite to stop Crowley and not Curt? But if Curt was fair game, why stop there? Where could I draw the line? And if no line made sense, why draw a line at all?

And below it all, behind every other reason, lurked the inescapable truth that I *wanted* to do it—I wanted to hurt him, to make him bleed, to make him scream, to make him lie still in the perfect peace of death.

I stepped toward Curt again, but something caught my eye—a tiny movement on the far edge of the room, no bigger than the wing of a moth. I looked and saw two eyes staring back at me, trapped and mute, watching. I stared back. Nobody knew who she was, maybe not even Forman. She blinked—the only form of communication she had.

Where was she from? What did she like, and what did she dislike? What did she love and hate? Who was she?

Who was I?

My name is John Cleaver. I live in Clayton County, in a mortuary on the edge of town. I have a mother and a sister and an aunt. I'm sixteen years old. I like reading, cooking, and a girl named Brooke. I want to do what's right, no matter what. I want to be a good person.

But that was only half of me.

My name is Mr. Monster. I show dozens of warning signs for serial killer behavior, and I fantasize about violence and death. I'm more comfortable around corpses than people. I killed a demon, and every day I feel the need to kill again, like a bottomless pit in the center of my soul.

Each half of me was a contradiction of the other, but each half was true. If I chose one I would be denying the other, and in doing so I would be denying myself. Was there a real me, somewhere in the middle?

There *was* another me—a me that I'd never seen for myself, only glimpsed through the eyes of others. It wasn't John the loser, or John the creep, or John the psycho. It was John the hero. Talking to Brooke and her friends, walking around at the Bonfire, looking at the eyes of the people I passed and seeing them look back with respect—I'd really felt like a hero. I wanted to feel that again.

And being a hero meant saving Curt, no matter how much I hated him. It meant saving all of the prisoners, no matter how hard it became. It meant stopping the villain—Forman—even if I had to break my rules to do it. Even if I had to hurt him, and even if I had to kill him.

But how could I kill him when I didn't know how he worked? What did he say about himself, and about the other demons? They define themselves by the things they lack.

So what did he lack?

He lacked emotions: he didn't have any of his own, so he stole them from others. He was a blank; a giant hole with nothing to fill it. Just like a serial killer, he had a need that demanded to be fed, and he had built his life around feeding it at the expense of everything else.

Mkhai was also defined by what he didn't have. He lacked an identity of his own, so he stole the bodies of others, over and over, moving from place to place and identity to identity until . . . until he stopped. Until one day he became Mr. Crowley, and he never switched bodies again. Something had changed in him, something profound, and on that day he ceased to be

Mkhai. He stopped defining himself by what he lacked, and started defining himself by what he had. So what did he have? He had Mrs. Crowley.

He had love.

I thought of him again, not as a demon but as the kind old man across the street. Love had pulled Mkhai away from his life of death and deception and into a life of near normality—a life that held so much less, but meant so much more. Forman didn't understand it; I didn't know if he could. And yet that's what this entire thing was all about: Forman wanted to know what happened to Mkhai. He didn't really want me to hurt Curt, he was just trying to turn me to his side and earn my trust. He wanted me to join him, at which point I would presumably tell him the secret he'd come to Clayton to discover.

He'd said before that love was weak and useless. Would he even understand when I told him? The demon Mkhai had almost beaten me because I didn't understand love; now Forman had the same weakness, and I might be able to use it against him. A plan started to form in my mind, but I had to do it carefully. Even the slightest emotional warble could give me away.

"You came to Clayton County searching for your friend," I said, turning to face Forman. "You said he'd disappeared forty years ago, and you didn't know why. Well I do. He did it for love."

"Don't play with me," said Forman, shaking his head.

"Trust me," I said, "from one sociopath to another: if you don't understand the reason for something, it's always love."

He considered me for a moment. What was he feeling from me? Did he know I had a plan? I wasn't lying to him—everything I planned to tell him was true. Could he still sense a trick? Could he detect my nervousness through the miasma of nervous fear that already filled the house? I watched him, trying to feel as honest and helpful as possible.

"All right, then," he said. "Try me."

"Food first," I said. "I haven't eaten in two days."

He glanced at Curt, his wild eyes watching us over his duct tape gag. I set the knife down on the dresser.

"There'll be time for him later," I said.

Forman nodded, and gestured behind him to the hallway. "In the kitchen, then. Let's hear what you have to say."

20

"Have a seat," said Forman, gesturing at the kitchen table. I sat down and he went to the fridge, opening it up to reveal not a collection of heads and arms but the mundane spread of a poorly-stocked bachelor: grapefruit juice, a bottle of mustard, half a loaf of bread, and a Styrofoam box of restaurant leftovers. In the back there was a jar half-full of pickle juice. I looked longingly at the restaurant box, but Forman pulled out the bread bag and tossed it onto the table.

"I don't eat in a lot," he said. "I prefer to enjoy my meals, instead of feeling how sad the toys are the whole time."

I opened the bag and pulled out a piece of hard brown bread, forcing myself to eat it slowly; I didn't want to eat too fast and get sick. It tasted delicious, but I was sure that was mostly a result of my hunger.

Forman leaned against the counter with his arms folded, watching me eat. After a few bites he spoke again.

"So I guess you know a lot more about Mkhai than you let on," he said. He was acting odd, like he should have been angry but wasn't, but then I remembered that he wouldn't be angry unless I was. Right now we were calm, and cautious, and ready.

He was a blank page, and it was time to write on him. I wanted him to trust me, so I focused on trusting him—not pretending to, since that was sure not to work, but trying instead to actually trust him, to rely on him, to feel like we were in this together. I found that if I focused on him it didn't work; I understood how he thought, but I couldn't identify with him. I couldn't empathize. Instead I focused on my own reaction to him and to the situation, trying to feel comfortable with the strictures that Forman had placed on our relationship. I put myself at ease and tried to treat him the way I treated my mom, or my friend Max.

"You told me in the car," I said, "that you thought Mkhai might have taken Mr. Crowley's body right before he died, which makes a lot of sense because Crowley was never found. If Crowley had died on his own, there would have been a corpse, but if Crowley died after Mkhai had his body, it would have dissolved into sludge and disappeared."

Forman nodded. "It seems you're familiar with his methods."

"What you didn't figure out," I continued, "is that Mkhai had been Crowley for the entire forty years when you couldn't find him."

Forman smiled snidely. "For love."

"Yes," I said, "for love. Forty years ago Mkhai came here in a brand-new body, ready to start a brand-new life just like he always did. How long did he usually stay in a body before moving on?"

"A year at the most," said Forman. "When you can go any-where, and be anyone, there's rarely any reason to stay longer."

"He found a reason here," I said. "Her name is Kay."

Forman laughed, an abrupt, derisive snort. "Kay Crowley? Mkhai is a being thousands of years old. He's had queens and empresses at his command; he's had slaves and fanatics, priest-esses and worshippers. What did Kay have that an entire his-tory of beautiful women couldn't offer?"

"Love."

"He's had love!"

"Not real love," I said, leaning forward. "You don't even know what real love is. If someone loved you, Forman, you'd love them back, and when they stopped, you'd stop. There's no com-mitment to anything, so it never really matters. It isn't real. But real love is pain. Real love is sacrifice. Real love is what Mkhai felt when he realized that Kay would never accept him as he was—only if he became something better. So he gave up the bad stuff and made himself better."

Forman stared at me intently. "How could a sociopath pos-sibly know anything about love?"

"Because I have a mother who gives her entire life to help children who don't notice it, don't appreciate it, and can't pos-sibly return it. That is love."

We watched each other, studying each other, thinking. This was the key moment, when I needed him to move from trust to longing. I needed him to feel there was a piece of him missing, because I knew exactly what he would do: the same thing he always did. He'd go out and find the missing piece and bring it back here to beat it into submission. It was his only way of dealing with the world. While he was gone, I would put the next phase of the plan into motion.

I thought about the people I missed.

"Humans aren't defined by death," I said, "and they're not defined by what they lack. They're defined by their connections."

I thought about my mother, and everything she did for me. I thought about the way she'd protected me six months ago when I killed the demon, and neither of us knew what to do. I thought about the way she'd turned her life upside down to accommodate me, to be the person she thought I needed. I hated it, but I knew she was trying to help.

"Mkhai knew it," I said. "He finally realized that there was more to life than running from one body to the next, from one life to the next, always escaping from everything without ever getting anywhere."

I thought about my sister, who wanted to watch out for me but didn't even know how to watch out for herself. I thought of her bruised and scared, and I thought about how she'd be even more scared tonight when she realized Curt was gone. She was an idiot, but she cared about people.

"Mkhai left your little community of demons because he didn't need it anymore," I said. "Thousands of years of meaningless existence, of existing without living, and finally he was free. He moved on, and the power he gained made him so much more than you will ever be. You called him a god, but he was more than that in the end. He was human."

I thought about Kay Crowley, the little old lady across the street, who smiled and helped and loved so unconditionally that she brought a demon in from the cold and made him a man—and I thought about that man, the old neighbor I'd grown up with, the demon who'd been more of an example to me than my father. What were his last words?

Remember me when I am gone. I remembered him, and I missed him.

Loss and longing.

"Stop it!" yelled Forman, standing up and pacing across the room—not toward me, but toward nothing; it was a nervous twitch.

My plan was working.

"You're not here for this," he said, waving his arms while he walked. "You're not here for sadness—this boring emotion." He walked into the living room, and his voice fluttered back in. "I don't need to miss things!" He barged back into the room and grabbed the sides of the table, leaning down to shout in my face. "You think I haven't felt this before? You think you can just shock me with some new emotion and I'll bow down and . . ." He stood up and turned around, then scratched his forehead, took a step toward the sink, then turned around again.

"I don't need this," he said. "I'm leaving." He came toward me around the table, and I backed up instinctively. "I'm not . . . just sit down. I'm locking you up so you don't do anything stupid. I'll be back." There was a thick length of chain under the table, with a manacle welded to the end, and Forman locked this securely around my ankle. "I'll be back," he said again, "and you'd better be feeling something more interesting when I get here."

He turned and walked out, going straight to the living room

and out the door, locking it carefully behind him. The car roared to life and drove away. I was alone.

Time for phase two.

Forman acted like he'd stormed off to escape my sadness, but I knew better—the last time we'd forced him to feel sad he'd come downstairs and attacked us. If all he'd wanted was a new emotion, he could have just attacked us again. No, Forman had left to kidnap someone, just like I thought he would— probably Kay Crowley, or maybe my mom. Once I understood him, he was easy to predict; I'd told him he was missing something, and now he'd gone to get it.

I had an hour, maybe less, assuming he went straight to Kay and brought her straight back. I needed to be ready when he returned, but I couldn't just attack him because he'd feel it coming—even when he was completely overwhelmed, as he had been in the basement, he could snap out of it in an instant. The only way to hurt him was to do it indirectly, by laying a trap. I stood up and tested the chain—it held fast, but it gave me about twenty feet of movement. I hoped it would be enough.

The kitchen was a good place for a trap because it had the strongest electrical outlet in the house: the oven's. All I needed to do was rig something to shock him when he came back, but what? I dragged my chain over to the cupboards, starting at the farthest edge where I had to stretch the chain to its fullest and reach out with my arm. Most of the cupboards were bare— what few dishes he had were mostly in the sink, waiting to be washed. One cupboard had a stack of paper plates and a box of plastic forks; another held a single ceramic mug, dusty with disuse. The cupboards below the counter were more fruitful, holding a number of rusted pots and pans, a coffeemaker, and, for some reason, a cardboard box full of old newspaper.

The counter itself held a number of items I might be able to use: a knife block, half-full; a toaster; a microwave. I opened the drawers and rooted through piles of mismatched silverware, old packs of batteries, and a random assortment of tools and wooden pencils. There were two screwdrivers; I might be able to take something apart . . .

There was blood on the screwdriver.

I looked closer; there was blood on all the tools. This wasn't just a utility drawer, it was another torture station. I pulled a knife from the block and examined it carefully. It had been washed, but not well; the serrations on the blade held brown remnants of old blood.

Of course I knew that he would try to torture whomever he brought back, but I considered now the possibility that he would do it here, in the kitchen. His basement was full, and his torture room was occupied; if he did it here he could force me to watch or even to help without even having to unchain me. And he had a full suite of tools—knives and screwdrivers, icepicks and pliers, even a hammer. All I needed to do, then, was electrify a tool I knew he would reach for, and then sit as still and emotionless as possible until he touched it—I couldn't let him know, through excitement or anxiety, that I was waiting for something. I had to be completely dead.

But what tool to electrify, and how?

I might be able to tie a wire to a tool in the drawer and run it out and back, into the oven outlet, but there was no way to guarantee which tool he'd reach for first. I looked around for a clock, but there wasn't anything; I had no idea how long he'd been gone, or how long before he came back. I had to move quickly, and I couldn't think of anything else, so the tool drawer it was.

I got the coffeemaker out of the cupboard and pulled a knife from the block. The coffeemaker cord was at least three feet long, maybe four; I hoped it was long enough to reach from the open drawer to the outlet behind the oven. I used the knife to cut the cord, right at the base of the coffeemaker, and started shaving away the plastic coating around the wires. While I was doing that, I noticed that the metal from the knife blade extended back into the handle—it was a long, single piece of metal, flanked on the end by pieces of wood riveted around it. A current at the tip of the knife would carry straight through to whomever touched the handle. I jumped up and looked at the wood block—there was a hole in the bottom where the tip of the biggest blade, a large butcher knife, peeked through. This could work so much better than the drawer—it was easier to rig, and easier to make sure he touched the right thing. I pulled out the huge knife, dumped the rest into the sink with the dirty dishes, and sat down to work.

First I needed a way to secure the wire to the knife. Bracing the butcher knife against the floor, back in the corner where any floor damage would be hidden by the coils of my chain, I lined up the icepick right at the tip and hit it with the hammer. Nothing. I hit it again, over and over, trading out the icepick for a Phillips screwdriver and still accomplishing nothing; the blade was too strong to puncture. I picked up the knife and chopped it against the heavy iron rim of a frying pan, again and again until it finally began to dent. When the dent looked deep enough to hold it, I looped the exposed wire around it and tied it off.

Using a smaller knife I cut the plug from the other end of the cord, and slipped the whole thing through the knife block. The cord came out the bottom just fine, and I shaved away about four inches of plastic coating from the end. I placed the block on the counter, passing the cord hanging off the side behind the oven, and looked out the window.

Nothing yet.

I pulled the oven away from the wall, unplugged the power cord, and wrapped my newly-exposed wire around one tine of the plug. Assuring myself that everything was ready, I plugged the oven into the wall, connecting a straight line of current from the wall outlet to the handle of the knife. I pushed the oven back against the wall and examined the scene. Everything looked normal—except for a few inches of cord running out from the bottom of the knife block to the gap by the stove.

I looked around for something to hide it with, and found a half-damp rag in the sink. I brought it up to the counter and set it on top of the cord; I just had to hope he wouldn't notice it was out of place.

I glanced out the window again and saw the car on the road, just coming around the nearest bend. *Don't panic*, I told myself. *Stay calm, but not too calm. He'll feel fear from the women, just like he always does when he gets here. Just blend in.* I allowed myself a touch of fear, but no nervousness, no desperation; I forced myself to walk slowly around the room, gathering the tools I had used, putting them back into their drawers with calm, measured precision. *Just enough fear to look normal, but not enough to stand out.*

I closed the drawers and walked to the fridge, pulling out the grapefruit juice and taking it back to the table—if I tried to look too innocent he'd get suspicious. I opened the juice and took a drink straight from the bottle; it was acidic and strong, and I grimaced at the shock. I heard the car park outside, and the engine went off. I took another drink and wiped my mouth with the back of my hand. The front door opened, though I couldn't see it from my seat at the table.

"Thank you again for coming," Forman said as he opened the door. "I'm sure you can appreciate the need for secrecy, and we normally wouldn't do this at all, but he did request you specifically."

"And you're sure he's okay?"

No. No! I knew that voice, and it wasn't Kay or Mom.

Forman stepped into the kitchen, grinning like the devil. "Hello John," he said. "I brought us a new toy."

The woman came around the corner. It was Brooke.

21

"John!" cried Brooke, half smiling and half staring in shock. I must have looked terrible. "You're alive!"

"Brooke," I said, standing up slowly, "you shouldn't be here."

"You should never trust a stranger," said Forman, "but everyone trusts a policeman."

Brooke frowned and wrinkled her brow. She was confused. "What?"

I can't do this, I thought. *I can't go through with it—not with Brooke.*

"Brooke," I said, taking a step toward Forman, "turn around and go." *He'll sense my emotions and attack me, but at least she can get out.* The chain scraped across the floor as I moved, and she tilted her head to see it moving slowly behind the table.

"What's going on?" she asked.

"Run!" I shouted, and lunged for Forman, but he was perfectly prepared for the attack and punched me straight in the face. I staggered back and Brooke shrieked. She turned to run, but Forman leapt and grabbed her by the hair, wrenching her to a stop with a violent yank that sent her sprawling to the ground. I ran toward him again but he had his gun out now, pointed straight at my stomach.

Back off, I told myself. *The plan can still work, but only if I'm empty. I can't feel anything. I'm completely empty.*

Brooke was crying, fighting to get away, but she stopped abruptly when Forman swung his gun around and pressed it up under her chin.

"Betrayal," he said. "It really is the sweetest, John, just like I told you."

Brooke looked at me, her eyes going wider, and Forman took a deep, luxurious breath.

"There it is again." He closed his eyes, gritting his teeth. Brooke and Forman began crying, almost perfectly in unison.

Brooke was mortified now, scared literally stiff, and Forman gripped her tighter, pulling harder on her hair. "No! No! No!" shouted Forman, then pulled his gun sharply to the side and swung it back powerfully, slamming it into the side of her head. He let go of her hair and she stumbled to the wall, grasping it desperately for balance.

Nothing, I thought, pushing down the anger. *Attacking him now won't do any good at all. Just wait, and feel nothing.*

"Please," said Forman, regaining his composure, "take a seat." He was using my neutrality to recover from Brooke's intense emotions of betrayal and fear. He waved his gun toward the table. Brooke clung to the wall with one hand, rubbing her face with the other. She didn't move.

"You will learn quickly," said Forman, "that I don't like to ask for things twice."

Brooke looked up at him, eyes wide with fear, then at me. After a moment she grabbed the back of a chair and pulled it out, sitting down warily.

"What are you doing with us?" she asked.

"Whatever I want," said Forman, gesturing for me to sit as well. I sat in the chair opposite Brooke, facing the living room. The counter, and the electrified butcher knife, were just in the corner of my vision.

"That's the short answer," said Forman. "The long answer is that I am teaching John a very important lesson about deception. You see, he wanted me to go out and get Kay Crowley—so I could learn some kind of valuable tripe about love, I believe— and he thought he was being very sly about it. He was manipulating me, and I don't like to be manipulated, so you, Miss Watson, are going to help demonstrate the consequences."

"I'm not going to help you do anything," said Brooke. I was a little surprised she had that much fight in her, and I shook my head, almost imperceptibly. The more she fought him, the more he'd enjoy it—just like with Radha.

"Actually you are," said Forman, opening one of the drawers. "But the nice thing about this kind of help is that you don't have to lift a finger." He pulled out a pair of snub-nose pliers and snapped them open and shut. "I'm going to do all the work."

Brooke's face paled, and I knew that she finally understood the situation. She jumped to her feet, pushing back the chair, and looked at me desperately. I shook my head.

Don't leave the room, I thought silently, *you've got to stay in this room.*

"Sit down," Forman demanded. He still had his gun in his other hand, and he used it now to persuade her back into her seat. Brooke shook her head and backed against the wall.

Forman smiled, wolfish and evil. "Can you talk some sense into her, John?"

I didn't want to have to do this to her. I could do it to Kay, to my mom, to anyone else in my life, but not to Brooke.

"Forman is a psychopath," I said, trying to keep my voice even. If I gave her any kind of hope—even if all I did was tell her to trust me—Forman would realize I had a plan. "He killed a woman yesterday, and he has four more in the basement. I've been trapped here for two days, and I know enough to tell you that the more you fight, the worse it gets."

"No," said Brooke, shaking her head. She was crying. "No."

"Please sit down," I said. "Please."

She sat down, and Forman threw me his keys.

"Unlock yourself, and put the chain on her."

I opened the lock on the manacle and brought it over to Brooke. She looked at me with vacant eyes, as if she couldn't understand what was happening.

"I'm so sorry," I said.

"Not just her ankle," said Forman, his breath speeding up. He was feeling the buzz of her emotions—the betrayal she felt with every command I followed, and every evil I went along with. "Wrap it around her," said Forman, "and loop it through the back of the chair. As many times as it will go around."

I wanted to say something—anything—but I didn't dare. I forced myself to stay calm. *Don't give anything away, even to her.*

"Why are you doing this?" asked Brooke. "Why are you helping him?"

"It's easier this way," I said. I didn't want to drag this out any more than I had to, so I tightened the chains firmly to make sure Brooke couldn't get away. Forman whimpered behind me, and I knew that Brooke felt even more betrayed. Even if we survived this, she'd probably hate me.

"Excellent," said Forman, his eyes half closed. His smile was broad and lecherous, like he was drunk. He picked up the pliers again. "Now, let's get this party started." He holstered his pistol and stepped toward Brooke, working the pliers eagerly.

I couldn't just let him hurt her. The idea was to shock him before the torture started, but how many tools would he go through before he got to the knife? I had to think of something.

"Wait," I said. Forman stopped. But what could I say? I wanted him to touch the knife, but anything I said to trick him would be false, and he'd detect the lie immediately.

"You want to stop me?" said Forman. His voice was sharper now; I was feeling anxious and worried, and that meant he was too. I didn't have much time.

There was only one thing I could say and mean it—only one thing that would lead him to the knife, and still be totally true. I looked at Brooke, pale and terrified and beautiful.

"I want to do it," I said.

Her face wilted, fear and confusion twisting it into a devastating grimace. Just like Forman, I pushed her emotions away; I pushed mine away. I ignored everything about the present and drew on the past. I remembered my dreams of her, of cutting her, of hurting her, of making her wholly and completely my own. Everything I'd ever tried to ignore and avoid I embraced now, filling myself with thoughts of Brooke's soft skin, of Brooke's bright scream, of Brooke's pale body lying still and motionless.

"Yes," said Forman. He was feeling it too—the forbidden anticipation, the pounding need of my desire, the sweet agony of her terror. This was what he'd wanted for days—to feel the emotions of a torturer, not just the victim. "Yes," said Forman, stepping back. "Do it. She's yours."

I stepped closer, watching her eyes as they watched me, feeling the electric buzz in the air as our minds connected—more closely and more purely than when we held hands, more completely than I'd ever connected with anyone. The thrill of fear was a like a tether between us, a conduit from one mind to another. No, it was deeper than the mind; there were no words, there were no thoughts, there was only *us*, Brooke and me, together at last.

I leaned in, smelling her—a hint of perfume, a touch of fruit from her shampoo, a clean, crisp scent of laundry soap. She was mine now. All mine.

"Hand me the knife."

"Yes," he hissed. He stepped behind me, once, twice, and then the lights dimmed and he screamed, a low-pitched grunt through gritted teeth. Brooke screamed with him in high counterpoint, and I savored the sound like a stream of crystal water.

There was a smell of burning meat, and Brooke shook her head.

"Help me, John, please help me."

Why did she need help? What was . . . ? There was something I was supposed to do. It was Brooke. I was supposed to cut her; she wanted me to cut. . . . No, no that wasn't it at all. I turned and saw Forman, his body rigid, his hand still on the butcher knife, and I remembered. *It was my trap. I didn't really want to hurt Brooke, right? It was only a trap for Forman.*

I couldn't touch him or I'd be shocked too. There was a pan in the lower cupboard with a plastic handle—I could use that. I skirted past him carefully, pulled the pan from the cupboard, and raised it up like a club.

Brooke spoke desperately. "John, what are you doing?"

"I'm making sure," I said, and slammed the pan into his face. It knocked him backward, pulling his hand away from the knife and sending him tumbling to the floor. Brooke screamed, and I jumped to follow Forman's body, standing over him with the pan raised. He looked up at me, his eyes barely open.

Slowly, painfully, he smiled.

"I beat you," I said. "You've lost."

"And for the . . ." he coughed, raspy and painful, his voice charred and black. "For the first time in . . . ten thousand years . . ." he coughed again. "I feel like I've won."

I hit him with the pan and knocked him unconscious.

"What's going on!" cried Brooke, hysterical. "What's going on?"

"I don't know how long he'll stay down," I said, dropping the pan. "We have to work fast."

"What?"

The keys were still on the table, and I ran to unlock her manacle and unwrap the chains. She struggled out of them like they were living things, tentacles trying to eat her alive.

"I know you're freaked out but you've got to trust me," I said. "Do you trust me?"

"You were going to . . ."

"No," I said, "it was just a trap for Forman. Now listen." I dragged the chains over to Forman and started wrapping him up, looping it through itself and under his arms and around his legs, doing my best to make sure that even if he woke up he'd stay completely immobilized. His hand was a blackened lump of cooked meat. "Everything I said about this house was true," I said to Brooke. "There's four women downstairs, and Lauren's boyfriend is tied up in the back. We need a knife."

I locked the manacle around Forman's leg and stood up, walking to the counter. Brooke was staring at the butcher knife in wonder, her hand half extended. I knocked the block over carefully and pointed at the cord in the bottom.

"Don't touch."

I pulled a steak knife from the sink and led Brooke into the back room where Curt hung from the ceiling. He was awake, but only barely; whatever Forman had drugged him with was powerful. I handed Brooke the keys and pointed at the handcuffs on Curt's feet; she dropped to her knees and fumbled with the key ring, still terrified, while I started sawing on the ropes.

"Wake up, Curt," I said, shaking his shoulder as I worked on the ropes. "We're cutting you loose, and we need you to stand up. Can you stand up?"

He didn't nod, but he pulled his feet closer and raised up, bracing himself against the sudden loss of support when the ropes gave way. I cut through the first rope and he dropped his arm like it weighed a ton, but he didn't fall. I cut through the other just as Brooke finished unlocking the handcuffs, Curt reached for the duct tape around his mouth. He was waking up.

"Let's get outside first," I said, pulling his arm over my shoulder. He was a huge man, and he leaned on me heavily, but I staggered with him through the door and down the hall. He stumbled in the kitchen, tripping over Forman's chained up body, and a few steps later doubled back to kick him solidly in the gut. I pulled him back.

"Let's get outside," I said, "I don't know how much time we have." There was more room here, and Brooke grabbed Curt's other arm to help guide him to the front door. I let her take him and stepped away. "Take him outside," I said, "I'm going for the women."

Brooke nodded, and I took the keys from her hand and went to the basement door. Forman was still unconscious. I opened the lock and started to throw it away, then thought better of it and locked it through two links of Forman's chain, keeping him that much tighter.

"Get up!" I shouted, throwing open the basement door and flipping on the lights. "We're leaving, and we're leaving right now. Can everybody walk?"

The four women looked at me in shock, climbing painfully to their feet. None of them had shoes, and their clothes hung thin and ragged on their emaciated bodies. Stephanie was healthier, but her wounds were more recent and she took the longest to stand.

"What's going on?" asked Carly. I unlocked her first.

"Forman's unconscious," I said, moving on to Jess, "and he's tied up. He might be down for good, or he might be back up any second; I don't know how he works."

"What do you mean?"

"Nevermind," I said, unlocking Melinda. "Just get upstairs and get out. We can take his car to town, and get you to the police and to the hospital. Go!" I unlocked Stephanie's chain and helped her to the stairs.

"Do you know why he did this?" she whispered.

I shook my head. "I don't."

I followed the women upstairs and met Brooke in the kitchen.

"Take them outside," I said, "I need to rescue one more."

"We need a phone for the police," said Brooke. "I don't have mine, and I can't find one here."

"Forman has a cell," I said, and dropped to the floor by his body. I reached in past the chains, struggling to reach his jacket pocket, and finally managed to fish out his phone. I handed it to Brooke along with the keys. "Start the car," I said. "Even after we call the police, we need to get out of here as fast as we can."

I started to head back to the torture room, but a distinct scent caught my attention. I'd smelled it before, several times, and I'd never forget it—acrid and thick, like an invisible caustic cloud. I turned around.

Forman was melting.

His body seemed to collapse inside the chains, hissing and sinking and curling in on itself like paper in a fire. In seconds the flesh was gone, leaving a blackened suit wrapped in chains and stained by greasy ash.

"Exactly like Crowley."

I hesitated, half-reaching out to touch it, then stepped back and turned again to the hall. I needed to rescue the woman in the wall. I started toward the back room again when another scent stopped me—woodsmoke and gasoline. Something was burning. I heard muffled shouts from outside, and suddenly the kitchen window shattered in a hail of splintered glass. The smell of gas was overwhelming, and I heard Brooke scream.

"John's still in there! You'll kill him!"

I raced to the front door and stumbled down the steps. The women were huddled together, crying and wailing as if they were more scared now than they'd ever been in the dungeon. I ran toward them but something hit me from behind, knocking me down.

"John!" cried Brooke.

"He's part of this!" shouted a deep voice. *Curt.* "He's working with him—they're partners!"

I tried to stand up but Curt hit me again, with something hard and metal. A gas can.

"He's trying to help!" shouted Brooke. "He's the one who got us all out of there!"

There were flames behind Curt—the house was on fire. He stepped toward me and raised the gas can over his head.

"He was going to cut me," said Curt. "He was going to torture me, both of them together. It was the same for you, too—I heard everything."

Brooke opened her mouth, but paused. I had been about to attack her, and she knew it. Her eyes were dark, and I knew that she was remembering: even if she knew it had been a trick she also knew, in that moment, that she wasn't sure if I was good or evil. Curt took advantage of her hesitation and slammed the gas can down on my head, making it ring with pain. My vision went black and I fell to the ground.

"You want to make sure that bastard's dead?" he said, his voice a thousand miles away. "Burn the damn place down." There was a crash and a new roar of flame.

"Not yet," I said, too weak to move. "There's a woman in the wall . . ."

And then the sound went dead, and the world spun around, and everything was gone.

22

This time, I dreamed of nothing. It was just me, floating, surrounded by endless stretches of . . . well, nothing. I guess it was black, if that counts as something, but in the dream that didn't occur to me—I *knew* it was nothing, and the strange thing was, I was fine with that. I wasn't scared or nervous or sad, I was content. And something else. I was excited.

I think I knew, somewhere in the back of my mind, that just because there was nothing at the moment, that didn't mean there would never be anything at all. It just meant that I got to choose.

I woke up in a hospital room, sometime in the middle of the night. It was dark and quiet. Lights were blinking behind me, reflected in the blank TV screen on the opposite wall. Soft voices drifted in from the hallway, hushed and distant. The curtains were open, and the moon shone faintly in the sky. Everything was still.

My mom was asleep on the chair next to me, curled up under a light hospital blanket that rose and fell softly as she breathed. Her hand was stretched out, bridging the gap between the chair and the bed, holding the side rail protectively. Her hair was pulled back, with a few loose strands that hung over her face like wisps of dark cloud. Her hair seemed grayer in the moonlight, and her face more lined and sad; her body small and fragile.

I wished, just for a moment, that I was like Forman—that I could reach out and feel what she was feeling. Was she sad? Happy? Did it matter? She was here. No matter what I did, no matter what anyone did, she would love me. She would never leave me.

I drifted back to sleep.

When I woke again the next morning Mom was still there, picking at a plate of hospital breakfast. There were other people in the room as well: a doctor and a policeman, conferring quietly in the corner.

"He's awake!"

I turned my head and saw Lauren, standing up from another chair and walking to the bed. Mom practically leapt out of her chair and grabbed my hand.

"John," she said, "can you hear me?"

"Yeah," I croaked. My throat was dry and raw, and it hurt to speak.

"Look who's up," said the doctor, coming over quickly. He shone a penlight into each of my eyes, holding each one open with his thumb. I blinked when he let go, and he nodded. "Good. Now I want you to say your name."

"John—" I swallowed and coughed. "John Wayne Cleaver."

"Excellent," said the doctor, and pointed at my mom. "Do you recognize this woman?"

"That's my mom."

"You're checking his memory?" asked Mom.

"His speech, mostly," said the doctor. "His memory seems to be good, though."

"What happened?" I rasped.

The policeman—it was Officer Jensen, Marci's father—glanced at my mother, then at Lauren, then back at me.

"Curt Halsey is in custody," he said, "for assaulting you, among other things. Clark Forman is, as near as we can tell, deceased."

"Not them," I said, "what happened to the girl?"

"Brooke's fine," said Mom, putting her hand on mine.

"No," I said, closing my eyes. I was getting too anxious, and I was starting to feel weak again. "There was another woman, trapped in the wall. What happened to her?"

"Remains were recovered from the ashes of the house," Officer Jensen said, "but we haven't identified them yet. One of them did appear to be imprisoned in a wall; she was surrounded by medical equipment, IVs and things. That's probably how he kept her alive." He paused. "I'm sorry."

I hadn't saved her. I opened my eyes again. "Is everyone else okay?"

"The women you rescued are here in the hospital," said the doctor, "though most of them will be transferred today. We're not a very big facility, unfortunately, and they can be cared for much better in the city."

"We're keeping you here," said Mom, patting my hand. "Don't worry."

"Technically," said Officer Jensen, "we're keeping you here in protective custody. We haven't confirmed that your kidnapper is dead, so it's partly for your own safety, but . . ." he glanced at my mom again. She frowned at him. "I'm afraid that you have been accused of a number of crimes yourself, including . . ." he paused, "the murder of Radha Behar."

"You can't possibly—" Mom said, but Officer Jensen cut her off.

"I've told your mother several times," he said, "and I'm telling you now, not to worry about this. The women you rescued have provided overwhelming testimony in your favor. We have a couple of things we're still looking at, but it's mostly just paperwork at this point. You're a hero, John. You should be proud." He smiled. "Now get some rest." He pulled the doctor aside again and they stepped into the hall, speaking in low voices.

"You're a hero," Mom repeated, squeezing my hand and kissing my forehead. "You saved six lives in that house! Six! Sure, one of them was a creep," she looked at Lauren, "but that's what makes it so good. 'Love thine enemies.'"

Lauren shook her head and smiled at me. "And don't worry about Curt," she said. "We are *so* broken up."

"Six lives," Mom repeated.

But I was trying to save seven.

I gave my statement several times, leaving out the part about Forman being a demon. Instead I told them everything I knew about Forman's history of torture, focusing specifically on the house—the chains in the basement, the pit in the floor, the torture room upstairs, and even the reinforced walls in the closet. The other prisoners gave corroborating statements, and as the police cross-referenced our testimonies—and as they discovered the identities of the other women Forman had killed—they began to piece together a strong sense of where and how he worked. They ended up linking him, in the end, to several dozen missing persons cases, all women, and postulated that he had kept it all hidden thanks to his position in the FBI. If they knew what I knew—that Forman was thousands, perhaps tens of thousands of years old—they would have known that the few dozen crimes they'd linked him to were only a fraction of his life's work. He'd been torturing and killing for ages.

But now he was gone.

I was released the next day, from both the hospital and from police custody. Curt's accusations that I was Forman's accomplice were thrown out almost immediately, based on a lack of proof. Even more redeeming were the eyewitness accounts from the women in the basement, who explained very convincingly that not only did Forman kill Radha, but that I had nearly been killed as well trying to stop him. It all added up to a very heroic depiction of John the Brave, the demon slayer, who ventured into the foul beast's darkest dungeon and rescued not one but five princesses. A story like that would normally make the news—it would probably make national news—but I was lucky. Jess and Carly's story about being held in another house, where a different person had come to feed them, made the police concerned that Forman's true accomplice, whoever he was, would come looking for revenge. They kept my name out of the story almost completely, and since I'd only been gone for forty-eight hours, very few people knew I'd been missing at all.

I was a hero, but nobody knew about it.

"Why can't normal things ever happen here?" asked Max, gazing out over the freeway. We were on the Route 12 bridge, leaning on the railing while cars sped past beneath us on the highway. He was tossing bits of gravel onto the tops of the semis.

"Plenty of normal things happen here," I said. "We get up, we eat breakfast, we have school, we have jobs. We watch TV."

"No, I don't mean normal boring things, I mean normal cool things."

"How can they be normal and cool at the same time?" I asked.

"Because cool things happen all the time," he said. "Cool is normal everywhere but here. Maybe someone could film a movie here, or open up a new comic shop, or we could finally get a good restaurant in town. I don't know, maybe a movie star could visit or something."

"They're probably at the shoe museum all the time," I said. "You just never hang out in the kinds of places movie stars visit, unless you're expecting Bruce Willis to come throw rocks off the bridge with us."

"Don't be an idiot," said Max, "you're missing the point. All I'm saying is that everything here is either boring or somebody dies. There's either nothing going on, or there's a dead body in the lake. Neither one is cool. I just want something to be excited about for once."

There was a gap in the traffic below us, and I tossed a rock onto the road. A moment later a truck zoomed by and clipped it with a tire, shooting the rock into the dead grass off the side of the highway. The truck, never even noticing, continued down the road.

"I held Brooke's hand," I said.

"Shut up."

"No, really."

Max looked at me, his face unreadable.

"Dude," he said. "You kissed her yet?"

"I think I would have led with that if I had."

"So kiss her already," said Max. "Are you an idiot? And then cop a feel while you're at it, because wow. She has got a butt I would love to get my hands on."

I shook my head. "How is it possible that an upstanding guy like you doesn't have a girlfriend?"

"The ladies love Max," said Max, turning back to the railing. "They just . . . you know."

"Yeah," I said. "I know."

Two days after I left the hospital, Brooke met me outside when I was walking to my car. It was nearly nine o'clock at night, and dark. It was the first time I'd seen her since Forman's house.

"Hey," she said. She was holding something in her hands.

"Hey."

And then she said nothing, for a long time, and I wasn't sure what to do. She was watching me, her mouth crooked, her eyes narrow and set. Her jaw kept moving, like she was about to talk, and after nearly a minute she did.

"I don't know what happened in that house," she said. "I don't know why he took me, or why he took you, or why that guy burned it down, or anything. I know there's reasons, because there's got to be reasons, but I just don't think I want to know what they are. I think that maybe you . . ." She stopped again. She looked away.

There were a lot of things I couldn't read from people, emotionally speaking, but "I'm leaving you" was one I knew pretty well.

"You're a really brave guy," she said. "And you're really nice." She paused. "I just don't want to remember what happened in there. I don't want it to be a part of my life."

It was just like my mom and the demon—she knew it had happened, but she didn't want to confront it. She was the one person in the world I could share this with, and she was walking away from it. And from me.

I wanted to speak, but . . . I couldn't. Sometimes you can't talk because there's nothing to say, and sometimes there's just too much.

"Here," she said, holding out something small and black. I took it, being careful our fingers didn't touch. It was a cell phone. "It's Agent Forman's," she said. "I forgot I even had it until I found it in my jacket pocket this afternoon. The police are going to want it, I guess, but I don't want to deal with it anymore. Can you give it to them?"

"Yeah," I said.

"Thanks. And thanks again for getting me out of there alive.

I don't know what I would have done if you hadn't . . ." Pause. "Well, I'll see you around."

"Yeah."

And then she walked away.

I was John the Brave, the demon slayer, who saved the kingdom and didn't get any glory; who braved the dungeon and didn't get any treasure; who rescued five princesses and ended up alone. I was John the Brave.

I knew who I was.

The phone in my hands was better than treasure—it was a map of the underworld. I flipped it open and scanned through the contact list, seeing name after name—people from the FBI, and from Forman's research network: doctors, psychologists, criminologists, and more. And interspersed throughout, buried in the middle under fake names I could only guess at, were the others. Demons. Crowley had been cut off, but Forman knew them all. If I could find the right numbers, then I could find them, too.

I stopped suddenly, scrolling through the list, my eyes catching on a name. There in the Ns between "NMH folk office" was a single word: "Nobody." In one calls I'd overheard, Forman had called one of the body," but I hadn't understood why. Apparently it name.

I dialed it.

A woman's voice answered, small and weak. "Kanta must have been Forman's other name, just like Crowley was Mkhai. "They're saying interesting things about you on the news," she said. "I wondered if you'd survived."

"He didn't," I said. "I killed him."

Silence.

"I killed Mkhai, too," I said. "Tens of thousands of years, gone in the blink of an eye."

"Why are you telling me this?" asked the voice.

"Because you're next," I said. "I'm the demon slayer. Come and get me."